Reviewers Love Meliss

"Melissa Brayden has become one of th[e]... of the genre, writing hit after hit of funny, relatable, and very sexy stories for women who love women."—*Afterellen.com*

Love Like This

"I really have to commend Melissa Brayden in her exceptional writing and especially in the way she writes not only the romance but the friendships between the group of women."—*Les Rêveur*

"Brayden upped her game. The characters are remarkably distinct from one another. The secondary characters are rich and wonderfully integrated into the story. The dialogue is crisp and witty."
—*Frivolous Reviews*

Sparks Like Ours

"Brayden sets up a flirtatious tit-for-tat that's honest, relatable, and passionate. The women's fears are real, but the loving support from the supporting cast helps them find their way to a happy future. This enjoyable romance is sure to interest readers in the other stories from Seven Shores."—*Publishers Weekly*

"*Sparks Like Ours* is made up of myriad bits of truth that make for a cozy, lovely summer read."—*Queerly Reads*

Hearts Like Hers

"*Hearts Like Hers* has all the ingredients that readers can expect from Ms. Brayden: witty dialogue, heartfelt relationships, hot chemistry and passionate romance."—*Lez Review Books*

"Once again Melissa Brayden stands at the top. She unequivocally is the queen of romance."—*Front Porch Romance*

"*Hearts Like Hers* has a breezy style that makes it a perfect beach read. The romance is paced well, the sex is super hot, and the conflict made perfect sense and honored Autumn and Kate's journeys."
—*The Lesbian Review*

Eyes Like Those

"Brayden's story of blossoming love behind the Hollywood scenes provides the right amount of warmth, camaraderie, and drama."
—*RT Book Reviews*

"Brayden's writing is just getting better and better. The story is well done, full of well-honed wit and humour, and the characters are complex and interesting."—*Lesbian Reading Room*

"Melissa Brayden knocks it out of the park once again with this fantastic and beautifully written novel."—*Les Reveur*

"Pure Melissa Brayden at her best…Another great read that won't disappoint Brayden's fans. Can't wait for the rest of the series."
—*Lez Review Books*

Strawberry Summer

"This small-town second-chance romance is full of tenderness and heart. The 10 Best Romance Books of 2017."—*Vulture*

"*Strawberry Summer* is a tribute to first love and soulmates and growing into the person you're meant to be. I feel like I say this each time I read a new Melissa Brayden offering, but I loved this book so much that I cannot wait to see what she delivers next."—*Smart Bitches, Trashy Books*

"*Strawberry Summer* will suck you in, rip out your heart, and put all the pieces back together by the end, maybe even a little better than they were before."—*The Lesbian Review*

"[A] sweet and charming small-town lesbian romance."—*Pretty Little Book Reviews*

First Position

"Brayden aptly develops the growing relationship between Ana and Natalie, making the emotional payoff that much sweeter. This ably plotted, moving offering will earn its place deep in readers' hearts."—*Publishers Weekly*

Praise for the Soho Loft Series

"The trilogy was enjoyable and definitely worth a read if you're looking for solid romance or interconnected stories about a group of friends."—*The Lesbrary*

Kiss the Girl

"There are romances and there are romances...Melissa Brayden can be relied on to write consistently very sweet, pure romances and delivers again with her newest book *Kiss the Girl*...There are scenes suffused with the sweetest love, some with great sadness or even anger—a whole gamut of emotions that take readers on a gentle roller coaster with a consistent upbeat tone. And at the heart of this book is a hymn to true friendship and human decency." —*C-Spot Reviews*

"Read it. Embrace it. Do yourself a favor and provide it to yourself as a reward for being awesome. There is nothing about this novel that won't delight any reader, I can guarantee this."—*FarNerdy Book Blog*

Just Three Words

"Another winner from Melissa Brayden. I really connected with Hunter and Sam, and enjoyed watching their relationship develop. The friendship between the four women was heart-warming and real. The dialogue in general was fun and contemporary. I look forward to reading the next book in the series, hope it will be about Mallory!"—*Melina Bickard, Librarian, Waterloo Library (London)*

"A beautiful and downright hilarious tale about two very relatable women looking for love."—*Sharing Is Caring Book Reviews*

Ready or Not

"The chemistry is off the charts. The swoon factor is high. I promise you this book will make you smile. I had such high hopes for this book, and Melissa Brayden leapt right over them."—*The Romantic Reader Blog*

By the Author

Waiting in the Wings

Heart Block

How Sweet It Is

First Position

Strawberry Summer

Beautiful Dreamer

Back to September

Soho Loft Romances:

Kiss the Girl

Just Three Words

Ready or Not

Seven Shores Romances:

Eyes Like Those

Hearts Like Hers

Sparks Like Ours

Love Like This

Visit us at www.boldstrokesbooks.com

BACK TO SEPTEMBER

by
Melissa Brayden

2019

BACK TO SEPTEMBER

ISBN 13: 978-1-63555-576-9

This Trade Paperback Original Is Published By
Bold Strokes Books, Inc.
P.O. Box 249
Valley Falls, NY 12185

First Edition: November 2019

CREDITS
Editors: Lynda Sandoval and Stacia Seaman
Production Design: Stacia Seaman
Cover Design by Jeanine Henning

Acknowledgments

I can't seem to get used to the magic I encounter when walking into a bookstore. I don't know if it's the crisp smell of the books themselves, or the idea that there are thousands of stories and adventures lining the shelves, just waiting to be snatched up and explored. Maybe it's all that creativity in one space, commingling and putting out the greatest energy ever. Whatever it is, I'm a big fan of the bookstore, and find the smaller shops have captured my heart exponentially. I hope A Likely Story will capture yours in a similar fashion. It was certainly fun spending my workdays there.

I'm grateful for my writing community and all the colleagues who have become so much more than just that. With each conference, I learn so much from you. With each conversation, I take in something new and valuable that enriches my storytelling. You're there for me when I have a rough writing day, and you cheer me on when I've had a particularly good one. I adore you all!

To those hard at work at Bold Strokes books, I say thank you for your efforts, guidance, and professionalism. I love my job and the people I work with. I realize how lucky I am in that capacity.

My editor on this book, Lynda Sandoval, is fantastic at phrasing things gently and rerouting me when I need it. She's also my very favorite cheerleader, who threatens violence when she loves a portion of the book. I adore our partnership and am forever grateful for your influence. Similarly, Stacia Seaman is a rock star of details. Her copy editing leaves me in awe with every book.

To my at home family, you make my life what it is. My hand is over my heart because you allow me to do what I do even when you sometimes need me to do the dishes. Thank you for holding my hand, making me laugh, and being my support system. I love you.

Lastly, dear reader, you make me happy to open my email and social media each morning. I treasure your messages and the relationship we share. I remark every day how cool it is that we bond over stories and plots and characters. I hope to keep writing, and I hope you'll keep reading. Let's go on many more journeys together.

For the Romantics

CHAPTER ONE

G ood morning, books," I whispered reverently. This was the first sentence that passed from my lips each day when I arrived at work. I flipped on the lights of the bookshop early that Monday morning at eight a.m. sharp, held my breath, and counted to three. The overhead lights took about that long to flicker to full vibrancy, bringing the store and the thousands of stories that lined its shelves to life. Incredibly satisfying, that moment. I exhaled at the pleasant squeeze my heart received and smiled in greeting at the space, my favorite in all of the world. I ran my hand along the spines of the mystery section as I passed, my own little version of a hello hug. Not that I was a sap. I wasn't. I just had a soft spot for books, even more than I had for people, and recognized the ability of books to change lives.

Today was going to be a good day. A brief pat on the spine for general fiction as I walked. Something important was going to happen. I could feel it prickle my skin and warm my midsection, almost as if the premonition had blown in with the impending fall temperatures, encapsulating me and giving me energy. Strangely, I felt like bouncing around. It was still late August, but with the thermostat only expected to brush seventy that afternoon, I welcomed the glimpse of autumn ahead.

I'd opened my bookshop, A Likely Story, eight years prior, snatching up the storefront in downtown Providence, Rhode Island, from an elderly man who'd been ready to close his flower shop and enter the glory years of golfing and fishing, having invested his retirement funds nicely. Because of the fair offer and quick close on the sale of the storefront, I'd gotten the shop for a steal, making me, Hannah Shephard, a small business owner for the first time at twenty-six years old. That felt like centuries ago now. I looked back in amusement at the idealism of that innocent youngster, who imagined the bookselling world at her feet.

The store's location was excellent, close to everything trendy and fun in downtown, but just off the beaten path by about two blocks, giving the shop its own quaint, away-from-the-hustle-and-bustle existence. The flower shop, Daisy Chain, had commanded a pretty steady business, and A Likely Story had followed in its footsteps…at least for the first few years I'd been in business. It would again, I told myself on the regular. That mantra had played like a broken record in my head this morning as I'd made the short walk to work from my apartment, only six and half blocks away. Things would be okay, I reminded myself again, while preparing the morning coffee with measured precision, taking each step in the process slowly to ensure the perfectly blended pot for my customers. Details mattered. If the coffee wasn't amazing, then I had failed to do a key part of my job, which was bait people into the store with the amazing aroma of fresh coffee—made every two hours—so I could match them to their book. That's right. I believed wholeheartedly that at any given moment, every human being had a book somewhere out there that was perfect for them and their headspace, if only they could find it. That's where I came in. Call it my gift. But I know firsthand how effective the perfect match can be. I've had plenty of perfect matches in my thirty-four years: a self-help book about human imperfection when I was feeling introspective and less than amazing, or Stephen King's dragon-slaying tale when my imagination was firing on all cylinders, or a fantastic Patricia Cornwell crime novel for a rainy night under a snug blanket. The key to a repeat customer was providing the ultimate escape, the perfect match, and so many had come to my store for that very reason. Fantastic coffee with a little bit of cinnamon helped grease the wheels, making my job easier.

"Morning, Hannah!" I heard Kurt, my employee, call from the front of the store. "It's cooler out, and I wore earmuffs. That might be premature, because I'm also wearing shorts, but I'm digging it."

"Morning right back. Today's gonna be a good one." I paused, then called again, "Shorts and earmuffs are maybe a weird thing to pair together, though." I was being too practical again, and knew it. Best to let Kurt be Kurt. He was lovable enough.

I hit Brew on the coffeemaker and headed to the front to greet him. Kurt had the morning shift most days, and Luna would be in midafternoon. I tried to work it so that I always had one employee in the shop in addition to myself, giving me time to take care of day-to-day upkeep, accounting, purchasing and, well, advertising, because we could definitely use new customer traffic. Our repeat clientele only went so far.

"Anything special to get started on, or just prep for opening?" Kurt asked. We'd open at nine, but the shop wouldn't pick up until close to eleven. I probably needed to do something about that.

"Well, we do have a new display to stage."

"Oh, okay. I'll get to it." Kurt nodded a lot. "I like a good book tower."

I couldn't hide my grin, aware of what was coming. "The boxes for the display arrived yesterday. You're gonna enjoy what's inside, if I'm not mistaken." I tossed that tidbit of information over my shoulder, knowing full well he was about to lose his mind.

He did a couple of shoulder rolls, his eyes scanning the room, as he pieced together my meaning. "No!" He looked up at me and paused midroll. "Is it Groffman's new release? It is, isn't it?" His hands moved to on top of his head. He rarely kept track of dates. Calendars were his kryptonite, which made surprises like today pretty simple to pull off. "I've been waiting on the new Groffman."

"No!"

He nodded earnestly, his chestnut floppy hair dancing around. "Yes, yes, I have."

"You only say so every other hour, so I wasn't sure." I winked at him. "I held back the boxes from Luna last night. Thought you might want to create the display yourself. They also sent some art and signage. I propped it up in the back. Looks like an action-packed book."

He was listening at the same time he tore into the first box, eyes gleaming like a six-year-old presented with a new bike at Christmas. With that kidlike smile, he held up a hardback copy to me in victory.

"Look at you two. I feel like it was meant to be," I said, over yesterday's receipts. "The perfect match."

"That's it. I'm canceling all plans tonight. I had a curling match. Forget it." He thumbed through the pages, seeming to inhale as he went. I completely identified. There was no smell as amazing as a brand-new book. No sound as breathtaking as the spine cracking for the first time.

"Take one," I told him. "On the house."

His eyes went wide, and if it was at all possible, his hair seemed to vibrate. "No, you don't have to do that. I put some cash away."

"But I don't want your cash. You've been here, what? Four years now? I can handle a free book when it's clearly a match. The two of you together is a thing of beauty. No arguing, and lend it to your mom as soon as you're done. She loves Groffman."

"Geez. Okay, but you're pretty awesome." He stared down at his new book happily.

It was the least I could do. None of us were making much money these days. Not me on the shop's bottom line, and not Kurt or Luna on their miniscule hourly checks. The only reason they worked here was because they loved the gig and the store as much as I did. I'd been able to offer them semiannual bonuses back in the more profitable days to help bolster their take-home, but not this year with the shop taking on water. We were all scraping by at best, adoring our jobs but watching the clock, wondering how much longer we had until A Likely Story shuttered for good. I wasn't sure what I would do with myself if that happened. These four walls, these books were my life, my family, and I had no intention of ever saying good-bye.

I shook myself right out of that line of thinking. Nope! No way. There would be no surrender nor submission on my part. Not when something I loved so dearly was at stake. I was prepared to fight this thing with every ounce of business sense I had or would have to learn. That last part was more likely. I tapped my lips in determination and headed off to make mugs of cinnamon coffee for myself and Kurt while he put together the Groffman display, which would hopefully sell like mad. *Thank God for long-awaited novels and please, oh, please let this one fly off the shelf.* I'd had several customers ask about the book's release date the week prior, which was a good sign.

"Looking sharp," I told Kurt as I surveyed his work still in progress and straightened a tilting copy. The shop would open in twenty-five minutes, and although Monday mornings were sleepy in general, I planned to be ready to wow any customers that came through the forest green door of the shop. I'd make them feel welcome, attended to, but not overly so, and excited to take home a few new fictional friends. Or nonfictional, if that's what they were into. I tried not to judge, but definitely favored getting lost in a make-believe tale myself.

By midafternoon, we'd had about eleven customers come through. Half had made purchases. All had accepted the complimentary coffee. The world had not been changed yet, nor had our finances. Maybe my premonition about today had been wrong after all. I stared at myself in the mirror of the small bathroom and attempted to scrub the noticeable worry lines from my face with a dousing of cold water. Double sigh. My brown hair needed to be cut. It hung too long and thick, well past my shoulders. I'd make an appointment for a few days from now and try to get my sass back. I lifted a strand and let it fall back into place, prompting me to give it a fluff. Unfortunately, I had not inherited the good curls from my father's side of the family, but I did get his blue eyes, which made me happy. "What are we going to do?" I asked my weary reflection. "What, indeed?"

"You're gonna stop talking to yourself in the bathroom like a semilunatic!" Luna shouted from the shop. "The universe will take care of you because you're a good human, and that's that."

I laughed, finished washing, and joined her. The store was currently empty and my employee Luna, who also happened to have become my friend, stood with her hands on her hips, surveying the Groffman display like she had a bad taste in her mouth. We'd sold three copies so far, though the day wasn't over. Luna held up a hand, palm up. "Hear me out about this thing."

"Uh-oh. Okay. Hearing you." Generally, when Luna started a sentence that way, she had passionate feelings about something. They weren't a rare occurrence. Sometimes her speeches were helpful and logical. Other times, they bordered on overly opinionated, whimsical, or silly. I tried to brace for all.

"Groffman is great."

I nodded. "He's good. I'll give him that. I thought his last one took a dip, but it's bound to happen after so many slam dunks. He's getting wordier to a fault, but maybe that's age."

Luna studied the display again. "And he sells pretty well. I'm not denying that. Let the record reflect." She placed her hands on her hips.

"The record so reflects that you acknowledge he's a definite best seller."

Luna now studied me, clearly preparing for book battle. I wasn't sure where she was headed with this, but it really could be anywhere. "We also got the new Parker Bristow yesterday." She gestured with her chin to the storage room, where the boxes were waiting to be unpacked. *"Traitorous Heart."*

"I know," I enthused. "I was hoping you'd get them on the shelves for tomorrow's release. Or I can, just as soon as I sort the mail."

Luna pointed at the display. Her medium-length strawberry-blond hair sported two blue streaks today. "That's the part I want to speak with you about, you fairy princess of a boss." I tried not to wince at the awful nickname I'd never heard before. There'd likely be a new one tomorrow. "Why not feature them up front? Scratch Groffman and go with Bristow? She's a powerhouse." Luna turned to me fully. "You know she sells fantastically. She just doesn't come in hardcover or with a penis. That's not a crime. People go nuts for her stuff, especially women, and we get a ton of them in here."

I scrunched my shoulders. Parker Bristow wrote romance and was at the top of the genre. I was grateful to her and the rest of Romancelandia for the dollars they brought into the store, but I couldn't really imagine featuring a romance novel in my one and only display, and the space wasn't large enough to support a second title. "I'm not sure that's the best idea."

Luna studied me some more. She wasn't done.

"What?" I asked. "You're looking at me with judgment, and I feel like ants are crawling all over me. Say what's on your mind."

"You're being a book snob."

I let my mouth fall open. "I am not. I would never do that. I'm being practical."

"If you were being practical, you would consider putting our best seller at the front of the store and letting everyone know the new book is out tomorrow. You're holding back because you think of the romance genre as lesser." Luna had a way of saying such matter-of-fact stuff without offending others in the slightest. Maybe it was her sweet, innocent face. Maybe it was the sheer earnestness of her delivery. Regardless, peaceful self-expression was her honest-to-goodness gift.

I exhaled, hating that she was right. My decisions had to take dollars and cents into consideration these days. No, I wasn't a huge romance fan. Those books were always so hyperbolic when it came to love and sex and perfection. They set unrealistic expectations and always had the formulaic "everything is going to be rainbows and unicorns" ending that I struggled with. I'd read a handful in my teens and enjoyed them well enough, that is, until I outgrew them. I just couldn't see the appeal anymore. I stared at the ceiling. "Why do people love these things?"

"Because they are amazing escapes and they offer a little glimpse of what could be when you finally meet the right person," Luna said, with a faraway glint in her eye. "We slog around going on all the wrong dates with all the wrong people, and these books nudge us to shoot for the stars. To find our true person. I can read one a night if I let myself."

"Are you dreaming about *what could be* in this very second?" I asked playfully. "Are you undressing *what could be* in your mind?"

Luna nodded slowly and deliberately. "I also have a date tonight with that hostess at Mementos. The one with the thingy always in her hair? God, it gets me going." She began to jog in place, suck in her cheeks, and take breaths.

"I think that's called a pencil." I hid my grin.

"Yes. Gandalf in sneakers, I love girls with pencils in their hair! I wish all of them came that way."

"That's specific. And why would Gandalf wear— You know what? Not important."

Luna wasn't fazed, and instead swooned a little. "She's so cute. Don't you think she's cute?"

I thought briefly on it. The hostess was less my type than Luna's. Loud, quirky, and fun. Those were the people I tended to bore after we spent a little time together. I was too reserved for them. Too pragmatic. Didn't matter if they were men or women, and I did date both. I gave Luna's blue strand a tug. "She's beautiful, pencil and all. You're gonna have a great time on this date. I beg you to tell me all about it afterward so I can live vicariously from my status as queen of couch potatoes."

Luna bounced her shoulders. "If we turn into anything even close to a Parker Bristow–caliber romance, I'll be thrilled and pepper you with every saucy detail I can muster. My heart would pitter-patter in the most luscious, lusty sense. Maybe we can get our palms read together. We should definitely do that. I hear there's a new psychic on Eighth." She gestured to the display. "Thoughts? A decision?"

My head was spinning trying to keep up with her twists and turns. Ah, the display. "A romance novel?" I sighed. I *was* being a book snob. I felt it that time, and the self-awareness was like a thump on the back.

"They've come a long way, Hannah. You should really pick one up again and start with a Bristow, because damn. She can rip my heart out with a few well-placed sentences. These aren't your mama's romances. Your mama would faint dead away at the angst, the love, the passion."

I blinked several times as indecision swirled. "That all sounds really great, the angst and such, and maybe I'll pick one up to read, but as for the display?"

"Yes?" Luna stared at me hard, as if daring me to make the right decision.

"I can't do it," I said, finally. "It would break Kurt's very fragile heart." I walked to the cashier's counter. "And go against my literary palate, snobbish or not."

Fire flared behind her eyes. Here came her feelings. "Your literary palate is wildly off when it comes to Groffman, by the way, who writes in sentences only containing thirty-five words or more."

I shrugged. "It's a stylistic choice. Not always a fun one for the reader, but it's his thing."

Luna blew out an exasperated breath. She was in her mid-twenties, putting her nearly ten years younger than me, but there were times she seemed even younger in her emotional displays. "Screw Kurt and his Groffman-loving heart."

I smiled. "You have deep-rooted feelings about this display. Look at you. You can't let it go."

"I can't. I'd also like to keep my job."

Okay, that one landed, and she meant it to. The air left the room, as I circled around the larger implications of these decisions. I nodded and remembered my plight, my vow to turn this place around, and maybe that meant, damn it, trying something different. I swallowed my own opinion about the Bristow books in the name of business. Luna was right. "You make a very valid point. I need to be smart about this."

Her eyes went wide as she predicted victory. "So, the display?"

I decided to bite the romance bullet then and there. Sometimes you had to make a drastic decision when times were tough. I needed to shake things up, and this could be stop one. "Sign me up for the sexy angst."

Luna beamed and nodded.

"Bring on the *Traitorous Heart*. I'll explain gently to Kurt. Maybe we can set up a secondary, smaller display on one of the shelves for Groffman."

Luna chuckled in triumph, as if Judge Judy had just awarded her three hundred dollars. She began to remove the Groffman copies, one by one, dancing a little as she went. "This is the right move, Hannah. Gonna be good. I promise you." While she went about constructing and tweaking a more romance-themed display, including some snaking ivy from somewhere in the storage room as well as art supplied by the publishing company, I began working on next week's orders.

"Oh, wow. Oh, wow. Oh, wow. Hannah Tropicana, would you look at this? It was tucked in with the promotional material." Luna came to the front of the counter and slid a flyer my way with wide, excited eyes.

I picked up the flyer and skimmed it. "Parker Bristow is doing a book signing tour. Very cool." I slid it back.

Luna slid the flyer my way again and landed a finger on the bold print. "They're still booking cities. It says so right here. We're a bookstore in a city. We should be a stop on that tour."

"I can't imagine they'd take us."

"We should try, at least. One tweet from Parker Bristow about the store and we're on the map. Do you know how many followers she has? She's like Twitter's unofficial queen of quip."

I blinked several times. It wasn't an awful idea, but they were likely hitting the big chain stores. "We're pretty small."

"The worst they could say is no, right? What if they're into quaint and desolate? We might be totally their jam."

"Very funny." I stared at her as I processed the possibilities. "You really think I should reach out to her people?"

"Hell, yeah. Parker's Posse—that's what her fans call themselves—will drive from wherever for a chance to meet her. She's not just another successful author. Think about it. She's a celebrity. She's made an entire brand for herself and has rabid fans. Throngs of them."

"It's true. She has throngs." I saw Luna's point. Parker Bristow had become the face of romance for a reason. She was beautiful and charismatic in addition to being their favorite storyteller. Once her books started hitting the big screen—and there had been two films at least that I knew of—her social media star rose rapidly. Her witty tweets garnered a lot of attention. After that, she'd even become a regular on the talk show circuit and on those podcasts that did things like top ten lists and what not to wear in June. I didn't want to go as far as to call her a sellout, but it seemed like the limelight carried more appeal for her than maybe the books did. Really, what did I know? People clamored for her, and Luna was right. An appearance at the shop would be a really, really big deal. I met Luna's hopeful gaze. "I'm doubtful about our chances, but I'll reach out and give it a shot."

Ten minutes later and I was still on hold with the publicist in charge of Bristow's book tour. I moved my head slightly in rhythm with the elevator music the firm had so kindly provided as I waved at the twelfth customer of the day. Luna quickly took it from there and escorted them to True Crime. When the agent finally took my call, he was clearly in a hurry.

"Yep. Where are you guys at, this bookstore of yours?" he asked, when I explained the reason for my call. He was clearly a New Yorker, with an accent and clipped tone. I stared at his name on the form: Hill Lawson. Sounded like a law firm to me.

"Providence, Rhode Island. Downtown. A very trendy area," I rushed to include. "Great restaurants and entertainment down here. Not to mention the water."

"Interesting." He asked some questions about the store itself. Square footage. Foot traffic. Parking opportunities. I cringed as I answered, hoping somehow, we'd be enough. When we were said and done with the Q&A, I asked the big question. "So, what do you think?"

"Gonna depend on Ms. Bristow's current itinerary and how we transition her from one city to the next. I appreciate the reach out. We'll be in touch." I opened my mouth to thank him, but he was gone. Not so much as a good-bye from Mr. Lawson, busy guy that he was.

"Well?" Luna asked, once her customer had made his purchase.

"Sounds like a 'no, thanks.' But he'll be in touch, which tells me to go back to the bag of tricks. What about a raffle? That could get people excited."

"For a Parker Bristow book bundle. I have a lot of friends who would die for a complete set."

"We could easily manage that." I studied the newly assembled display at the front of the store, with the cover of the starry-eyed girl looking off into the abyss. Likely, some alpha male had swooped in and put that dreamy look on her face. I tried not to grimace and instead embrace this new release, *Traitorous Heart*, as my new cash cow.

❖

I loved the newly billowed ceiling in my bedroom. It seemed like such a simple thing, but it made me want to spin in circles like I lived in *The Sound of Music*. I didn't actually *do that*. But I thought about it in detail.

Instead, I stood with my hands on my hips, blew a loose strand of hair from my eyes, and stared up at the project I'd poured my weekend into. I was a champion of the billowed ceiling and never even knew it. Project mode served as my true happy place. Fabric selection, placement, and the right amount of billow had been the perfect antidote to keep my mind off A Likely Story's financial woes. I'd taken Saturday afternoon off, leaving the store in Kurt and Luna's capable hands, and with shortened Sunday hours, I'd given myself lots of extra time to billow that weekend, and billow I did.

"Well, look at you," I murmured to my beautiful ceiling. The finished product was breathtaking, if I did say so myself. I'd gone with a beige fabric that came with a little bit of a gold shimmer and billowed it moderately from the ceiling, with each section meeting just shy of the small chandelier in the center. "I can most certainly get used to sleeping under this."

The fabric matched my curtains, which I'd also designed for maximum swoop. My entire bedroom now looked like the fluffiest place I knew, complete with lush ivory pillows. I felt damn proud about that. So much so that I let my phone continue to ring while I took it all in. Finally, I clicked onto the call.

"Hey, Kurt."

"Hey, boss lady."

"I thought we agreed you weren't going to call me that anymore."

"We did. I'm phasing it out slowly. Feels better that way."

I accepted the small win. "What's up?"

"A woman from Barrow House called to set up details for the Parker Bristow appearance."

"What?"

"That's what I'm saying over here. We're getting Parker Bristow? I had no idea. This is like the day they added that raspberry donut to the lineup at Ralph's. Well, maybe not as big, but had I known about that raspberry donut, I would have been there right—"

"Kurt, focus." I paused and walked down the hall of my apartment to the living room, which sadly had no billowing ceiling. "They've actually put us on the calendar? I put in a request to be included on her tour but didn't expect they'd actually book us." Kurt was muttering to himself on the other end of the line. It was something he did when he had a lot of feelings. "Kurt, I can't understand you. Can you enunciate?"

"I was just saying that I was going to need a new outfit if Parker Bristow is coming to town. She's a hottie and I'd want to be at my best, so she'll at least think I'm not a schlub. What do you think of my light blue linen pants?" I imagined him ruffling his hair. He had a tendency to run his fingers through it until it puffed up, wavy and tall.

"The linen pants are great." I smiled into the phone. "So, you have a crush on Parker Bristow?"

"She's so pretty. Did you see her on *Lip Sync Battle*? I recorded it."

"Perfect," I said, with a laugh. "This signing is really great news. We need to get the word out to our customers, social media it, publicize the hell out of this thing. My head is spinning with possibility now."

"The voice mail says they'll be sending press releases to all local news outlets."

I couldn't dim the smile that crept onto my face if I'd tried. At last, I'd been granted a true shot at putting A Likely Story on the Providence map. The day we'd set up the display had been an important one after all.

"Kurt, can you jot down the details and then save the voice mail so I can listen in the morning?"

"On it, Hannah. Sans boss woman." A pause. "This is really excellent news."

"I couldn't agree more."

I clicked off the call and turned to the pair of bookends also known as my cats, Bacon and Tomato, who sat on either end of my sofa. "Parker Bristow, unlikely savior of bookstores, has agreed to come in for a signing." I waited for their response, which consisted of some blinking, and a yawn from Bacon. "This is big," I told them with a nod and headed for my much-anticipated bath after billowing. It was the most relaxing bath of my adult life. I had hope, a lifeline, and a shot at something important.

❖

"Really? The romance novelist?" Brandon asked, with a pretentious smile that said he was humoring me.

This was our third date, and he'd upped his game and taken me to somewhere that had white tablecloths and something called a waiter's captain. We'd been finished with our meal for a good twenty minutes now and had ordered more wine to continue our conversation. I always relaxed with a little wine and contributed more to the conversation. I wasn't drunk, but the tipsy line had been breached.

Brandon's dark hair was extra wavy tonight, which made me want to run my hands through it and watch it bounce a little. Not in a sexual way, more like a kid exploring an interesting museum. "Yes, and before you say it, I know what you're thinking. It's fluffy. It's gimmicky." I held my hands up. "I get it, completely. But we could use the extra attention. We've been a little light on traffic lately, and with fall coming and the temperatures dropping, that trend will only increase as people stay home more."

"You don't have to explain yourself to me." But he said it with a sidecar of judgment. Brandon and I had matched on Hearts Aflutter the month prior, more than likely because we both had a long-abiding love of literature. Given, his tastes fell on the extra-literary side of things, but it was nice to converse with someone who understood my passion. "But let me ask you, do *you* read romance novels, Hannah?" He finished the rest of his wine and let the glass linger on his lips in a move I think he believed to be sexy. It was only so-so.

"I've read them before, sure. They're not my go-to." I paused, and set my glass down. "I don't think I've picked one up in the last, what? Ten years?"

He fell back against his chair. "Thank God." He laughed. "I didn't want to say anything, but if you've cried your way through those trivial fairy tales, I was about to lose a little respect for you."

"Really?" I wasn't a huge romance fanatic either, but I'd never count it as a deal breaker. "Oh, c'mon. You have to give them some credit. They sell like crazy."

Brandon wasn't having it. "Regardless, they're the epitome of ridiculous."

"The *epitome*." I repeated the word, because it was harsh. "'Ouch,' said billions of humans across the world."

"I apologize to them, but it's true." He poured more wine and leaned forward, gesturing with his glass like he owned the world. His opinions sure blossomed when he drank. The thick hair seemed less interesting the more pretentious he became. "If you told me you lived with your nose in a string of romance novels that all had the same singular, formulaic ending, I'd have a hard time with that. That's all I'm saying."

"Then you're a book snob," I said, and dropped my jaw. "Sitting right here in front of me." I was playful in my delivery, but I also didn't think it was cool to judge someone else for what they liked to read, even if I slightly agreed with him about the genre. Without the wine, I would have nodded and avoided the debate altogether.

"I guess I am." He nodded several times, as if lost in the examination of the concept. "There are too many good books out there to fall into a pit of Parker Bristow." He raised an eyebrow. "Though she is beautiful."

"All of America sure thinks so."

"You don't? You're into women. What do you think of her?"

I guess I had put that on my profile. "She's very pretty."

He leaned close and I felt his palm just above my knee on my bare skin. "Though I'm not opposed to acting out our own sex scene."

Nope. Wasn't feeling it. I picked up his hand by the wrist and returned it to his lap.

"I don't think we're a good fit. I'm very sorry about that."

He blinked. "Then why did you go out with me again?"

I scrunched up one eye. "You have nice hair."

CHAPTER TWO

Y ou dropped him? The book guy with the luscious locks?" Luna shrieked, actually shrieked, from atop the twelve-foot ladder. She was up there stocking our highest shelf full of graphic novels, which had seen quite a surge lately. I'd made a note to up our order for next month. "Hannah, you have no life. This was the first actual incident of socializing on your part in months. Years. Probably ten."

"Easy."

"It's true." She placed the last copy and scurried down. "Talk to me about what went wrong, and maybe in the evaluation we can find the heart and soul of the problem."

"He's really high on his own opinion."

She nodded as if chewing on this new information. "Well, that does suck. So, you disagreed with him and it didn't go well. Did he yell or get violent?"

"What? No." I slid back onto the stool behind the counter. "We actually agreed. We just did so differently."

"Oh." Confusion struck Luna's features. The blue strands in her hair were pink today, always keeping me guessing. "You might have to explain that one."

The bell above the door rang and we turned. "What's up, working people?" Instead of a customer, it was my stepsister, Bo. Her real name was Belinda, but that seemed cruel. We called her Bo, which fit her much better. When my mother married her father back when I was six and she was eight, we thought we'd hit the jackpot, each gaining a ready-made sister. I still felt that way. Bo was great. Today she had straightened her curly red hair and wore sophisticated heels and a killer blazer, which meant she'd had an important client meeting at the family law firm she worked for. That or a court appearance.

Luna turned to Bo with her hands on her hips, really working the incredulous angle hard. "Your sister ditched the one potential suitor she's indulged in decades and is going to die alone in the corner of her apartment if we don't do something."

I turned to her in utter shock. "Severe. Even for you."

Luna raised her hands and let them drop. "Someone's got to do something."

"Nooo. The wavy-haired guy?" Bo asked and looked to Luna. "We had such hope for him. I'd already Instagram stalked the hell out of him and imagined where he'd go in our family Christmas photos."

I rolled my eyes, and Luna shook her finger at Bo, reenergized. "I'm not convinced this thing isn't salvageable."

"You guys talk about me behind my back? Interesting. I need to remember to be aghast later. Putting it on my to-do list." I didn't look up from my paperwork.

Bo sidled up next to me. Her perfume smelled nice. I never thought to wear perfume, just scented lotion. Putting that on the to-do list, too. "It's a good thing we're fired up on your behalf, then. Maybe you shouldn't give up so quickly."

I shook my head. "Not going to happen. He hates people who read romance novels."

Luna gasped. "Good riddance, Douche-Meister-Crazy-Hair."

"See?" I held my hand outstretched. "My good judgment remains intact."

"Sorry about the date." Bo dropped her briefcase on the counter. "I'm here for a breather before court. This is my lunch break and it's only about fifteen minutes long." Hearing my cue, I slid her a Snickers from the drawer, which she happily tore into.

"What's this one about?" I asked. Her cases always intrigued me.

"Child custody hearing. Amazing mom. Loser dad. Abusive, too. We're going to wipe the floor with this guy."

"Child support payments?" I knew the drill.

"He's behind by close to two years, yet taking vacations with his new girlfriend every three months. He uses the money as power to hold over her head. He hasn't stopped trying to control her, even post-divorce."

I nodded. "Lovely fellow, but I like these odds." My sister fought the good fight, and I loved her for it. Not only that, but Bo was damn good at her job, put in the time, and rarely lost a case. We bonded over our complementary work ethics in school, grappling for the highest grade point average. Yeah, she won.

"As for your dating life"—Bo placed a hand on my shoulder— "don't die alone in the corner of your apartment. The cats will eat you. There are other solutions."

"Bo! Stop that." I looked between her and Luna. "What has gotten into you two? I like my life on my own. Genuinely. Therefore, the fact that Brandon didn't work out is honestly not an awful thing."

My sister passed me a sympathetic look that I wanted to hurl right back at her. It was true I didn't date much and that I spent most of my free time alone in my apartment, but I wasn't antisocial. I just... did my own thing. "We both feel it's time we give you a little shove. Knock you out of the nest. You get hit on all the time. Stop being so hyperselective."

"I'm not in any kind of nest, and I'm hyperselective because it would take a lot to make me want to share what I have going. I'm happy, Bo."

"There's a definite nest." Luna made a sweeping, round gesture. "A nest of your own twiglike construction that insulates you in a snuggly cocoon of comfort but holds you back from your true womanly destiny." She finished with some flowy arm movements. She'd been reading too many new-age books and was inching her way closer to flower child status by the day.

"Well, now I'm confused." I stared at her, waiting for her demonstration to trail off. "Is it a nest or a cocoon? You lost me." I blinked.

"You're missing the point."

The bell above the green door rang and Kurt appeared. He pointed at Luna, who repeated her performance silently for reasons I was unclear on.

"Hannah's cocoon demonstration?"

"Aha, so it is a cocoon," I said, pleased with myself, and nodded to Bo.

"She's out of the cocoon," Kurt said. "At least, I thought she was. With the guy with the..." He pointed at his head.

I tossed Kurt a look. "Yes, the guy with the nice hair had me out of my perceived cocoon, but I'm going back in because I really, really prefer it. Dating sucks, and honestly? I like my life and my time alone. Nothing is missing. I went out with hair guy because you," I said, gesturing to Bo, "made me feel like I was missing out on a fundamental part of life, when really, I just think I'm not at all. I'm happy. I'm solitary. My cocoon is comfortable."

"But—" Bo started.

"Not everyone has the same need for day-to-day companionship," I reminded my sister. "I think having to deal with someone else would exhaust me. No, I know it would." Yeah, I tended to get wordy when I felt strongly about something. My mother thought I should have been an attorney myself. But she retired to Tampa with my stepfather, and I opened a bookshop, so the rest was history. Bo and I visited them once a year and hit the beach.

"Are you done?" Bo asked.

"Yes."

She continued. "You're drop dead gorgeous."

"Thank you." I sipped my coffee. "That's a non sequitur. How was your chocolate lunch?"

"I know what it is," Bo said. "My lunch was fine, but you're deflecting. My point is that you can literally have your pick of lots of people. You have to go on a ton of dates, Hannah, to find someone worthy, and with those blue eyes and a face like yours? You're gonna score big. You just have to put in the time."

"You do have the best eyes," Kurt said. "Is that weird to say to your boss?" He looked worried. "I shouldn't say things like that."

"I'll let it slide." I sent him a smile.

I'd never paid much attention to my looks. My style of dress was fairly understated and simple. Shoes were my favorite and I owned a ton, yet most were practical, comfortable, like old friends. I brushed my hair and kept it neat but didn't get caught up with fancy, intricate styles. I wore lip gloss and mascara on occasion, preferring to keep it subtle. Glamour and fashion had never been my thing. But yes, I'd grown up with people commenting on my looks since I was small, so Bo's declaration was not the first time I'd heard the sentence. I accepted my fortunate genetics, and the smiles and open doors they'd afforded me, but I also believed I had two feet planted firmly on the ground. Looks were superficial. Plus, if I *was* pretty, I definitely wasn't the *prettiest*. There were degrees to everything.

Luna tousled my hair and grabbed a second box of new books for stocking. "She's got a point. That face is going to waste in your apartment, plastered to the squawking box."

"I think they call that a television these days. Are you eighty now?" Luna didn't pause. "It's sucking all of your good energy dry."

"You don't want to go dry," Kurt said with a grimace. "Energy has got to be kept aloft. Luna's taught me a lot."

"Too much, I'd say." I flipped open my ledger. "Your concern has been noted for the record." I turned to Bo. "I learned that sentence from you, Counselor."

She touched her chest. "Because as your sister, I could not fail you." Her eyes landed on the display and the corresponding poster advertising the upcoming signing. "Get out. You march right out of this store and don't come back, you secretive minx."

I narrowed my gaze. "Well, I own the place, so that might be problematic from a logistics perspective."

Bo stared wide-eyed, as if she couldn't quite believe it. "Focus. Are you telling me that Parker Bristow is coming here, to this shop? No."

"Yes. Next Saturday," Luna said, smugly. She took great pride in having been the catalyst for making it all come together, and honestly, she deserved that credit.

Bo seemed to marvel at the information and then erupted in an uncharacteristic flutter. "I have to meet her. I've read everything she's ever written. I love her stuff."

"Rewind." I frowned. "You have? How did I not know this?"

"Maybe because I tend to buy them up when you're out of the shop." Bo high-fived Luna, who was clearly her romance novel dealer. They were doing back-alley romance deals, and I'd had no clue. "I don't need to advertise my reading habits to a sister who has strong opinions on books and their hierarchy."

"I'd never judge you for what you read, even if it is romance, sappy as it is. I just love that you read in general." To help that comment along, I kissed her cheek as I passed. "Speaking of which, do we all have our assignments for Saturday in order?" I asked my tiny team. The PR people for Bristow had sent over a list of requests—I called them demands—to help the signing go smoothly. They'd also done a great job of putting the word out there to hard-core romance fans. Bo must have been elbow-deep reading case law to have missed this.

"I'll be sweeping, scouring, and scrubbing this place until it shines," Kurt said, and cracked his knuckles.

"I'll be clearing a space for the throngs of fans to line up on that wall, that will lead out onto the sidewalk for overflow. Plus, moving some shelves so the readers have a clear exit through the back of the store after having their book signed."

"Overflow," I said, tasting the word. "I never thought A Likely Story would have a possible overflow issue. Not that I'm complaining. Time to introduce the city of Providence to the store they hopefully can't get enough of."

Bo hugged me. "I'm so happy for you, little Hannah-pants, and you will see me next Saturday, books in hand." She checked her watch. "Now I'm off to court to save the world."

I waved. "We're going to stay here and sell books."

My sister grinned. "You always have the best damn ideas."

❖

Why in the world was I nervous? It was Saturday afternoon and the Parker Bristow signing was set to begin at three p.m., and my stomach was flip-floppy, my mouth was dry, and I couldn't quite seem to settle into one spot, because they all seemed to suck. I was normally a jittery type on special occasions and reminded myself that it wasn't as if there would be much participation on my part. Our job was to sell copies of the book, make sure that the signing ran smoothly, and to make sure that the "talent"—that's how the paperwork referred to Parker Bristow—was provided for. We'd obtained all the items on the rider, including Diet Coke, bottled water specifically manufactured by Fiji, a very hard to find brand of tea, and popcorn. Yes, popcorn. I couldn't make this stuff up. Apparently, Parker Bristow would drink obscure tea and eat handfuls of buttery popcorn as she signed books and took photos. Who was I to judge? I didn't have throngs or a publishing contract. I did enjoy feeling a part of it for a little while, though.

"They here yet?" Kurt whispered, peeking his head out from the

Intrigue section, where he was helping a gaggle of college kids find something "scary, but not *really* scary."

"Not yet," I said, after handing a friendly woman her bag of purchases. It had been a high-volume day in the store, as folks seemed to want to peruse the place in advance of lining up for the signing. Exactly what I was hoping for. It was just past one, and we'd already broken all sorts of sales records. I owed Luna big-time for this one.

An hour and a half later, two well-dressed women, who didn't look like they were here for a signed copy, entered the shop. "Ms. Shephard?" the brunette asked. She wore a black suit, and yeah, that had to be designer. A week's salary of mine, at least. I fought the urge to handle the fabric of the lapel.

"That's me." I extended my hand and she shook it firmly, as I'd been taught to do from a young age.

"So nice to meet you." The brunette glanced around the shop while the other woman, a tiny blonde, began walking through the space, clearly in investigation mode. What they were searching for I was unsure. "I'm Bernadette Hall. You can call me Bernie, and we're here to prep for the signing."

"We'll want to set up here, Bernie," the blonde said, pointing at a spot not far from the cashier's counter.

I half raised my hand to be polite before speaking. "Actually, I was thinking that over there near the display might work best because—"

"No, I think Pinky is right." Pinky? Really? Okay. Pinky and Bernie, it was. "This is the spot. We can drag some of the promo art over, and we've brought some of our own for a photo backdrop." She walked a few feet to the right. "We'll need a table of books here."

"On it!" Luna said, scurrying in from the break room, where she'd been on lunch. She'd informed me earlier that the streaks in her hair were red today in honor of romance, passion, and fire.

"What else can we do?" I asked. It turned out, a lot. They had us dragging shelves out of the way, and setting up "the most comfortable chair possible," brewing coffee, prepping hot water for tea, opening the snacks, popping the popcorn, and handing out numbered cards to the masses waiting in line on the sidewalk. It was a whirlwind of a half hour, and at 3:00 on the dot, I heard a roar of applause. Sounded like the talent had arrived.

"All right, everyone. I think it's go time," Bernie announced.

And then there she was. The most beautiful woman I'd ever seen in my life.

I hadn't expected that. My breath caught and released. Parker Bristow was attractive on television and in photos, but I now realized that they'd not done her justice. Not even in the realm of reality.

"Parker, we have you over here," Bernie said, and gestured to the comfy chair we'd pulled in from the break room. I smiled but stayed out of the way. That didn't deter her.

"Hi, there," she said with a bright smile. She walked out of her way, in my direction. "I'm Parker."

I took her offered hand. "Shephard. Hannah." I made a circular gesture. "But the other way around. I don't know why I said it that way."

"Both are good names," she said, with a laugh. Her long blond hair fell across her eye in the way it never seemed to on normal people, only characters in movies. Yet hers did. I swallowed and attempted to rebound.

"We're so excited you're here." I gestured outside. "As you can see from the incredibly long line."

"I just hope they like the book," she said, and took a sharp inhale. She looked, dare I say, nervous? How was that possible when she was…her?

I pushed forward. "Well, my sister already read it and can't stop gushing. She'll be here soon."

She turned around and faced me. "Well, please don't make her wait in line. You're lending out your store to us for the afternoon, so I'd be happy to sign her book without a delay."

"Oh, that's okay. You don't have to—"

"I want to."

I paused, feeling a heated blush inch in on my cheeks. Did I mention her hair was actually shiny? "Thank you so much. I'll tell her." I came around the table to where she'd settled. "Is there anything you'd like to drink? Or eat? I could pop some fresh popcorn." God, that felt weird to say.

She laughed. "I'm so sorry that's still on the rider." She glanced at her people. "Bernie, can we get that updated, please?" She turned back in my direction, and her hair swung like a shampoo commercial.

If I'd had a rewind button, I would have utilized it. "I had an ex who ate nothing but popcorn to lose weight. Crazy and unhealthy, I know. She used to come to these things with me, and as a courtesy, we added popcorn. I'm really sorry." Her eyes carried sincerity.

"It's not a problem. We have some spare popcorn now for the break room. Silver lining, right?"

"Well, there is that." She held my gaze, and I held hers. It only lasted a few seconds, but they felt important. Everything about her did.

"Well," Pinky said, snapping us back on course. "Here's the pen you like to sign with, and here's a backup. You've got your water, lip gloss. Anything else?"

Parker uncapped the pen with flourish. "Just the readers. I don't like to keep them waiting, so let's be sure we start on time."

Bernie jumped to attention and I exchanged a thumbs-up sign with Kurt and Luna, who watched from some distance away with big grins on their faces. This was such a big day for all of us. I would be sure to introduce them later. Parker seemed approachable and kind, and I don't know why, but I hadn't expected that. At all. If anything, her team seemed higher on themselves than she did.

The afternoon flew by in a flurry of smiling readers, small talk, snapped photos, laughter, and the best of all? Lots and lots of sales. We had it set up where the readers entered through the main door of the shop to buy their copy of the book from me before being ushered to Parker for a few moments of conversation and a signature. Because they would exit through the back of the store, they'd pass through the many shelves of possible matches, which more often than not resulted in *more* sales, rung up by Kurt and Luna. I had to pinch myself. Today couldn't have gone any better. From my spot behind my register, I watched as each reader, most of them women, were treated with the utmost respect and enthusiasm from someone they clearly admired so much. Parker made each one of them feel special, which, after hundreds had gone through, had to have exhausted her. Maybe I did need to read me a Parker Bristow novel. She'd won me over today.

"She's amazing," Bo whispered in my ear after having her copy signed. "She smells like baked goods and said my favorite book of hers, *Willing to Fall*, is also her favorite she's written, and that I was right about there needing to be an additional book in the *Angry Tears* series."

"Well, you've always had good taste, Bo-Bo."

She scrunched her shoulders, which was Bo for "I'm so giddy right now."

I laughed. "I'm glad you've had a good day."

"Haven't you?" she asked. "I've never seen more people between these four walls. You gotta have cash coming out of your ears by now."

"Well, it is hard to hear you." I laughed. "This has all been fantastic for the shop. You're dead, aren't you? Meeting her."

"I'm talking to you from the grave." Bo squeezed my arm. "Just so you know, there's also a news crew out front covering the whole thing."

My jaw dropped. "You're making that up."

"I'm happy to report I'm not."

She wasn't! As soon as the signing wrapped—and it ran over because Parker wanted to make sure she signed for everyone who came out to support her—Marta Jenkins, the very spunky reporter I watched every night at ten, appeared in my store and asked to interview Parker, who was nice enough to suggest they stand in front of my sign during the interview. Bernie and Pinky stood off to the side, nodding at everything Parker had to say.

"It's been a fantastic day here in Providence, and I'm so blessed to have met so many readers," Parker told the reporter, grinning broadly. "And this bookstore is one of the most awesome I've seen anywhere on the tour. Quaint and comfortable. Everyone should be sure to check out A Likely Story. I hope to be back someday. In the meantime, I'll be buying a few books for my next flight."

I closed my eyes in gratitude, hopeful that the unexpected plug would transfer to customer acquisition. I held a glimmer of hope that it just might.

"Well, I count today a big success," Bernie said, as she helped me carry the signing table to the back of the store. "I wasn't sure what to expect, but Providence sure showed up today for Parker. Just goes to show you that every city loves her."

"Everyone was so sweet."

I turned at the sound of Parker's voice and found that she'd followed us, carrying the comfy chair I'd pulled from the break room. Apparently, she wasn't above helping or physical labor. Strong, too. Kurt and Luna had moved it together.

"Well, you were a hit, and we sold hundreds of your new one, and tons more from your backlist." We set the table down gently and Bernie dashed off to the front to gather the promotional artwork they'd brought with them.

Parker relaxed into a smile. "That's good to hear. The sales. You never know how these things are going to go. Is anyone going to show up? Will they be disappointed when they do?"

"Why would they be disappointed?" I asked, confused. I had no concept of what in the world she was talking about.

"Well, if they have an idea of what I'm going to be like and I don't live up to it. That's always a fear. Keeps me up at night sometimes. Insomnia has been an issue lately because of it."

"Really?" I just couldn't imagine someone like Parker Bristow being nervous about what a stranger thought of her. I pushed the table against the wall of the break room. It was usually where we kept the coffee supplies, but it felt infinitely more important now that it had fulfilled its celebrity signing destiny. I gave it a "good table" pat and straightened. "Well, everyone loved you, just like Bernie said. Even I was impressed."

"Even you?"

I hesitated. "Well, you're pretty famous, and—"

"It was the popcorn on the rider, wasn't it? Set the bar kind of low."

I smiled. "It made me wonder who'd be walking through that door."

"Let's have dinner."

I stared at her. I had definitely heard wrong and replayed the sentence for its actual meaning. I came up empty-handed and glanced behind me to find we were alone in the room. "Why?"

She laughed. "Why?" She glanced at the ceiling and back to me. Her green eyes were so big and expressive. She had lashes for days. "Because I'm hungry. You might be, too, though one can't be sure. Hence, the asking."

I immediately came up with eighteen reasons why I wasn't available. There was the shop to reassemble after the slight redesign for the signing. I'm a quieter person who'd been looking forward to heading home and curling up under a blanket to decompress. The cats

MELISSA BRAYDEN

probably missed me. I wanted to watch the news that night and see the story about the signing. Yet none of them toppled the insane offer that had just been extended to me to have dinner with Parker Bristow, who'd been so kind all day.

"Okay. I could eat." Bo was gonna flip. So was Luna.

Parker smiled, this time bigger. "Where should we go?"

CHAPTER THREE

There weren't too many authors who had recognizable faces. Parker Bristow, due to her relationship with the media and insane Twitter following, was one of them. She wasn't just an author, she was a personality, and the looks we got at Harry's Bar & Burger, one of my favorite haunts, only proved my point.

"So many choices. What do you recommend?" Parker asked, flipping through the menu. She'd pulled her hair up as we'd walked the three blocks to the restaurant, and made it look gorgeous without so much as a mirror. I'd have failed that test miserably.

"I usually get the sliders without onions," I said, wondering if those might be too basic for her. I wasn't exactly clear on what people with tons of money liked to eat. Surely their taste buds were different, as ludicrous as that sounded.

"I love a good burger," she said, holding her fingers together and shaking them for emphasis. "You have no idea. That's why I was so jazzed when you suggested this place."

Okay, so apparently Parker appreciated the simpler things in life and I hadn't embarrassed myself with my restaurant choice. Harry's was close to the shop and my apartment, making the place an easy go-to. "You think Bernadette and Pinky are okay?" I asked, noticing that she hadn't invited them with us.

She waved off the question. "We spend way too much time together on the road, and sometimes I just need a little space." She sipped her water. "I have no doubt that they're stressing over hotel reservations for the next stop and working through logistics of travel. I just really need a break from that, you know?"

"I can imagine."

"And you're so nice to indulge me."

"Hi, there." We turned to see a woman standing at our table, smiling at us with a spark of excitement in her eyes. "I just want to say that I love your tweets, especially the one about Hallmark commercials sabotaging your right to emotional autonomy. That GIF still kills me."

"Thank you," Parker said, and extended her hand. "Nice to meet you. Parker."

"I'm Vicki. I love your books, too. If I were more put together, I probably would have led with that."

"That's okay!" Parker said, and laughed. "They're all me, regardless."

"Would you mind taking a photo with me? I can be quick."

Parker glanced over at me, perhaps asking permission.

I reached out for the phone. "I can take it. I don't mind."

"Thank you." Parker pointed at me. "This is Hannah. She owns A Likely Story, the bookstore three blocks that way. Do you know it?"

Vicki slipped in next to Parker for the photo. "I don't, but I promise to check it out."

I snapped the photo, Vicki gushed a few moments more, and we were left on our own again to figure out our orders. Joe, the generally low-key server, had no idea who Parker was and it showed as he blandly took our order. Sliders for me and Harry's Double Wide for Parker, which I found impressive. Double meat, double cheese, all the way. She had shown up for Harry's. No phoning it in.

"I'm sorry we were interrupted earlier," Parker said.

I smiled. "You don't have to apologize to me. You have a public. I have cats."

"You do? What are their names?"

"Well, there's Bacon, who prefers his head to be scratched constantly, and Tomato, who pretends she hates me until Bacon is getting said head scratched. Then we replay it."

"I'm jealous. I wish I had a pet. I'd take a Bacon or a Tomato. Maybe mine should be Lettuce."

I smiled. "You should get one. Maybe a little dog you could carry around in a purse."

She looked thoughtful. "Is that really the persona I give off?"

I smiled and placed my thumb and forefinger close together. "In a good way."

She rested her chin on her hand. "I feel so bad for those dogs in the bags. Like little props carted around."

I loved hearing that. "I was actually only joking when I suggested it, because I feel the same way. I always cringe a little bit and want to take them home with me and let them play in the yard. Well, if I had a yard."

"Right?" A pause. "Have you always lived in Providence? It's a beautiful city. I had no idea."

"Yep. My stepsister, Bo, who you met today—"

"She was so sweet. Honestly, her enthusiasm made me smile."

"I'll be telling her that. Well, we were raised here by our parents before they fled south for warmer weather. Apparently, Tampa is the place to be when you retire. Where do you live?"

"New York mostly, but I have a house on the lake near Austin that I like to sneak away to when I need downtime. It's my favorite spot of any spot."

I imagined such a place. "That sounds really peaceful. The lake."

"I love it." She lit up and my stomach fluttered uncomfortably. I shifted in my chair. "One day I'd like to move down there permanently. I'm going to do it, too." Her smile faltered. "At least I always tell myself that."

Our food arrived, and for the next fifteen minutes, I had the pleasure of watching Parker Bristow, who'd only been a famous name and face to me in the past, grapple with a big old messy cheeseburger. It might have been the most glorious thing I'd witnessed to date. She attacked the thing both delicately and aggressively, depending on the moment. The dichotomy had me struck. With sauce running from the burger onto her wrist, she smiled at me gleefully, and I knew then and there, she was more than happy in this moment. That emotion was contagious and I wished I could bottle it.

"Hey, Hannah?"

"Yep." I fought the urge to dab the bit of mustard from the corner of her mouth. God, I wanted to, though. I think I'd developed a very fast and unexpected crush, which caught me off guard, because that kind of thing didn't happen to me. At least, not on the very first meeting with someone. My crushes had always been gradual, contemplated, analyzed, and accepted—the way most of my life was.

"Thanks for bringing me here. I know you don't know my life or my stresses, but I needed this. In a big way."

"No problem." I took a risk and got personal. Why the hell not? We'd likely never see each other again. "Rough time lately, or…"

She set down the remainder of her burger and reached for a napkin to wipe her hands. I slid the whole dispenser to her side of the table, which earned a laugh. "Let's see. I've been on the road for seven weeks now. A different hotel room every two days, with very little time to see any of the places we visit because my publishing company has a very tight budget."

"Right. You don't see as many book tours these days, so I imagine they're being frugal even with the bigger names."

"That's exactly the case." She dabbed the mustard herself, and I grieved for the moment that would never be. "So, I count myself lucky that they're invested at all. But it can be a lot. I have trouble being…I don't know…on. At least, for quite so many days at one time."

"Well, as a quieter person, I can certainly identify with the sentiment."

"Right? And all I really want is a pair of comfy socks, some yoga pants, and a damned cheeseburger that's so good it gets all over my face."

I inclined my head in the direction of the pertinent evidence. "One out of three. You're off to a nice start."

"It's fucking amazing. Let me tell you."

We laughed together at that.

When the bill came, Parker snatched it up without hesitation, and though I didn't want to be overly nosy, I did catch that she'd left an incredibly generous tip. I wondered what that must be like, having money to share with others so freely. "I don't know what your situation is tonight, if you have somewhere to be, but do you want to grab a drink at the bar? I'm having a really nice time."

I followed her gaze to Harry's well-stocked bar behind me and didn't have to give it much thought. I was having a nice time as well. The nicest in a long time, actually. "Let's do it." We picked out two stools, and the muscular barkeep tossed two coasters in front of us. "What are we drinking?"

"Old fashioned, extra cherries," Parker told him without hesitation. "Oh, um…" I glanced around for a menu, but there wasn't one within reach. I wasn't good at this. I wanted to have a signature cocktail the way Parker did to just toss out there like a boss. Unfortunately, I was more simplistic in my choices. Less cool. "I'll take a boring red wine."

"You find red wine boring?" Parker asked, and swiveled her stool so she faced me, our knees staggered. Yep, she was definitely in my space, and I could feel the warmth from her leg against mine. I swallowed. My everything tightened.

"I don't, actually. I don't know why I said that. Probably because your drink sounds more exciting."

"Oh, it's not. I love wine. Have you been to Napa in the spring?"

"I've not been at all. But wine has recently been a new hobby of mine. I'm trying to learn as I go." I tucked my hair behind my ear.

She paused and met my gaze. "One day, you'll go." She said it like she knew it would happen, and I realized that her personality was infectious because I started to believe it, too. Was this how she sold so many books? "Tell me, what does the owner of a bookstore like to read?"

This was an answer I didn't have to grapple for. "The classics are always a comfortable place for me. Jane Austen, F. Scott Fitzgerald, even his early stuff. I know." I gave my head a shake, then began to count off on my fingers. "Mary Shelley. Harper Lee. More recently, Margaret Atwood, like the rest of modern society. Oh, and Toni Morrison. I've also been known to lose myself in a good Grisham on a rainy weekend, and I'm a big J.K. Rowling fan." I was smiling, because I loved talking about my favorites, who almost felt like old friends to me. It's what made me want to open a bookstore in the first place, so I could be surrounded by their stories every day and introduce them to others.

"Those are all great choices." Parker accepted her drink from the bartender and raised her glass to him. After a long sip, "This is really good." That's when I realized I hadn't mentioned her books at all, which I felt really awful about.

"I like your work, too." It sounded lame now, an afterthought, because it was.

She laughed with kindness. "No need to say that. You don't have to read my books to be my friend. That's never been a requirement of mine."

"Well…" I wasn't sure what to say. "You're great at your job. The romance genre is huge. It keeps my lights on, so really I should say thank you."

"I love my job. That's thanks enough." She touched her cocktail glass to my wine goblet. "Cheers to good books and new friends." We smiled at each other. "You're really beautiful, you know that? Stunning." She turned back to her drink.

I took a moment to swallow my wine, delaying the process because I wasn't clear on what smart, flirtatious, or alluring thing would sound okay leaving my lips. "Thank you," was all I managed. I sipped my wine again and set it on the bar. "And I don't have a situation. The thing you said about it earlier? If I had somewhere to be, or a situation. I don't." Oh, man. Why did I say that? I had no idea why I couldn't just be a normal human, cool when I needed to be, laid back other times.

Parker's grin started slowly and grew. "Good to know." I felt a warm shiver move up my back, because it was clear she meant it. "You can be honest. You've never read a book of mine, have you?"

"Um, I probably have. I've read romance."

She shook her head, amused. "You have not."

"Read romance? I have."

"One of mine."

"Oh. Well. I will. This week."

"You definitely don't have to. But what do you have against it?" She downed her drink and signaled for another round. I needed to catch up, and thereby took a big gulp from my glass. Then another. Apparently, the stuff was working fast because I felt extra warm all of a sudden and touched my own cheeks. Luckily, it was a good, relaxing warm.

"I don't have anything against it." I paused, wanting to be honest yet polite. Definitely not wanting to sound like Brandon from the other night. "I think there's an idealism there, however."

"Ah, a cynic. Are you a part of the love sucks club?"

"What? Oh, no. I wouldn't go that far. I just think real relationships are maybe a little less wonderful than romance novels would have us believe. I think they're nice for an escape, though. They serve a great purpose."

I saw a fire ignite in her eyes. "This is where you and I differ. I believe love in the real world can be just as amazing, just as transformative."

"Ah, a romantic," I said, mirroring her earlier delivery.

"Touché." She clinked our glasses as round two arrived. "But don't you want it to be real? The longing, the passion, the connection to another human to the point that you just can't breathe without them?"

"Of course I want it, but do you believe that truly exists off the page? Have you ever experienced it?"

"No, but I want to. And I believe I just might one day." She tapped the top of the bar with her finger. "Love like that exists."

"If you say so. It wouldn't be awful to be wrong on this one."

She turned to the bartender and raised her hand. "Excuse me, sir? Yes, sorry. I don't mean to bother you. What is your name?"

He ambled over and I noticed him subtly flex his biceps as his gaze swept over Parker and then me. I smothered a smile. "Arlo."

"Arlo, have you ever been in love?" Parker leaned in, chin resting on her palm.

His whole face softened and he got an unexpected faraway look in his eye. "Yeah. I had a girl once." It was like his whole body sighed in surrender.

"How did you feel about her?" Parker asked.

"She was my whole world. Sun, moon, all of it."

Parker nodded, engrossed. "So, you believe in a 'love conquers all' mentality?"

"Nope." He frowned. "Fuck that. She cheated on me with my best buddy, but it was pretty fucking great while it lasted."

I didn't hold back my laughter this time. Arlo glanced over at me, and I held up a hand. "That's awful. I'm so sorry for what happened."

"Thanks," he said, still sulking a bit. He tossed a towel onto his shoulder. "I'll find another one day. What is it they say? Back in the saddle." He knocked on the bar and walked away to serve another customer.

"I don't know whose point he just proved," Parker said, looking confused.

"Definitely mine. The relationship went up in a ball of flames." I shook my head. "Not a romance novel kind of conclusion. Score one for me."

Parker didn't look like she bought it. "Oh, I don't know about that. If it hadn't ended badly, it would have definitely been a win in my column."

I looked at her. "We have columns. Things are getting serious between us." Yeah, the wine was definitely loosening me up. That sounded halfway coquettish.

"Are you flirting with me?" Parker narrowed her gaze in a playful manner. Parker Bristow was gay and made no secret of that in the media. I'd known before she arrived. That part wasn't news. The fact that I was now feeling comfortable with her was.

"Half flirting." I raised a shoulder, which was half of the shoulders I had.

"Damn. What am I supposed to do with that? Halfway recipro-cate?"

I didn't know how to answer, so instead drank a little more, all the while feeling her watching me. I liked it. I felt alive and playful and courageous. All things I didn't feel very often.

"I have an idea," she said, finally. "You can shoot me down. I'll find a way to heal."

"Okay," I swiveled around in my stool so that our legs were once again staggered.

"Show me these cats of yours. The sandwich cats."

She wanted to go back to my place. A quick inventory had me nervous as hell, but also not ready to say good-bye to this woman quite yet. I still couldn't get over her hair and how beautiful it was with its long, subtle curls. I just wanted to slide my fingers through its thick strands. Her eyes, wide and expressive, had held me captive all night. I could stare into them forever. The daydream made me warmer than the wine had. "All right. They'd love to meet you and then promptly ignore you." I signaled Arlo. "I'm paying for these."

She grinned. "If you insist."

❖

My apartment was dim when we entered, but through the slight illumination, I scanned the living room for any kind of clutter or embarrassing laundry items I should promptly throw my body upon to hide. Luckily, the only thing askew was a fluffy white blanket unfolded on the couch from last night's TV watching. Surely she'd get over that.

Parker wasn't shy about exploring and moved right past me into the living room. "Oh, I love it. This is beautiful."

"Thank you." I placed my hands on my hips, watching her gaze move across the worn, brown leather couch, the plush white throw rug that matched the curtains I'd hung several feet above the windows themselves to make the small room feel much bigger than it was. Thank goodness for old buildings with high ceilings. "It's not fancy or large, but I've tried to make it home."

"I don't know you very well, Hannah, but at the same time? This feels like you. At least, everything I've seen about you so far."

I shrugged. "Then I've not done too bad."

She pointed at Bacon, my large gray and white guy, who sat perched on the back of my oversized leather armchair. "Friendly?"

"The friendliest. If you scratch his head, he's your soulmate for life, so choose wisely."

I watched as she ignored my warning, pulling a low purr from Bacon. She got a little closer and nuzzled his neck. He loved it, and I loved watching him get such fearless attention. The purring escalated to motor status. Right on cue, Tomato appeared from the small hallway that led to my bedroom to check out why her brother was getting attention when she, the superior feline, was not first in line. I inclined my head. "Now you've done it."

Parker paused midnuzzle and glanced up. Her makeup from the signing earlier had faded, and though she was every bit as gorgeous, there was a youthful quality present now, too. "Hey there, little girl." Parker knelt and allowed Tomato, my orange and white striped cat, to approach her slowly. All the while, Tomato tossed sideways glances at Bacon, as if to say, "you stay right there, putz." She allowed Parker to pet her exactly three times before continuing on her way slowly, head high, like the royalty she believed herself to be. Sometimes I imagined her waving to her imaginary subjects.

I leaned forward. "Tomato says, 'You're welcome.'"

"I got that impression," Parker said, straightening. Her gaze landed on the couch and she all but fell back onto it with a weary sigh. "Two old fashioneds, and I'm feeling the effects of the long day."

"You talked to a lot of readers. That's understandable. Tired?"

She nodded and held out her hand for me. I didn't hesitate long before sliding into the spot next to her. The surreal quality from earlier, the one that kept reminding me I was having dinner with Parker Bristow, of all people, had faded into the recesses of my brain. Now I simply enjoyed her company and the little hints of tension I felt vibrating between us. We felt like two people, enjoying each other on an unexpected Saturday night. With her forefinger, she traced a circle on the back of my hand. "Do you date women, Hannah?"

The question was late in the game, but valid. "Yes. I've dated men, too."

She nodded and continued to tickle my hand with her fingertips, causing a very primal reaction that started in my chest and crept lower. She pulled my hand into her lap, turned it over, and kissed my palm. It was a simple gesture but sent a shiver through my body in the most wonderful sense. And that was all. She placed my hand on her chest, held it there, and closed her eyes. I laid my cheek against the cool leather of the couch cushion and studied her. My heart pounded, but my head took over. "Parker. You okay?"

A faint smile appeared. She opened her eyes and turned her cheek, mirroring my position. "I am. It's been a really nice day. I feel like I've escaped everything in my world that's been weighing on me. Being here with you is really nice."

"For me, too."

But her eyes closed again, and her breathing shifted to the relaxed, long breaths one takes when they're asleep. I smiled. Perhaps that streak of insomnia had reached its end. I watched her sleep for a few moments and then slowly pulled my hand away, careful not to wake her. I walked quietly into my kitchen where I prepared dinner for the cats and glanced at the clock, surprised by how much time we'd killed together between dinner, drinks, and our walk home. It was later than I thought, which explained Parker's exhaustion. When I returned to the couch, she'd slumped to the side with her feet now tucked beneath her, perfectly content with where she was. How was I supposed to disturb her now? I couldn't. I wouldn't.

Instead, I smiled and took the blanket from the edge of the couch and covered her. The weight of the fabric and the soft comfort it likely provided prompted her to stretch out a bit more. I didn't understand quite how, but I knew that Parker needed this. A night away. "Hey, Parker?" I asked quietly, adjusting the blanket around her.

She blinked a couple of times and looked up at me. "I'm sorry. I guess I feel asleep. I never do that. Ever." Another glance around to orient herself. "I can go."

"It's okay," I said. "You can stay right where you are tonight, if you'd like."

"I can? Are you sure?"

"Definitely."

She smiled up at me. "Okay."

I nodded. "I'll text Bernie and let her know where you are."

"Thank you," she said in a sleepy voice, and drifted off again. I waited a moment, feeling out of sorts, because there was a strange, wonderful woman, who was also kind of a celebrity, asleep on my couch. Mine. I quietly went about my nightly routine around her, turning off lights, locking the door, pouring myself a glass of water. I set one out for Parker on the coffee table next to the couch, just in case, and then tiptoed off to my own room, hoping Bacon wouldn't try to sleep on her head or anything. After sending a text to Bernie and updating her on Parker's whereabouts, I slipped into bed and lost myself in a haze of details. The flirting, the good conversation, the hand touching. I didn't have a ton of noteworthy nights, but I hadn't minded this one at all. I'd remember it forever.

When I awoke the next morning and headed to the living room to check on my guest, I found the white blanket folded neatly on the couch. The glass of water had been rinsed and left in the sink. On the counter, I found a note.

You are a saint for letting me stay last night. Best sleep in ages. Take care, Hannah. It was a fantastic night.—Parker

She'd signed her name in swirly script, and it occurred to me that she'd perfected the hell out of that signature over time. Ah, well. It had been a fun little adventure. I smiled to myself, folded the note, and decided to keep it as a memento. I held it to my chest for a moment first and savored the unexpected connection. I'd probably never see Parker Bristow again, but I hoped only good things for her.

Time to get back to the grind of the real world.

CHAPTER FOUR

The grind wound up a little easier that week. As I inputted the sales from the signing into the books, I was over the moon at the chunk of change we'd pulled in. It was a temporary shot in the arm, yes, but if we kept the momentum rolling, we could capitalize on this attention and turn things around permanently. I just had to keep the forward progress.

"I feel like we've had double the traffic today," Luna said, coming around the counter. "Several of the faces looked familiar, too, from the Bristow event."

It was the Thursday after the Saturday signing, and I still hadn't told anyone about my evening with Parker. Somehow, I'd wanted to hold it close and keep it for myself for just a little while. "She's been great for business. We're giving her the display for every new release from now on."

Luna shot a hand in the air in victory. "That's huge. This is gonna make a big difference. Just wait."

"Have you read the new one?" I asked, scratching my neck in nonchalance, totally selling it. No biggie. Just a girl wondering about a particular book in the store she owned.

"I read it before the signing, and again once I had her signature, all the while live texting Bo. It's a good one. Lots of unadulterated angst. I love it when authors rip my heart out and stomp on it like a slug."

"And she does that? Stomps on the reader's heart?"

"Yes, but she puts it back together again, piece by lovely piece, which is the whole point of the—"

"Romantic journey. Right." I walked over to the display, which held only a handful of books. Not that I hadn't ordered more and eagerly awaited their arrival. Sales had been excellent. "Maybe I should read it. Give it a shot. I am curious now."

"You're going to indulge in a sexy romp? Whoa, Hannah Atlanta, I didn't see this coming." She eyed me suspiciously, but I gave nothing away regarding my newfound interest in Parker Bristow's take on romance. I certainly didn't dish on my personal motivation.

"I'm trying to branch out," I said, and thumbed through the pages like a breezy person.

"She wrote a more lighthearted one last year if that's more your thing. I think we still have it," Luna said, hooking her thumb in the direction of the romance section.

"Don't worry about it," I said, and held up the new release. "This one is fine." And while I did want to check out Parker's newest and very much sought-after new release, I also wondered about the book Luna mentioned, and all the others for that matter. Parker had piqued my interest in a lot of different ways.

"Cool. Very cool. I'm going to check on this customer," Luna said. She eyed me suspiciously as she passed.

That night, as I sat in bed and furiously turned the pages of *Traitorous Heart*, I clutched the fabric of the pillowcase for support. Thomas had just learned that Whitney gave birth to his child six years back and never said a word. Not one damn word. Yet he loved that little boy with all his heart, and he hadn't even met him. Hell, he loved Whitney, too, and should have made sure she knew that before he headed off to war. What had he been thinking? He'd been very, very wrong. Yet the chances of reuniting with her were slim but not impossible.

I closed the book, needing a moment to catch my breath. How had she done this? Parker Bristow had tossed my heart into treacherous waters. Hell, now I sounded like a dramatic romance novel myself. I flipped the book back open, unable to stay away for too long, read a few pages, and then clutched it to my stomach before pressing forward once again. The journey was full of twists and turns. I wept silently as I read of Thomas's and Whitney's emotional reconciliation and nearly couldn't take it when he met his son for the first time. When I turned off the lamp at 3:32 in the morning after finishing the novel, my heart was full of love for the couple and the life they would now lead together. What the hell had Parker done to me? Who, exactly, was I?

The next morning, after whispering my customary greeting to the books and pausing for the lights to hum to life in the shop, I skipped over making the coffee and instead headed straight to the romance section and plucked *Move Through Me*, one of two copies, off the shelf. That puppy was going home with me tonight. I contemplated starting it on my lunch break because tonight seemed so very far away. I stared down at the book, enjoying the weight of it in my hands, marveling at all of the unexplored pages, and wondering if I just might have found my very own perfect match.

❖

"What I'm looking for is something that will challenge me intellectually. Do you know what I mean?"

I nodded, doing my best to interpret. If there was a perfect match out there for this young woman, I was determined to find it. I'd watched her peruse the aisles for over thirty minutes, refusing my help each step of the way. I'd only just now got her talking and wasn't going to fail her.

"Are you thinking classical fiction, or something more contemporary?"

"Definitely contemporary. I don't like dusty books, you know? I don't like the way the characters speak. I don't identify."

"Fair enough. Nothing from too far back."

"And if possible, I'd like it to have animals." She blinked at me, happy with her addition. "And dancing."

Okay, we were making progress. "Modern day animal book with dancing. Follow me." The wheels were turning, but I had a section of contemporary fiction that would likely be our saving grace. I scanned the titles, many of which I'd read firsthand, and the rest I'd made a point to acquaint myself with. Aha, and there was the book I sought, *Little Bit*. I scooped it up and showed her the cover: a teenage girl, who couldn't have been much younger than my customer, standing in a field with a golden retriever. "It's a coming of age novel about a young woman and a dog who grow up together. She's a cheerleader, so there's maybe a little bit of dancing tossed in. Heavier on the dog, though."

She snatched it from my hands and stared at the cover with a newly displayed hunger. "Yes. I'll take this one."

I smiled. "I really think you'll enjoy it. It has comedy, a strong plot, and will tug on your heartstrings."

She nodded, her eyes still glued to the cover.

"Anything else I can help you find?"

"No, just this one." She held the book against her body in a manner one could almost classify as a hug.

"Let me know what you think once you're finished. If you like it, there's more where that one came from."

"Thank you. I will," the girl said, beaming.

"Kurt can check you out up front."

I set off for the children's section because I'd caught sight of a preschooler wreaking havoc on the lower shelves earlier that morning. As I walked, my phone dinged in my pocket. I winced. I hated people who let their notifications ring or ping in public spaces, but I'd been waiting to hear from Bo on the outcome of her custody case that would likely be decided today. However, the message wasn't from Bo.

Hannah Shephard, come meet me in Mystic. Please?—Parker

I took a moment to work that through. Surely this wasn't a text from Parker Bristow. Yet I didn't know any other Parkers. I glanced around the shop to see if Luna had popped in early and was playing a joke on me. No such evidence. I ran my thumb over the screen. The words didn't disappear, as I somehow suspected they might. Mystic? As in Connecticut? I slid the phone back into my pocket because I didn't know what else to do. Then I pulled it right back out again.

Parker Bristow? I typed back.

It was only a moment or two before a selfie of her in yet another bookstore popped up, validating her identity. I could see Pinky in the background, setting up for a signing. Parker was smiling and I found the happiness infectious, mirroring her expression. *I had Bernie send me your number. Come to Mystic. Say yes. I want to see you.*

"What has you so happy?" Kurt asked, as he passed me in the central aisle. "It's nice."

"I happen to like Fridays in the shop." I shrugged. "It always feels like the weekend starts early. People have a buzz about them. They seem excited."

"You *should* like this Friday," he said, lowering his voice. "Sales are climbing already." Apparently, the shot in the arm had worked, and it hadn't just been a fluke. It seemed that once a customer discovered our store, they actually came back. "Are you a fan of hummus?"

I squinted. "I'm sorry. Hummus?" My mind was on Parker and the text. I wanted to get back to it without appearing obvious.

"Have you heard of it? I bought some for lunch," he said, as if this were premium information. "I found it yesterday at a health food store on Twelfth. It's good stuff. If you haven't tried it, you really should. Hummus. This one has red peppers."

That was Kurt, loveably unique, with a sprinkling of naïveté. His book knowledge couldn't be beat, especially when it came to obscure fiction, which was why I treasured him at the shop. He had a list of titles in his head that no one could compete with. That, and the fact that he and Luna were now family. I patted his shoulder. "I have heard of hummus, and I'm so happy you've found it for yourself."

I walked on and considered the offer on the table. Mystic, Connecticut, as far as I knew, was a cute little town on the water, less than two hours away. A jolt of excited energy zapped me at just the thought of driving over and seeing Parker today. Was it even logistically possible? It was. I wasn't scheduled again at the shop until Sunday, opting to take an occasional Saturday off for myself. I typed back a tentative reply. *This is an unexpected invite.* Maybe. I wasn't really the spontaneous type. Dinner? Sure. But a day trip at the drop of a hat? That was a bigger leap.

My phone buzzed. *Pack a bag.* Make that an *overnight* trip. I rolled my head in a circle, loosening my neck as I considered my options. "As if I have one," I mumbled, knowing full well I wasn't going to say no. No one had snagged my attention the way Parker had. The whole thing made me nervous, but it also felt like something I couldn't turn away from. What was it my friends had called it? My cocoon of comfort? Maybe it was time to break the heck out of that and see if I had wings.

My fingers went to work. *I've always wanted to explore Mystic.*

CHAPTER FIVE

The signing still had another thirty minutes when I arrived, and the line for Parker's signature still stretched around the small building. I looked up at the sign above the store that read "Little Red Riding Book." Catchy name. I tried not to be too jealous that they'd thought of it. The bookstore also had actual window displays, showcasing cozy little reading scenes. I had to give them more credit for a clever way to snag the attention of pedestrians walking by. I filed that away, always learning. I could borrow that easily enough.

Not wanting to be any bother, I joined the line and pulled my own copy of *Traitorous Heart* from the messenger bag on my shoulder. I'd been waiting about fifteen minutes before nearing the entrance.

"Are you as nervous as I am?" the young woman in front of me asked. She held four books of Parker's in a stack. Each copy showed heavy signs of rereading, which I now completely understood.

"I'm sorry?"

"To meet Parker Bristow. I'm like freaking out right now. She's my favorite. I've read every word she's ever written. In books and online."

The line moved forward and I smiled. "Yes. I'm very excited." I held my copy up. "I loved this one."

"Everyone says she's so nice in person. I'm hoping they'll let me take a photo."

I nodded. "She's very nice, and I have a feeling she'd be happy to take one with you."

The girl fanned herself as she rounded the corner into the store. "Here we go." Her eyes went wide and she clutched her books. Parker sat behind a table with Bernie to her left, helping keep things organized. Pinky stood behind Parker, likely ready to move any lingerers along politely, the way she'd done at A Likely Story. I will say one thing for the road team—they were a well-oiled machine.

The girl in front of me was next. She handed the first book in the stack to Parker, who smiled up at her warmly, set down the book, and offered her hand. "I'm Parker. Thank you so much for coming."

The woman shook it several times past what was standard. "I'm Tegan, and I love you. A lot. I always have."

"Oh, well, thank you. I mean that sincerely. I appreciate the support."

Tegan held her palm out like the stop signal to correct herself. "I love the books, too. Not just you. This one is my favorite," she said, sliding forward a title I'd yet to read. I filed it away, knowing I'd be binging more in the future, and recommendations mattered.

Parker took a moment to sign each of the four books, handed them back to their very grateful owner, and then turned her gaze to the next in line, which just so happened to be me.

"Hi," I said, and handed over my copy. Bernie smiled at me. Pinky relaxed, understanding she had a moment or two free from her pseudo security detail.

Parker stared up at me. "Hannah. What in the world are you doing?"

I slid my book a little closer to her. "Having my book signed. To Hannah, please."

She pulled her face back in confusion. "You don't read romance."

"Oh, but I do." I pointed down at the book. "I read that one just recently. Loved it." I tapped the cover. "Hannah with two ns."

Parker opened the book to its title page with hesitation, as if she wasn't quite sure if I was messing with her or not. Moments later, she slid the book back to me and turned to the next person in line. I walked farther into the store and took a moment to peruse its aisles. The space was adorable and had a children's reading competition advertised. Another brilliant idea. If I followed Parker around the country, from city to city, I'd likely come up with a million new concepts to bring back home. I shook my head at the far-fetched notion. I skipped the romance section, as it was swarming with the romance readers who'd come to see Parker, and walked along the poetry aisle instead. I touched the cover of a collection on the topic of lasting love. The intertwining hearts made of what looked to be dandelions on the cover made me smile. I looked down at the book I'd had signed by Parker and opened it.

Hannah, welcome to the romance club. P.S. I think about you more than I should. There, in formal script, between the two, was her name. I reread the postscript, and my heart filled and sped up. I'd thought of her, too, but felt sure I'd been alone in that. Today proved otherwise. I peeked around the corner and stole a glimpse of her finishing the last of her signing.

"There you are," she said, ten minutes later. I dropped the book of poetry I was thumbing through like the graceful human being I was and leaned down to retrieve it. She beat me there and held it out to me. We were both still crouched on the floor. I hadn't moved because I was staring into the very green eyes I'd not thought I'd see again. I wasn't sure why she hadn't stood up.

"You didn't have to wait in line," she said, quietly, and pushed herself into a standing position. She wore all black with the exception of a green leather jacket with a zipper. Today, in heels, she was taller than me. An illusion. I had the slight height advantage between us.

"I know, but I wanted to. I loved the book and I wanted your signature in my copy, just like everyone else who showed up here today."

"I'd have signed your book anytime you wanted, you know."

I met her gaze. "I didn't. I do now." The air between us held a rare charge. I wanted to bottle it and save it for always, get drunk on it when I needed to. Why couldn't more moments be like this one? As nice as it was, there were eyes on us, and I could tell Parker was aware of them, too. Fans of hers were observing our conversation with interest, all the while feigning preoccupation with random books upon the shelves. "Wanna get out of here now?" she asked, quietly. "Just us?"

I nodded. "Lead the way." The truth was that I'd have followed her anywhere, happily. She tossed a wave over her shoulder to her team, thanked them, took my hand, and led me through a storage room and down some steps to the back of the building that spilled us out into an alley.

"This is very glamorous," I said, of the trash heap we stood next to.

"Well, I wanted to show you a little bit of Mystic. I thought that was the idea."

I laughed. "It's breathtaking." The only problem was that my gaze never drifted from her face when I said it, making my inner thoughts now public knowledge.

Her mouth, possibly the most expressive part of her face, relaxed into a lazy smile. "Were you surprised to get my text?"

I nodded. "I didn't think I'd see you again."

"Well, I couldn't let that happen. You left me intrigued." She raised one shoulder. "When I saw we were doubling back to the Northeast, I took a chance you'd be free."

"And here I am. In a dirty alley in Connecticut."

She laughed. "Let's remedy that. Walk with me by the water, and intrigue me some more. I'll try to be half as interesting."

"I'm in."

On our way, we strolled among the tiny shops in the very quaint town, ducking into a pet boutique that had food and water on the sidewalk for passing dogs, of which there were quite a few. "I feel like Bacon would like this guy," Parker said, and held up a mouse with glasses.

"He definitely would." I picked up a magnet with a cat wearing hair curlers and set it back down absently. "You remember my cats' names? Wow. Ten points for Gryffindor."

Parker winced. "I'm Hufflepuff, but I'm very appreciative of the sentiment." She kept hold of the mouse and walked farther down the aisle.

I had to pause right then and there because I'd just spouted off a Harry Potter reference, and Parker hadn't missed a beat. I couldn't properly explain how much of a turn-on that was. I gawked after her. Yes, gawked. Ten points for Hufflepuff, indeed.

"Oh, and for Tomato," she exclaimed, turning around, glowing with pride. She held up a round catnip-infused tomato.

I shook my head. "Get out of town. I can't believe that exists. That's hysterical."

"My gift to them."

"They're going to love those. Thank you."

She reached out and squeezed my hand. "My pleasure."

I stood close to Parker as she paid for the cat toys, giddy to spend more time with her, thrilled that I'd done the unexpected and traveled to meet her, yet nervous as hell as to where this all might lead. She accepted the bag from the attendant, who stared at Parker like he couldn't quite place how he knew her, and slid it into my messenger bag.

I turned to her as we continued our perusal of the town, now down another side street. "Do you think my overnight bag is okay in my car? I left it at the lot near the bookstore."

"We can double back for it later. Don't you think? You're staying with me, by the way. I owe you after last time. My suite has an extra bedroom that's all yours. A zillion pillows. You're going to love it."

"I don't mind renting a room. There are a thousand bed-and-breakfasts in this area."

Parker paused on the sidewalk and stared off at the water in the distance. "Seems like a shame to do that. Don't you think?" She passed me a glance. "I won't bite, I promise."

"Okay, then." I heated all over, and was pretty sure it showed.

She walked on. "Unless you want me to."

Breathe in. Breathe out. "Negotiable." That earned a laugh.

We hadn't made it to the water yet, despite our best efforts. There was the hat shop next, where Parker tried on upward of ten, modeling them for me to help her decide which one worked best. "You have hat face," I told her, in amusement.

"What's hat face?" She placed the fedora, which had looked beyond sexy on her, back on the rack.

"It's when you do this." I pushed my lips out, dropped my eyebrows, and smoldered slightly to the best of my ability.

"I don't do that," Parker said, and proceeded to pop on a newsboy cap and make the exact same hat face as before.

"Do so. You're doing it now. Look at you and your hat face." I laughed because how could one not?

"What are you talking about?" She checked herself again in the mirror. "Oh. I do make hat face. Well, hell. Why stop now?" She exaggerated her hat face, which had me laughing all the more.

"People are staring at you." They weren't. There were two other people in the store, tops.

"Why?" she asked through exaggerated duck lips. "Why would they stare? I don't understand."

"Because you're acting like a weirdo, and you're famous." I

pointed at the newsboy cap and moved in closer. "That's also the best hat of the day." I snatched it from her head. "This time, it's my treat."

"Hannah. No. You don't have to do that. Let me."

"Doing it." I headed to the register and could feel her on my heels.

"You're buying me a hat, huh? Things are getting interesting. I really feel like they're heating up between us now that hats are involved. Feels like a new level of intimacy."

I frowned on purpose. "Oh, I don't know about that. I'm buying this hat for you because I need you to make hat face every time you put it on. Strictly an amusement-based decision and very selfish."

Parker shook her head. "Well, now I have to fulfill my destiny. I can't stand to be a disappointment."

"The world will thank me for that lip action." I winked at her, feeling playful and confident. The look that came over her said that I'd affected her. I handed the cap to the shop owner. "One hat, please." The fact that it was forty-five dollars plus tax made me swallow a surge of panic, but I reminded myself that this was a special occasion. I'd make up for it in other ways. Maybe skip a few luxury items at the grocery store. I didn't actually need ice cream. We declined the bag, and Parker popped the cap back onto her head as we hit the sidewalk. I stood by my earlier opinion. She looked amazing in it. Cute, yet sophisticated.

"Thank you," she said, touching the cap's bill. "I think we're going to be great friends, me and my new hat. I'll think of you each time I wear it."

"Good." I liked that a lot, actually. I stole glances at her in my cap as we walked.

The September weather was crisp, and the tree branches swayed slightly, making me happy I'd worn my light jacket. It was a fitted utility jacket that I'd always considered stylish until I met Parker. My wardrobe paled in comparison. Not that I minded. With the sun on its way down, I snuggled into it as Parker watched me.

"It will be colder near the water."

I shrugged. "I'm okay with cold."

"Are you sure? We don't have to walk down. I just happen to be a sucker for scenic views when I'm with someone I happen to like spending time with. Okay, you're not bad on the eyes either."

"Flatterer."

"Hey, I'm not a romance writer for nothing."

I slid my hands into the pockets of my jacket. "You don't have to sell me, Parker. What do you think? I drove all the way down here just to see *you*? Bring on the money shot already."

Though we both knew I *had* dropped everything and showed up when she asked, she had the decency to laugh at my unilateral demand. "Your wish is my command, and I mean that." Hell, she really looked like she meant it, too. That comment inspired a shiver as I thought of a few other wishes. Parker was beautiful, smart, and fun. Why was she spending her time with someone as unexciting as me? I decided to shut the hell up, shelve the recriminations, and enjoy the moment for what it was. She liked me. I should accept that. I would, in fact.

When we arrived on the dock, the entire seaport came into view. I nearly hugged myself at how quaint it all seemed. A little village of boats of all shapes and sizes bobbed away in their respective slips. "I wonder what that kind of life must be like, you know? Setting sail on the water for an afternoon, or a weekend even, if we're talking about the yacht down at the end."

Parker followed my gaze. "I don't own a boat, but I've chartered quite a few."

I turned to her, eyes wide. "A yacht? Have you rented a yacht? You have, haven't you?"

"Only twice. I can confirm that it made for a fantastic time. I recommend it."

I shook my head and followed her to the edge of the dock, where we took a seat and let our feet dangle. "One minute I remember how fancy your life must be, and then another I completely forget you're... you. Have you passed Nora Roberts in sales yet? Never mind. Don't answer that. I'll get a complex."

"First of all, I have no idea. I don't keep up with sales and charts. I have people for that. I just want to write books. Second of all, why should you get a complex? You're the one who gives me a complex. You're really beautiful, Hannah, in case you haven't noticed, and incredibly smart, and well-spoken. I'm honored you're choosing to spend your day with me."

I gaped. "You are *not* nervous around me. Do not even pretend. You just signed books for hundreds, and if that didn't make you nervous then I certainly don't."

"You do, too. I'm nervous right now, but in a good way." The wind lifted the portion of blond hair outside of the cap, and it settled down her back again. I could tell she'd curled it expertly that morning, and now it had a very sexy windblown quality that had me preoccupied even beyond her ridiculous declaration.

"Well, there is no way you're going to be able to convince me of that." I folded my arms and stared out at an incoming sailboat. And then back at her newsboy cap and sexy hair, which won the competition for beautiful visual.

"You can remain unconvinced all you want, but it's true," Parker said. "You give me butterflies. Good thing I happen to like them." I wondered what it was like to kiss Parker, to take her face in my hands, pull her in, and sink slowly into those lips. I exhaled. The exercise in control helped. "What are you thinking about?" she asked.

"The shop," I said automatically. There was no way I was confessing. "It's seen better days financially." Really? I'd skipped one admission for one easily as embarrassing.

"Your store's not doing well? Oh, no."

I shrugged. "No bookstore is, I would imagine. But I owed you that hat, because ever since your signing, we've had a definite uptick. People know we're there now. The media attention helped a ton."

She beamed. "Then it was well worth it. Invite me back sometime. I'll come."

"You have a standing invitation."

"Dangerous," she said, took her cap off, ran her hands through her hair, tousling it all over the place, and put the cap back on her head.

I grinned.

"What?" she asked.

"You're a walking hair commercial nearly all the time. I can't believe some company hasn't snatched you up for that."

"I've had offers to endorse certain products on social media. They pay way too much for that kind of thing. I don't think I could stomach being an influencer, at least on purpose."

"They'd pay you to post about a conditioner or hand lotion?"

She nodded. "Exactly. Feels like selling out, though, and so much of my success has been because of my brand, and I want that to remain true. I'm not sure pimping moisturizer is…me."

I admired that. She could likely make a killing from one tweet alone, given her gigantic following. I dropped my palms to my knees with a slap. "Well, I for one don't think you need it. Your books do enough for you."

She studied me with a dubious expression. "Says the non-romance reader. It was nice of you to have a book signed, though."

"I've read that book three times now."

She barely moved. "I can't tell if you're lying or not."

"I especially enjoyed page eighty-three when Thomas caught Whitney by the waist, but then she turned the tables and got a little handsy herself. I liked her take-charge attitude. We can all learn from Whitney."

She stared at me, not moving at first. "Well, color me shocked. You read the book."

I held up the number three. "That's what I've been trying to say. I loved the book."

Parker blinked, as if still not fully buying in. "You're not into romance, though."

"Well, it's—"

She held up a hand. "I have questions. But they can wait."

"They can?" I laughed. "This sounds serious."

"It's everything. But we need food first, and this conversation is too important to be had while we're hangry and squinting."

"Who squints when they're hangry?" I tilted my head in confusion.

"I squint when I'm nervous. The hangry is in addition."

Well, that was new information. "Does that mean you're nervous as to what I thought of your book? That's insane." It was also incredibly flattering. I was no one important in the scheme of publishing, and she was a blockbuster. Parker adjusted her sitting position. She *was* nervous and not sure what to do with herself. The extra fidgeting only highlighted it all the more. I couldn't wrap my mind around it.

"It's not important," she said, deflecting. It was adorable, and I felt my midsection flutter pleasantly. "What kind of food makes you happy? I very much like seeing you smile."

I laughed, because it was a really smooth line. She was good. I'd give her that. "I hear the pizza in Mystic is pretty good."

CHAPTER SIX

When a perfect pizza like the Grecian Delight does what it promises and delights your taste buds, you pay attention. It was those little bursts of special that I had learned to pay attention to over the years. They mattered. Maybe it was because my bursts were generally small that I collected them so reverently. I didn't mind. I'd always liked my small life. Somehow, it suited me. Big things didn't happen to Hannah Shephard. Small ones did.

"What are you thinking about with that faraway look in those baby blues?" Parker asked, slice of pizza in midair.

I pulled myself back to the moment, the pizza, the woman before me. I set down my knife and fork. "Just that this food is amazing, and the company's not half bad either. Okay, better than that."

"Then we're in agreement." She took a bite, and I watched as a string of cheese stretched from her mouth to the slice. Somehow, she made it look good. This was the second messy meal I'd watched her skillfully embrace and master. Color me impressed.

"Excuse me." We glanced up. "I'm Maureen, the assistant manager. How are things tonight?"

"Fantastic." Parker held out her hand. "Parker. So nice to meet you. This is my friend, Hannah."

Maureen smiled warmly. "Hello." She then shifted her focus to Parker, and why wouldn't she? "We know who you are. I heard you were in town for the signing at the bookstore."

"Yes. Earlier today. Everyone was so friendly."

Maureen placed her hand on her heart. "I'm an avid reader, and most of the staff knows you from your top ten tweet lists. We're so happy you're here, so dinner's on us tonight. Oh, and would you mind taking a photo for our wall before you leave?" She pointed behind her. "We have a collection."

"That's very sweet of you, and I don't mind at all," Parker said. She turned to me. "Be right back." I watched her follow the manager across the small restaurant to an appropriate backdrop that featured the name of the restaurant, Mystic Pizza. Parker smiled her gorgeous smile alongside a radiating Maureen. I took a sip of my wine and watched her return to the table, hips swaying slightly, tiniest hint of cleavage glimpsable. God almighty, help me.

"You're back." I stole a pepperoni.

"Miss me?"

"Maybe a little."

"I love the progress we're making." She snagged another slice of pizza, and I watched her eat it, enjoying the show. It was dark outside now, and we sat by the window watching people pass. The night came with a new and a very palpable charge that moved and swirled in the air all around us. Maybe it was anticipation, possibility, or the unknown. I didn't know what the rest of the evening had in store, and I liked it that way. I was trying hard not to think too far ahead, because I was known to shy away from things outside of my comfort zone. Instead, I floated along, enjoying myself.

"So, lay it on me," Parker said, as she slid back into the booth across from me.

"I think you're going to have to be more specific."

She swallowed. "What did you think of the book?"

"Ah." I sat back. "Your new release or another one? I've read a handful."

She inhaled and exhaled slowly. "Any. All. You pick."

I grinned at the obvious tension that had overtaken her body. "I started with the new one, *Traitorous Heart*, and loved it so much that I went from there. I've loved every book I've read, and that is not in any way an inflation. You know your craft."

She nodded several times, her eyebrows drawn in. "Are you just saying that because we're here together, and you're being nice?"

"I'm not that nice."

"Yes, you are."

"But I'm also highly opinionated. Sometimes to a fault. Ask around."

She laughed. "I did see that side of you in Providence. You can be feisty." She raised her wineglass and peered at me over the top. "It's sexy as hell."

I blinked several times and did my best to keep the blush off my face, but the heat that hit my cheeks told me I'd lost that battle. "Can I ask a personal question?"

She folded her arms. Her foot touched mine under the table. I wasn't sure if it was accidental or on purpose. "Go for it."

"Well, you came out publicly years ago."

Parker met my gaze. "True."

"And pretty much everyone loves and adores you."

"I don't know that I'd go that far."

"Trust me on this." I pressed forward, shrugging "So, why not write a book about a lesbian couple?"

She nodded and seemed to mull over the suggestion. "I've considered it. Trust me."

"But?"

Parker sighed and eased a strand of wavy blond hair behind her ear. She made even simple gestures seem extra attractive. "I worry my audience won't follow me. I've made my career on the alpha male and the every girl. It's what I'm known for."

"And don't get me wrong, you do it well. I just can't help but wonder what you'd be capable of doing with a couple you had more of a firsthand investment in."

She smiled. "Well, when you say it like that…"

"Just something to think about." I met her gaze. "You'd have one built-in reader."

"I feel like a challenge has just been extended to me."

I shook my head. "I wouldn't dare presume to know more about your job than you do. I just would love to get my hands on that book once you write it."

She nodded slowly. "On that very thought-provoking note, why don't we get out of here? We can take the long way to the bookshop for your car. Soak up a few more minutes with the adorable town of Mystic."

As we left, Parker took another photo with a nearby table of women, and then Maureen generously sent us home with a bottle of red wine. "That's the good stuff, too," she whispered and patted me on the back.

"What's that like?" I asked, when we hit the streets. The effects of the wine were present and accounted for, but I was the good kind of tipsy. Far enough in to be at ease and warm, but not yet drunk. The perfect buzz.

"What?"

"To have people know who you are and buy you dinner. On one hand, it has to be awesome. On another, I would imagine it's unnerving."

"It used to be unnerving. Now it's just part of the job." She held up the wine bottle. "Perks are nice, though. Do you think you have another glass in you? We could pop this thing back in the suite. Unless you're sleepy. In that case, I won't keep you up."

I stared at her. "Are you trying to get me drunk?"

She smiled. "No way. I don't want you drunk. I want you happy."

I nodded as we walked the now darkened sidewalk. "Oh, I am."

"Good." We looked at each other and then away like a couple of eighth graders. Parker, I was learning, was confident and friendly and bold, until the moment she wasn't. There was something to that dichotomy that I couldn't quite grasp just yet. Yes, I'd said *yet*. I was interested in learning more.

After swinging by the bookshop to pick up my car, I met Parker in the lobby of the Hilton, where we encountered Pinky having a drink at the restaurant's bar. Parker waved, Pinky waved back and then regarded us with noticeable interest before finally turning back to her drink. Did Parker do this a lot? Meet some local and befriend her, invite her back to her hotel room? I hoped not, but the world was faster paced than my everyday life indicated, and I was aware that such things happened.

"She's nursing a broken heart," Parker told me, and inclined her head in Pinky's direction. "Husband left her for his secretary, and I'm not even making that up."

"Ouch," I said.

Parker nodded with a wince.

I looked behind me back to the bar. "Maybe we should donate our wine."

"Not a chance."

We stepped onto the elevator together and our words seemed to fade. I stood on one side, watching her. She stood on the other, watching me. Hell, undressing me with her eyes was a better description, and I felt it all over. I knew right then and there, as the elevator climbed higher and higher, that I wanted this woman. My fingertips tingled to touch her. My body wanted to lie pressed against hers. We weren't a couple, and I had no idea what it was that we were doing with each other tonight or back in Providence. However, I'd never felt such noticeable chemistry with another person before. When Parker sat across from me, I didn't just see her. I felt her. When we walked the streets that afternoon, I was aware of her proximity at any given moment. Two steps ahead, or three behind. I always knew.

The elevator dinged, and we stepped out. Parker carried the wine, and I carried my bag.

"I'm down here," she said, and took the bag from my hand. The hallway seemed extra quiet, so our voices followed the trend. "I'll get this."

"Thank you." I appreciated the small gesture. Those kinds of things resonated with me and made me feel important. Parker let us into her hotel room, correction, hotel suite and I gaped. This had to be some kind of penthouse for VIPs, because I'd never seen this kind of a setup at a run-of-the-mill hotel chain.

"Not bad, huh?" Parker asked.

"I think that's an understatement."

She took off her jacket, dropped it over the back of the chair, and opened the wine. I used the time to explore the main living room. There was an open door to the right through which I glimpsed a luxurious king-sized bed with way too many pillows for any one person. Behind me, there was a second bedroom, with a more modest approach. Likely meant to be mine. Maybe.

"For you," she said, and handed me a glass of the Chianti Maureen sent home with us. I drank from the glass, rather than sipped, which earned a laugh.

"Well, okay," she said, and touched her glass to mine. "Bottoms up, then." She also took a healthy swallow in solidarity. I hadn't been fully nervous until that moment, but standing there in Parker Bristow's hotel room had me jittery. I took another swallow and watched as she set down her own glass and took three steps toward me, leaving her in my space. She smelled amazing, like peaches and sugar.

"Where in the world did you come from?" she asked quietly, and touched my bottom lip with her thumb.

"I just run a bookshop," I said, lamely. I trembled, not caring if she noticed.

She took my glass and set it on the end table next to hers, making her intentions clear. "There's nothing *just* about you, Hannah." I liked the sound of my name on her lips. I wanted her to say it some more but didn't dare ask. I watched as she took my face in her hands and leaned in slowly. She was giving me an out, taking her time in case I wanted to say no, step away. I didn't. I met her halfway, my eyes fluttering closed as our lips met.

Nothing was the same after that.

The rush hit. I'd never experienced anything like it. A cascade of unexpected sensations were upon me as her lips, warm, soft, and insistent, clung to mine. She tasted sweet, like the wine. I adjusted the angle to deepen the kiss and heard her murmur quietly in appreciation. I parted my lips and let her tongue explore. My legs shook, and my center ached, but it was Parker I focused on. My hand crept from her waist to her neck and down to the edge of her neckline. The bottom of my palm could feel the curve of her breast. It made me wet. It made me crave.

"Oh, my," she whispered against my lips, and went in for more.

Everything in me surrendered to her, while at the same time asking for more.

With her tongue battling mine, her lips kissing me expertly, my whole body vibrated with longing. I dropped my hand a tad, allowing it to settle on the top of her breast, and felt her react beneath my fingertips. Feeling encouraged and assertive from the wine, I dropped that hand all the way and palmed her breast more forcefully, infinitely aroused now. She wrenched her mouth from mine and sucked in air. With her eyes still closed, the expression on her face could only be described as tantalized. I loved the word but loved her depiction of it more.

She placed her mouth next to my ear. "Take it off me," she whispered. I didn't hesitate. I grabbed the hem and pulled the shirt up and over her head, exposing a low-cut lacy pink bra. My mouth watered.

Part of her nipple peeked out and I wanted to lick it, swirl it with my tongue. She watched me with a hooded gaze. "That, too." She glanced down. She wanted me to take off her bra. Invited me to. I pulled the straps down first, exposing more of her shape, and both nipples. Her breasts, I could tell, were full and round. I bit the inside of my lip to steady myself, a reminder to go slow. She was gorgeous. I undid the front clasp and took in the sight of her breasts fully exposed. Holding her by the waist, I dipped my head and drew one of those nipples into my mouth, sucking slightly. She pulled me to her and threaded her fingers through my hair while making quiet sounds of satisfaction that I planned to memorize forever. I moved on to the second nipple, licking it, moving my tongue in a circle over its expanse. I was drunk on her already. "I think I'm going to want you to do wonderful things to me."

I raised my head, met her gaze, and nodded. Her lips were parted and her breathing accelerated.

"Here?" I asked.

She smiled. "Or the bedroom. What would you think of going into my bedroom with me, Hannah?"

Staring at her topless, I thought that sounded like the best idea I'd ever heard in my life. But to Parker, I simply said, "Lead the way."

She did, and when we arrived in the spacious master bedroom, Parker climbed on the bed, knelt, and waited for me. I walked to the side of the bed and faced her. The lights were low but not off. I could hear the quiet whir of the heater behind us. Her eyes never left mine as she moved in for a kiss that scorched and encouraged. Parker's lips parted for me eagerly, and my tongue was in her mouth without delay. The intimacy of the kiss turned me inside out. I barely noticed that she was undoing the buttons on my shirt until it hung open. She pulled back and stared at my bra, my breasts, and ran her hands down from my shoulder blades, over the black fabric and to my stomach. "You are so fucking hot," she breathed. "I thought so the moment I laid eyes on you. God, just look at you."

I grinned, trying to imagine that first moment playing out without my knowledge. My brain wasn't exactly working, though. I blinked back to the present. She pulled the shirt down my arms and caught me around my waist as she kissed me once again. She kissed her way to my neck and then up to my ear. "Can I touch you, Hannah?"

Her breath tickled, and my arousal at her words went through the roof. I had a feeling that had been her goal. I noticed my hips were moving all on their own.

She'd noticed, too, and smiled against my cheek. "I think that might be a yes."

I nodded. It was all I could manage. As I stood alongside the bed, a still kneeling and topless Parker flicked open the button on my jeans, slowly lowered my zipper, and reached inside. When she touched me, I trembled, sucking in a breath. When she touched me with more determination, I groaned and pressed myself into her hand.

"Do you like that?" she asked, stroking me steadily. "Because I do."

I couldn't answer, but the noises I made, the insistence of my hips, surely told her everything she needed to know.

"I love that you're so wet for me," she said quietly. She kissed my neck and she continued to work. Her hands were magic. I was convinced. I was moments from coming when she slid her hand out of my jeans and eased back on the bed, resting on her forearms and elbows, waiting for me.

I shrugged out of the open shirt altogether and as I joined her on the bed, she made quick work of my bra. Very quick. I watched her drop it quickly next to us on the floor. "You're good at that."

"We all have our special skills." But she was preoccupied with my breasts. Touching them. Massaging them, softly. When she flipped me onto my back and covered my nipple entirely with her mouth, my hips bucked. To accommodate me, she slid a knee between my legs and pressed upward with her thigh against the ridge of my jeans. I saw stars. *Yes, I need that.* I cupped her ass and rocked up into her leg.

She paused and grinned down at me. "What are you doing to me?" she asked, in a breathy voice. "I can barely see straight."

"Come here," I said, and pulled her head down to me so we could make out. Except I really wanted to do so without these clothes and went about removing them through the haze of our kissing. Her pants first. My jeans. Her underwear.

"Let me do it," she said, pausing to ease my blue bikinis down my legs. She did so very slowly, and the hunger on her face as she watched my body revealed to her upped my anticipation. My legs quivered as her heated gaze took me in. I swallowed as she lowered herself on top. Skin on skin. Automatically, my eyes closed so I could savor the feeling of us pressed against each other with absolutely no barrier—there was nothing more satisfying.

She pushed my legs apart, slid herself between, and rocked her hips.

Except maybe that. I bit my lip.

I matched her rhythm and we moved together like this was what we were made to do. It startled me how perfectly we fit. As she thrust into me, I felt the pressure between my legs climb and climb. She slipped a hand between us and pushed her fingers inside.

"Oh, God," I said, finding no words more original. I had a gorgeous view of her breasts swaying as she worked me over with her hand. Her thumb circled my most sensitive spot, torturing me endlessly, as her fingers moved in and out. I was seconds from exploding. When her thumb pressed down firmly, I all but lifted off the bed as the orgasm crashed hard and then slow, if both were even possible. I'd never felt anything like it. The pleasure, already intense when it debuted, seemed to grow with each passing second, and I couldn't take much more. Easily the longest lasting orgasm of my life and I wasn't complaining. As the surge began to ebb, I relaxed onto the bedspread beneath me. I was done for, and loving every minute of it.

Parker collapsed to my side with a wide grin on her face. "You are so responsive, Hannah," she said, kissing my cheek and running her fingers gently across my breasts. "And these, I can't get enough of."

I chewed on my cheek because the attention she paid my breasts felt entirely too good. Yet I had other ideas about the next few minutes. I turned my face and kissed her deeply, wanting nothing more than to have my hands and mouth all over her. I was different with Parker than I'd ever been in bed with anyone else. Ravenous and unafraid. Somehow, she'd rubbed off on me.

I pulled her to me and rolled onto my back, taking her with me. She sat up and straddled my stomach, which was sexy as hell from my vantage point. Her hair fell around her shoulders, touching the tops of her breasts, and she rolled her hips in a slow rhythm.

The urgency hadn't abated in me, orgasm or not. I took both breasts in my hands. As she rocked, she pushed them farther against my palms and then away. I was turned on again in a big way. I twisted her nipples with the tips of my fingers and watched her toss her head back at what it did to her. She had sensitive breasts.

"Please," she said, covering my hands with hers, picking up the pace with her hips.

I slipped my hands out from beneath hers and stared as she cradled her own breasts above me. Driven by the image, I had her on her back in moments, and slid down the bed. I parted her legs and heard her murmur, "God, yes," from above. I traced a gentle pattern with my tongue, exercising enormous restraint, and from the whimpering sounds I heard floating my way, the soft touches served their purpose. I wanted Parker craving more and then I wanted to deliver. I took my time, paying close attention to what worked for her, which was just about everything I did. She was writhing beneath my mouth, my tongue. With two fingers, I entered her slowly, pulling a moan. I rested my other hand low on her abdomen so I could slowly drop my fingers over her, prompting her hips to buck. I replaced that hand with my mouth again and flicked her firmly with my tongue. That did it. Parker tensed all over and cried out. I held her in place, in spite of her frantic movements, and continued to lavish her with attention until she fell back in a flushed heap. As she recovered, I stole another moment to appreciate all of Parker.

"I just experienced things that I don't quite know how to handle," she said, with a chuckle. "Wow. That was really good."

"I think so, too." It was an understatement, because I was hesitant to gush even when gushing was called for. It had been the best sex of my life, but I didn't want to assume the same for Parker, who was surely a lot more experienced than I was in that department.

"More wine? At least let's finish the glass we started." Parker didn't wait for me to answer and was quickly up off the bed and walked naked into the living room to retrieve our abandoned glasses. I watched in much appreciation, impressed by her body and her apparent confidence. She set the glasses on the nightstand and slipped beneath the covers of the bed, propped up in a sitting position with the sheet tucked under her arms. Following her lead, I did the same. Once settled, she handed me my glass.

She took my hand and kissed the back of it. "I feel like I want to know so much more about you."

"You do? I'm not sure there's that much to tell. I was on the swim team in high school."

"That makes a lot of sense, actually," she said with a raised eyebrow, indicating she'd liked what she'd seen. "Why Providence?"

"I grew up there and have always kind of been someone who shies away from too much change in my life, so I stayed. Where did you grow up?"

"New Braunfels, Texas. It's not far from San Antonio. I still have family down that way."

"A Southern girl. I wouldn't have guessed."

She sipped her wine. "I don't really think of myself that way, but sure."

"That's why you have that place out in Austin. Hanging on to your roots, like me." I set down my glass, feeling like I'd had my fill of alcohol for the evening.

She nodded. "You got me there." She didn't say anything further, and I couldn't help but wonder if maybe she didn't like speaking too much about herself. She was open in so many ways, yet, it seemed, private in others.

I offered her a soft smile. "I had a nice time tonight."

"Nice? Nice?" She leaned forward. "That was insanely hot, and I write this stuff for a living. Nice is not the word I would use."

I laughed, feeling a little taller. "We have chemistry, you and I. A lot of it."

Another wine sip. "We so do." Parker glanced at the clock and I remembered my manners.

"What time do you head out tomorrow?"

"Our flight is at seven a.m.," she said with a grimace. "I don't know why they book them so early. Headed to Memphis. But you're welcome to stay until checkout. Order some breakfast if you'd like. On me."

"Will you see the Elvis sights? Wear a jumpsuit?" I liked the thought of her exploring the city, having fun. I felt sad I couldn't explore it with her.

"I doubt there will be time." Her eyelids looked heavy.

"Want me to get out of your hair so you can get some sleep?"

"Only if you send me to bed good and kissed."

I had no problem honoring this request, and crawled across the bed to her.

"Hi," she said quietly, when my lips hovered just shy of hers.

"I think you mean good night."

"Yes. Well. Or…hello again," she said, finishing the distance between our mouths. I could say that we ended that amazing good-night kiss and went straight to sleep, because that's what a good-night kiss was by definition. What an utter lie that would be, because Parker and I came together a second time, playful and earnest, with the same mind-blowing results as the first time. An hour later, I kissed her one final time, left her naked under the covers, and headed across the living room to what would be my room for the night. I could have stayed in her bed, but for reasons I couldn't quite zero in on, it didn't feel like the right decision. Not that Parker had ordered me to leave. But we weren't a couple, and it felt like her space. We'd not spoken of any kind of next time, and that was kind of what made today so awesome. There was something about Parker that felt wild and untamed. Dangerous even, and I valued my safety a lot. I found it between the covers of my own bed across the hall.

Exhausted, satisfied, and happy, I flipped off the light and allowed my tired brain to reminisce about the night I'd just shared with a wonderful woman. I pulled the ridiculously soft down comforter up to my chin and grinned as I relived each and every amazing second. The walk we'd taken, the beach, the pizza dinner, and finally the best part of all, her. I sighed dreamily. I didn't know if I'd see Parker again, but I hoped maybe someday. My phone vibrated on the nightstand. *Where the hell are you?* a text from Bo read.

I shook my head and fired off a reply. *You wouldn't believe me if I told you.*

CHAPTER SEVEN

For reasons that are unknown to me to this day, Bo's pantry remained pretty much empty at all times. She subsisted on giant containers of salad from the grocery store down the street from her house. In fact, when you opened her fridge, there was a stack of them, lined up like athletes on the bench, just waiting to be called into the game.

"I don't know how you live this way. You're a rabbit set on repeat."

Bo came up behind me and shut the refrigerator door. "It's what happens when you work ungodly hours for the good of the world. You sacrifice creature comforts for quick and accessible."

"Then grab a burger from any of the fast food restaurants five minutes from here. At least that would be a hot meal."

"Do you know what kind of preservatives they shovel into those things?" With her expression dialed to aghast, I knew this was a losing battle.

I covered my eyes at my health food nut of a sister, who still wore heels and a business suit when she'd been home for over an hour now. Another anomaly. "And why are you still dressed for work? Take your bra off. Walk around barefoot. Let's get crazy!" I was already in my worn-in jeans, long-sleeved T-shirt, and white Chucks. We'd made plans for dinner but decided to stay in when we realized we were both too exhausted to sit upright at a table in public. I'd been pulling extra hours at the shop to turn the place into more of a common area for my customers. After visiting the bookstore in Mystic two months prior, I'd come back with new ideas to implement. Once I started on window displays and a nook for reading in the children's section, I moved onto other ideas. I was fired up and excited about the changes I already saw working.

"You can take your bra off if you want. Mine is staying on. My girls demand maintenance." She said it with a playful smile. It didn't hang out on her face long, which told me she was tired or stressed. Maybe both.

"Were you in court today?" I asked, and slid onto her countertop.

She scrunched her nose, a telltale sign that Bo was frustrated. "A motion didn't go our way. I'm representing a woman trying to get a custody agreement in place for her six-year-old son, fearing that the abusive father might try to take him and hit the road as payback for the child support order that came down recently. I think I told you about this one."

"You did. And what was the ruling?"

"The court granted him a continuance to get his documentation in order, and that just puts everyone at risk. My client is worried that without a custody order in place, he's going to demand the child, and when he doesn't get what he wants, he gets violent."

I shook my head, not understanding how Bo didn't just leap across the table and demand to be heard. "So, now what?"

"We hope that doesn't happen, and she keeps her phone close by in case something does."

I walked to Bo and pulled her in for a hug. I didn't have a million skills, but hugging was something I'd grown pretty good at, and my sister was my favorite target. When we released each other, her expression seemed to relax, leaving me to believe that my theory that hugs do cure all was firmly proven.

"Hey, I saw Parker Bristow, your author friend," Bo said, using air quotes, "is dating that woman from the radio. The one with the repetitive song they play nonstop?"

I furrowed my brow. "Which woman from the radio?" I tried not to bristle noticeably that Parker was dating someone. I hadn't seen or heard from her since the morning she'd kissed my cheek in the darkened hotel room in Mystic before leaving for the airport at zero dark thirty. That didn't mean I hadn't thought about her, wondered what she was up to. I'd followed her on Twitter and smiled at her witty observations about life, and the millions of likes and retweets they always pulled in. But I'd seen nothing about a romance, which had been fine by me. More than fine.

Bo snapped her fingers a few times, trying to remember her name. "The woman, what's her face. The one who sings about the back of the club, and then repeats that phrase a bunch." She broke into a hypnotic, repetitive chant. "Back of the club with you. Back of the club for two. Back of the club. Back of the club. Back, back, back of the club." She rolled her hips on that last part, her big finish. "Bam. Done. That was my back of the club shake. Got it now? You have to know this song. It's impossible to escape."

Unfortunately, I did. Kurt loved to play the radio in the employee kitchen on his break, and that song was on way too often. It got in your head and refused to leave, like a cat you happened to feed just the one time, damning you to a lifelong duty. "Carissa Swain. You're telling me Parker's dating Carissa Swain?" Nooo. Couldn't be. I took a minute to metabolize this information. I'd seen a photo of Carissa at one point and had a vague mental image but was already on my phone and pulling up a recent one.

"You seem huffy," Bo said, with a sly smile. I'd told her everything about the night with Parker, minus a few of the more intimate details. I'd also framed it like two consenting adults enjoying an evening before returning to their respective lives. And that's what it was. I just hadn't exactly shelved the experience yet.

"I'm not huffy," I said, waiting for the page to load. "I just didn't peg Parker as someone who'd be into that kind of person. It doesn't match what I know of her."

"A pop star? Who isn't into a scantily clad woman with lots of money and fans? I'm not gay, but she's a looker." Bo snagged a handful of grapes from the fruit bowl on her counter.

Where were some good old-fashioned heal-thyself-Cheetos when you needed them? "Oh, here we go." The image populated on my screen and I stared. Carissa Swain was definitely beautiful, and could fill out a dress. I glared at her ridiculously large amounts of cleavage, beautiful smile, and luxurious platinum hair, probably styled by a professional moments before she left the house, or more accurately, blinged-out mansion. I disliked her then and there, a reaction that surprised even me, given that I had no knowledge of her caliber of character. I swiped for more images and unwittingly landed on one of her and

Parker outside a ritzy restaurant in New York from just two nights prior. While Parker wasn't the brand of celebrity to have paparazzi follow her too often, Carissa definitely was. In the photo, Parker was exiting the restaurant first, and Carissa had her hand on the small of Parker's back. The headline read "Carissa Swain Steps Out with New Lady Love." I closed the browser, having seen enough to make me uneasy. I glanced up at Bo, who watched me with a combination of amusement and pity.

"So, you have a few lingering feelings for Parker Bristow?"

I scoffed. Ridiculous. Except I was beginning to understand that perhaps it really wasn't. She'd made an impact on me, and I hadn't assigned the impact enough credit. I swallowed. "Maybe a few, but I didn't realize it until now."

"You don't like seeing her with someone else," Bo said, pointing at me, as if she'd discovered the murderer in a high-stakes game of Clue. "This is a big day for me, because the last time you showed undeniable interest in someone was Mitch Brady your junior year of college, and I hated that guy. Way too much corduroy, for one."

I thought on Mitch. "He had a nice collection of classics, and he let me read them whenever I wanted."

"If only you'd make out with him," she said in an overly sweet voice.

I frowned. "I appreciated his mind more than his kissing abilities." If Mitch could have figured out what to do with his tongue, we might have had a better time of it. I cringed.

"Then there was Audra Hudson the year before. You were all about her for a minute."

I sighed. "Fantastic ability to kiss. No intellect."

"And Parker Bristow?"

Her name alone dropped me into fantasy land. "Equipped in both areas…generously. I can admit that."

"I knew it," Bo said. "You downplayed your little overnighter so hard, but underneath it all, you were taken with her, and how could you not be? She's an amazing writer, and incredibly sweet. I love everything about her, especially the way she's woken you up to the world."

"In many ways, I wish she hadn't. Then maybe there'd be less blowback from a Carissa Swain pairing."

"Aww, sweetie," Bo said, closing the distance between us so she could look me in the eye. Bo had always been good at using intimacy to communicate how much she cared. I appreciated that about her. "I'm sorry I slammed you with bad news. You seemed so breezy about the whole thing. I didn't realize it would matter to you so much."

"It shouldn't. It won't. Just gonna shrug it off."

"Sounds like a sound plan." Bo grabbed a pizza delivery menu from the drawer next to the sink, which was good because I had no plans to eat one of those ready-to-go salad soldiers. She paused. "I'm gonna backtrack. I think you should text her. Test the waters. You never know. Hamburger and onion?"

"Yes, and fresh tomato." I shook my head and went about pulling my hair into a ponytail for maximum relaxing time with my sister. "No way. That ship has sailed, and I have a great story to tell. Pure bonus."

She studied me and paused. "Except I feel like it's not. Hold on a sec." She dialed, ordered our pie, and turned back to me, phone in hand. "What can it hurt?"

"Well," I gestured in a circle to the air all around us, "it will upset the balance, and I'm big on balance. I learned all about it from Luna. It's important to me to keep my life in order and not wildly—"

"You hate anything messy." Bo headed to her living room. "Just say it. That's why your life is boring. You take very few risks because you're afraid of the big bad word."

"What's the big bad word?"

"Complicated."

"No, no, no. Unfair. I'm not afraid of complicated." Bo blinked, clearly not buying it. I pressed on, defending myself hard-core because I was debating with a seasoned attorney. "I take *wise* risks that come with probable reward. I think about things. I calculate the chances that they'll go my way before leaping. This thing with Parker? Isn't a smart bet."

"Oh my God. You're such a justifier." She collapsed onto the couch and located the remote. But I wasn't done.

"Our lives are radically different. Parker's doesn't fit into mine, and vice versa. She wants to live in a lake house in Austin, for God's sake."

"Fine. You win. You and Parker should stay far away from each other. Take out a restraining order. I'll file it for you." She lifted her head. "I think I am going to take off these shoes."

"Oh, wow, Bo. That's huge. Now who's a risk taker?"

She inhaled from an imaginary cigarette. "Oh, it's me." I adored this woman.

We had a nice night of pizza scarfing and catching up, followed by a marathon of *Married at First Sight*, which had us both screaming and cringing in happy horror. All the while, I could feel the photo of Parker and Carissa Swain burning a hole in my pocket, closed browser or not. On my drive home, I sorted through my feelings, making a point to be dead honest with myself. I made peace with the fact that whatever fleeting moment in time Parker and I had shared, it was over and meant to be short-lived. I mentally wished her well, and made the choice not to dwell on what couldn't be. There was plenty to occupy my time and attention, and in fact, dating was still a viable option. In fact, yes. I nodded several times. What I'd experienced with Parker had jump-started my desire to recapture that same feeling somehow. I probably just needed to look a little harder, exactly what Luna and Bo had been saying all along. Maybe life was a lot more fulfilling alongside another person, and maybe I just needed to put in the time. In fact, I couldn't wait to dive back in.

❖

"'Tis the season to be jolly." I switched from singing to humming and finished the rest of the song. The late morning was overcast and frigid, ushering in mid-December with only a mild amount of fanfare. I didn't care. I was in great spirits these days, and there was one very particular reason. I scrunched my shoulders to my ears and smiled.

Her name was Sheila and she'd been born and raised in Germany. Only you wouldn't know it because her accent had apparently faded in her teenage years, though I did hear a slim affectation on occasion. Sexy. She was four years older than me with brown hair that fell a little above her shoulders, and she had a way of pursing her lips when she was thoughtful. I envisioned it now. We'd had exactly 2.5 dates, because I definitely included the coffee we'd met for initially in my calculation. It was early in our burgeoning relationship, yes, but things felt promising. I thought about Sheila as I worked that afternoon, and smiled when she sent me occasional texts to say hello or update me about what she had going at work.

"What does she do for a living? Sheila, the woman you talk to, I mean," Kurt asked. He lay upside down beneath the new puppet theater, screwdriver in hand. The children's section was really coming along nicely. I'd put my billowing fabric design skills to use and added a tented ceiling to make it feel like the perfect reading hideaway. I'd noticed that parents perused the shelves longer, and thereby made more purchases, if their kids were happy and occupied nearby. The puppet theater and the rack of puppets we'd leave out would hopefully only add to that. I was planning on scheduled puppet shows, too, twice a week, and a more formalized events calendar I could Instagram the hell out of. The ball was really rolling now at A Likely Story, and that had me smiling just as much as Sheila did.

I grinned and handed Kurt a screw. "Sheila, since you asked, is a CPA. She works at Hargraves and Scott. The firm," I informed him, feeling proud of Sheila's businessy side. It was one of the things that had attracted me to her right off. In fact, when she'd first shown up for our coffee, she was still wearing her buttoned-up work clothes. A white blouse beneath a blue sweater and slacks. Her hair had been in a loose bun that told me she didn't mess around at work. Prim and proper was a good look on her.

"I'm so sorry that I'm not more casual," Sheila had said, depositing her briefcase and extending her hand for a shake. I stood from where I sat at the small table and accepted it. Her grip was extra firm. Maybe too firm for a date, but she was a career woman. I got that. That handshake probably helped establish her presence in a male-dominated field. I'd bet anything.

"Are you kidding?" I glanced down at my outfit. "I wish I'd dressed up more now." We smiled at each other for that weighted moment that happens after you'd talked to someone on a dating app for a week, gotten to know them a bit, and were now seeing them in 3-D. She looked up. I liked her brown eyes, and small number of freckles.

"What can I get for you?" she asked with a smile, and gestured to the counter. "My treat."

"Oh. I'll take a vanilla latte with skim milk," I said. "And thank you."

"My pleasure."

And that's how it started. The following two dates had only gotten better from there, and we shared our first kiss over dinner two nights back. It was also the first time I'd seen Sheila with her hair down. She'd looked so pretty underneath the halo of my porch light.

I shook myself back into the present and the shop, and extinguished the smile that pulled at the corners of my mouth just thinking about it. About her.

"A CPA, huh?" Kurt said, sliding out from inside the puppet theater. "Maybe she'll do your taxes for free. That'd really be a score. I can't imagine that kind of convenience at my fingertips."

"Well, it depends on what you do for her in return," Luna said from behind. We turned at the sound of her voice. She was early for her shift, but ever since she'd been dating the pencil-haired hostess, she'd developed a zest for life. I identified.

I held up a hand. "We'll get there eventually."

"When's eventually?" she asked, with a mischievous grin. Since we'd both started dating new people, our girl talk quotient was definitely on the rise.

Kurt covered his ears and stalked down the aisle. "Do not think of your boss having sex. Never do that. Nope. Not right. Think of Bugs Bunny. Recite some Browning." He gave his head a firm shake and I laughed at his inadvertent traumatization.

I turned back to Luna and shrugged one shoulder like I was the most casual of individuals. "Just taking it slow. If things go well, we'll get there, you know?"

"You seem sassy today. I feel it all over you." She made a gesture as if to outline my aura, or my chi, or something I wasn't quite clear on. She made it hard to know. "I like sassy Hannah."

"I feel sassy, too." I retrieved a box of bookmarks for the carousel near the cash register and swayed my hips as I walked toward the front of the store, earning a laugh and catcall from Luna. I took out my phone to fire off a semiflirtatious text to Sheila, only to find a message waiting for me.

I had a burger today. Not quite as good as Harry's. The message was from Parker. I froze. It had been nearly three months now since we'd seen each other, and I'd purposefully not allowed myself to think about her after the Carissa Swain photos went up. I hadn't been all that successful at first, but as one week had turned into two, and then three, I'd gotten better. She'd receded from my thoughts bit by bit, as did our time together. Now I blinked at my screen, her message, her words lit up for me. Now what? I shook my head. I knew exactly what, I just wouldn't answer. Probably for the best.

Two hours later, I'd lost all my sass. My hips weren't swaying. I was preoccupied with that text. Wondering about it. I dove into my own head and remained there. Kurt had gone home for the day and Luna was tending to what would likely be the last batch of customers before we closed. Luckily, they were big purchasers, and I spent my time at the register, smiling and remarking at each book. Two women in a row had accepted my book recommendation based on what they seemed most interested in. I was confident we'd found them the perfect match, and that cheered me up. Perfect matches made my job awesome.

Each time the door opened and closed, I'd hear the winter winds bluster and want to shrug farther into my sweater. Finally, as we said our good-byes to our last customer, Luna locked the door and turned back to me.

"You good? You seem quiet. Did something happen?"

"No. I'm great. Just thinking about plans for the weekend."

Luna nodded. "Hit up Sheila. Do something fun. I'm thinking ice skating for us, though I swear to God, if I break one of my precious ankles, I'll never forgive myself."

I had no idea Luna considered her ankles so precious, but I also preferred she stay upright for both selfish entrepreneur and caring friend reasons. Once she headed to the back for the vacuum cleaner and left me alone, I fired off a text. It wasn't to Sheila. *Burgers come in all shapes and sizes. I try not to discriminate.*

An hour and a half later, once I was home, I flipped the fried egg I planned to eat for dinner, along with a platter of bacon. Mid-flip, she answered. *So, now that we got that difficult burger talk out of the way, how are you? Tell me all about it.*

All about it? I waited half an hour. I wasn't a pushover. *Great! I'm doing well. I see you're happy.* Parker now had a very public girlfriend, and I needed to get that information out into the ether of our correspondence. Straightforward communication was best.

Twenty minutes passed. *It's been a whirlwind but in a good way. She makes life...fun.*

I waited fifteen. Why did people play these games? We weren't fourteen years old, but there was something therapeutic about the illusion of control. A defense mechanism? Maybe. I picked up my phone to text, but it rang in my hands. Parker was calling, and I picked right up, not wanting to continue my ridiculous overthinking. I needed to stop analyzing every little thing. My brain hurt.

Her voice was just as I remembered it, and something in me responded noticeably to the sound. I had goose bumps and a hit of adrenaline. "It's silly to keep going back and forth when we can just talk."

I chuckled. "Okay. That's true, I suppose. What made you reach out?" I carried my empty breakfast-for-dinner plate to my kitchen table.

"I just hadn't had my recent dose of Hannah the quiet bookshop owner."

"I'm not that quiet."

"No, not always." I couldn't tell if that was innuendo. If so, I didn't appreciate it because she was with someone. I decided to give her the benefit of the doubt. "So, how's your girlfriend?"

A pause. "She's fantastic. Currently in Santa Fe for a gig. She's trying out some new material before recording next month."

"Oh. That's why you're calling me." It was the equivalent of a sigh. She was bored and alone.

"I'm calling you because we get along well. We click. I want us to be…friends, if that's possible. Of course, you can say no."

She wasn't wrong about the getting along part. We were as different as could be, but yes, somehow, we clicked. Whether I wanted to or not, I missed her. September felt like such a long time ago now. "Friends is doable. What are you writing these days?"

She seemed to relax right then and there. "It's a friends-to-lovers story about an upstairs/downstairs pair of neighbors. I'm on the last third and starting to find my stride."

Her voice sounded the tiniest bit scratchy. Maybe the evening air had done that. Maybe she'd been out late the night before. It tickled my ear. I liked it. "When do I get to read it?"

"Um, when everyone else does."

"What? No sneak peek? We're friends now. You said so yourself." I made a point of sounding aghast. We were falling back into our old rhythm, teasing each other, comfortable and exciting at the same time. "What are the perks of friendship if I don't get a first glimpse?"

She paused. "I never let anyone but my editor see the book before it's out, but I will see if I can make a mental concession." She paused. "Since we're friends."

And we turned out to be. I heard from Parker several times a week and began to feel comfortable enough calling her on my own. We'd stayed true to our plan and kept everything about our relationship firmly in the friendship column. It turned out, Parker was a really good friend. The day of the first official live puppet show, she called to wish me a fantastic turnout. She was in San Francisco for a charity wine tasting event, which had me a little jealous. I was developing my own fascination with wine, gravitating toward the big reds, mostly, and doing everything I could to learn about pairing. "What would be a good number for the turnout today?"

I had her on speakerphone in my car, deciding to drive that day in case I needed to dash off for any last-minute errands. "Honestly? If we had ten children, each with a parent, I'd be thrilled with the day. If they like it, they'll tell their friends, and we can go from there."

"Okay, I'm going to send good vibes into the universe so you get your ten."

"Thanks, Parker."

"You're welcome, Hannah. Bye for now."

It was loud when Parker called later that night to find out how it went. "Sorry," she said, struggling to rise above the noise. "I'm at the event but wanted to find out about the puppet debut. How'd it go? I was rooting for you all day."

Hearing that I'd been supported from afar made me warm and happy. Parker was a good egg. "It was amazing. The woman I hired did a fantastic job. She had all of these amazing voices, and we had fourteen kids all gathered in the children's section. I was thrilled. Plus, we sold a lot of books. Well worth it."

"That's the best news I've had all day."

I could hear her smiling through the phone, and now I could picture it. "How's your thing?"

"Not as riveting as a multivoiced puppet show, but we've raised a lot of money for charity. Plus, the wine is fantastic. I bought a case of my favorite. I'll send you a bottle." A pause. "And how's Sheila?"

I smiled. "She's great. Working late tonight, but we're getting together tomorrow for Thai food. It's her favorite, and there's a dish she wants me to try." Over the course of the past month, things with

Sheila had steadily progressed at a very appropriate and comfortable rate. She'd stayed over a few times, and I'd stayed at her place twice. Christmas Eve was next week, and I was thinking maybe it wouldn't be too much to have her over for our traditional dinner. My parents wouldn't be there, but Bo, Luna, Kurt, and their dates would be.

"And Carissa?"

"She's here with me, though I'm not sure she's a fan of the wine. She's mainly putting up with it. I'm going to have to take her somewhere later so she can get what she calls 'a real drink.'"

I laughed. "Well, thank you for checking in on today."

"No problem. I had my fingers crossed for you."

Our conversations were a lot like that at first. Short check-ins. But once Parker came off her book tour in January, settled into her life in New York, and started writing her next manuscript, we talked for longer stretches.

"So, I need this character to do something drastic to be seen by the other one, who is a firefighter."

"You're gesturing a lot right now, aren't you?"

She laughed. "How do you know that about me?"

"I just happen to remember." I squinted as I set my pasta water to boil. I had Parker on speakerphone as I made myself dinner. It was snowing out, and I had mellow tunes playing on low in the background. "She could set her house on fire."

"Hannah, no. I'm thinking criminal activity might be hard to come back from."

She had a point. "Throw herself in front of a moving vehicle and hope they send fire and rescue? Namely her hottie in turnout gear?"

"Negative. You're awful at this. How can someone who reads so much, who sells books for a living be so bad at plotting?" She was teasing me, as she so often did.

"I like my idea. Throw her into traffic. She'll recover." I tasted my meat sauce and tried not to melt. God, I made good sauce, and I wasn't the type to brag. "You're the one who asked me for advice. You're the famous author. Shouldn't you have this down?"

"You'd think." We'd been on the phone for close to an hour now, and she'd done a great job of keeping me company. I was starting to look forward to our conversations more and more. She had a great way of helping me talk things out, and I hoped I did the same for her. I'd been skeptical about our ability to remain in the friend zone, but it had worked. We did well in the zone. Hell, we rocked it. I still rolled my eyes at the photos of Parker and Carissa that showed up online. She deserved someone…more cultured, in my opinion. I was being petty, yes, but I was allowed a moment of immaturity now and again, and Carissa Swain wore outfits that left little to the imagination and tweeted things like, "Gettin' lit tooo-nite." I wasn't able to connect the dots to someone like Parker, who seemed together and intelligent, if not a little lost. That part hadn't eluded me, the lost.

"I'm thinking of having my main character make a move, but crash and burn horribly. Embarrassment will set in. She'll retreat into her cave. That will give her a lot to recover from."

"I like that idea." I tossed the pasta into the water and winked at Tomato, who watched from on top of the cabinet overhead. "See? There's a reason you are incredibly rich."

"I don't know about incredibly." There was a muffling sound, and then I heard a female voice in the background.

"Do you have company right now?"

She went quiet on the line and then came back. "Carissa just got here. She had a rough day apparently, so I should go."

"Is that your friend Hannah?" the voice asked. It was surreal that a pop star as famous as Carissa knew my name. "Tell her what up for me."

"Carissa says hello."

That's not at all what she'd said, but Parker was helpful enough to translate.

"Tell her I said hi back. I'll let you go. Dinner plans of my own, and all."

"Fancypants. That's always been you."

I grinned. "That's my middle name. Always has been."

"Bye-bye, Hannah."

"Bye, Parker. Be good, and give that wallflower her happily ever after. Oh, and don't drag it out."

"Well, I have to drag it out. My job. Bye, again."

I clicked off the call on somewhat of a high and caught Tomato staring. "What?" I asked. "It's nice to have a good friend."

There was a knock at the door, and I sang to the radio on my way to open it. "Well, hello," I said after swinging open the door.

Sheila handed me a bottle of wine and pointed at it. "It's the good stuff. Gift from a client." She leaned in for a kiss, but we bumped lips, misjudging in the dim entryway of my apartment. "Ow," she said, laughing and rubbing her bottom lip. "That was my fault."

"Pretty sure it was mine." We laughed it off and tried again, this time landing the kiss successfully. Sheila was a very pleasant kisser, I'd found. Never too much or too little, and that was nice, wasn't it? Yes, definitely. Nice. "Come inside for pasta and tell me about your day. I want details."

"Well, it started with an angry staff meeting and ended with an impatient client."

"Oh, no," I said sympathetically. I poured two glasses of wine, handed her one, and went about plating our dinner while Sheila told me all about the ugly details. I truly felt bad for her, as it sounded like her job just really never let up.

"That's crazy," I said, when she told me all about the new email system. "Not at all fair," I said over dinner, when she explained how her counterpart, Sven, always got the better assignments. "You've really been going hard," I told her sympathetically when she explained that she'd forgotten what it was like just to have a solid few days off in a row. By the time we slid into bed and had what I would describe as neat and orderly sex, much like Sheila, I realized we wouldn't be talking much about my day, or what I had going on at the shop.

That was okay. We'd get to it.

I threw my arm around Sheila's waist and settled in for the night.

CHAPTER EIGHT

W hat do you think about the color green?" Parker asked.
I pondered her question as I switched my phone to my other ear. "I've never had reason to fight with it."

"I agree. It's not an aggressive color, but maybe, and hear me out on this, maybe it's overrated. It bores me."

I picked Bacon up off the stove and set him on the floor. I had no idea why he had such an affinity for stove sleeping. It freaked me out. "Run and frolic."

"Excuse me?" Parker asked, with a chuckle.

"Sorry. Bacon. Well, you can run and frolic, too, but watch out for overvalued green stuff."

"Honestly, think about a forest, how much prettier it would be if the trees were a light blue or a warm red. What's something that's better green?"

I plopped into my comfy armchair and slipped out of my shoes after a long Friday at work. My toes rejoiced at the soft carpet beneath, and I scrunched them in and out in celebration. "I happen to be partial to your eyes. They're green." I heard myself say the words but didn't proof them before leaving my lips. The feet relaxation had distracted me and interfered with my normally sound judgment. Parker went silent on the line.

Then, finally, "I had a thought."

"Okay," I said meekly, fully aware that she'd completely sidestepped my line-crossing comment. Embarrassment crept in, and I fought it with everything I had.

"There's a resort in South Carolina, very rustic, that I just love. I go there to get away and really focus on my work. It's on a lake, and the cabins are set back from each other. There's a beautiful restaurant attached."

I tried to imagine the place. I loved everything about the words "cabin," "lake," and "rustic." "It sounds so picturesque, so tranquil."

"Want to go next weekend?"

"Us?" My heart began to thud, and my brain tried to catch up. This had taken an inadvisable turn and somehow, I needed us to get back on the Parker/Hannah friendship train before it pulled out of the station without us. There was Sheila to think about, who I was very much involved with now. Plus, Parker had that wild child pop star to—

"Well, with Sheila and Carissa, of course. Would you guys be game? Would be nice to see you again, and for everyone to meet. Could be a really fun weekend for the four of us."

The panic that moved in zigzags through my system came screeching to a halt. I immediately relaxed. "Oh, you mean all of us. I was confused."

"You thought I was inviting you for a whirlwind sex weekend?" She said it playfully, but the concept prompted me to swallow. I'd never had someone affect me quite the way Parker did. I couldn't put my finger on what it was about her that got under my skin so effortlessly. She could rattle me one minute, comfort me the next, and frustrate me entirely with just a slight insinuation. When she said things like "sex weekend," my face went hot.

"No, no. I didn't think that. Not at all."

"You did. You thought I was trying to whisk you away."

I frowned into my living room. "I was just trying to understand what you were asking. We're on the same page."

"Are we?" she asked. "Good."

She had the upper hand, damn it, and I was frustrated now. *She* had frustrated me. How quickly she could do that. I blinked. Didn't matter. I was moving us out of it. "I think the resort sounds fun. It's short notice, though. I'd have to rearrange some special scheduling at the shop and check with Sheila about her work schedule."

"You have to Hannah-fy it. I understand entirely. Meanwhile, I'm booking a two-bedroom and will get back to you with details. Sound good?"

"Um. Yeah, I'm game. *We* are," I amended, sure to include my plus one.

"I can't wait to meet her," Parker said. "You've said so many good things."

"Likewise, I can't wait to meet Carissa. Learn more about the back of that club." I'd meant it as a joke, but somehow it didn't land as jovially as I'd hoped. I needed to work on my delivery.

"She'd be happy to enlighten you, I'm sure."

"Ha ha," I said, overdoing it. I should just stay quiet. Always.

"Take care, Hannah. Talk to you tomorrow with more details."

"Good night, Parker."

I set my phone on the counter, feeling like I'd just run a marathon. Now, alone with my thoughts, I wondered what the hell I'd just done. I'd be face-to-face with Parker again, only this time on very different terms. As long as I kept all of my thoughts, perceptions, and expectations in separate boxes, and didn't allow them to touch, a four-person weekend would likely be a lot of fun. I'd bring some board games and some wine. I'd make a homemade breakfast for everyone. We could look out at the lake and talk about the world, and books, and anything under the sun. When it was time to sleep, we'd break off into our respective pairs. I could be a grown-up about Carissa in Parker's room. I'd never even slept in the same bed with Parker, so there'd be nothing to be jealous of.

In fact, the more I thought about it, the more I was really looking forward to the weekend. Parker was becoming a new and very valuable friend, and this getaway would likely help us solidify our new dynamic. I shrugged and began to think of a mental packing list.

To a cabin in South Carolina we go!

❖

"Oh, wow," Sheila said, as we pulled onto the property of the Coral Lake Resort. The heavily wooded drive made me feel like we were leaving civilization behind us. The narrow road snaked around a handful of cabins, a volleyball court, and a playscape, all nestled near a gorgeous lake. I followed Parker's instructions and directed Sheila to pass the main lodge and head to the back of the campus, where Parker and Carissa were already checked in and waiting at the cabin.

"Over there," I said to Sheila. "Number seventeen, she said."

"I'm a little nervous to meet them." Sheila looked at me with wide eyes. "They're both so…well-known."

I leaned over and kissed her cheek. "Don't be. They're going to love you. Parker's great, very friendly, and Carissa…might be." I bounced my eyebrows. "I guess we're about to find out."

I came around Sheila's SUV to help with the luggage but paused when the door to the cabin opened. Parker. She stood atop the small flight of steps that led up to the porch, grinning at me. She held her hands out. "You're here."

"We made it." I grinned back. Parker looked amazing as always. She had her blond hair partially swept back with the bottom portion loose and down. She wore hunter green shorts and a form-fitting white T-shirt, more casual than I'd ever seen her. If it was possible, she glowed.

"Hi, there," Sheila called up, friendly as always.

"Hey, you two!" Parker raced down the steps. "Here, let me help with some of that." She gathered a couple of extra bags and lugged them alongside our haul. We were a trio of pack mules. I wasn't one to pack light, too fearful I'd forget something important. I had food, games, bug repellent, extra clothes, hiking attire, a first aid kit. You name it, I'd thought of it and shoved it into Sheila's car like a Tetris whiz. Parker surveyed all the bags. "You two don't mess around when it comes to travel."

"All Hannah," Sheila said, with a laugh, carrying four bags herself. "I'm simply a foot soldier." Parker glanced back at me with a smile. When her gaze found mine, I warmed all over and couldn't help but smile back. A private, friendly moment. As we climbed the steps, Carissa came onto the porch, and with that, the temperature changed.

"Hey, guys," she said. Oh, wow. She was even more beautiful in person.

"Hi, I'm Hannah," I said back. "I'd shake your hand if I could." I tried to juggle something to my left side to free up my right, but it just wasn't happening.

"Don't sweat it," Carissa said, and took a seat on the porch swing. She didn't offer to help at all, even Parker, who'd taken a large share of the load.

"Hi," she said to Sheila with a wave and went about gently swinging. "I like your flip-flops." Carissa had very blond hair, the type that didn't exist in real life and was colored to look almost white. She ran her fingers through it slowly. I had to admit she was striking. She wore short-shorts and a pink halter top with a myriad of zippers heading in several different directions. If you asked me to spot the pop star in the wild, I'd have zeroed in pretty quick.

We did that thing for the next hour where we were all extra polite to each other, and Sheila and I explored the cabin, remarking on all the cool features, along with Parker.

"I love the garden tub in our room."

"Do these blinds go up? Oh, they do."

"There's a hot tub on the deck!"

"I could get used to this."

And so on and so forth. All of this minus Carissa, who took to curling her hair in the main bathroom off the living area. It wasn't until late afternoon when we popped a bottle of Rosé that we all seemed to take a moment to breathe and relax around the outdoor table.

"You're an accountant?" Parker asked, handing Sheila a full glass.

She nodded. "Numbers have always made more sense to me than anything else. There's something reliable about them."

Parker nodded. "I can see that. I'm just happy we have you, because my brain couldn't hack it." They touched glasses in what was a nice but surreal moment for me. My friend and my girlfriend were hobnobbing for the first time. Okay, my friend that I had had amazing sex with and my girlfriend. That was the surreal part.

"I could say the same back to you," Sheila said after sipping from her glass. "I could never write a book, yet you've written hit after hit."

"Do you read romance?" Parker asked.

"No, but this one," she placed her hand just above my knee, "says I should give yours a try. They made a believer out of her."

"Isn't that amazing?" Parker asked, absently. Her gaze flitted to Sheila's hand and back to her own glass. "You know what? I'm going to check on Carissa."

Once we were alone, Sheila turned to me with a grin. "She's really wonderful, just like you said." She gestured in the air as if searching for the right word. "She has a presence about her."

"That's Parker." I leaned forward. "Think about it. She's known for more than just her books these days, and that's for a reason. People gravitate to her, want to hear what she has to say, even if it's just a sarcastic quip online."

"I saw her on that morning talk show just a few months ago, the one with the crazy cooking segment midway through?"

I nodded. "Exactly. How many authors are invited onto talk shows? She's invented her own category." Since our newfound friendship, I'd been paying attention to Parker's career and the track she'd established for herself. Television, social media, and the book world all clamored for her.

"Well, she apparently thinks the world of you. You've only been friends since August and we're vacationing with them already. Not that I'm surprised."

I scoffed and drank my wine. "Oh, I don't know about that."

"I do. Plus, she beams every time you speak. Have you noticed that? Her head swivels in your direction."

"No, actually I haven't." I shrugged. "We haven't seen each other since September." My cheeks felt hot, and I wasn't sure why. I touched my glass to one, just as Parker reappeared with Carissa.

"Hi, gang," Carissa said, sliding into a chair and accepting a glass from Parker. "I was on the phone all morning and didn't get to do my hair, which was atrocious." She flashed her million-dollar smile that likely solved any and all problems for her.

"Oh," I said, waving off the apology, "we've been just fine. I've never been out this way, so I'm just enjoying the ambience." From the back deck, we had a gorgeous view of the lake stretched out beautifully in front of us, which was surrounded by an army of tall oak trees. The light jacket I wore was plenty for the sixty-degree temperatures, especially with the sun shining down on us. "It's really awesome meeting you. Of course, I know of your music."

"Which is your favorite?" Carissa asked, without hesitation.

I looked to Sheila for assistance, scrambling to remember the name of the song I always just referred to as "Back of the Club." It was the only Carissa Swain song I knew, though I was well aware she'd had more than one chart topper.

"Hannah likes 'Club Nights,'" Parker supplied. She met my gaze knowingly. Yep, she'd saved me.

"I do. That one is really catchy."

She nodded. "I consider it my most artful."

I nearly choked on my wine. "Well, people love it." That was general enough to pass as a compliment, right?

"I need to get back to writing soon," Carissa said, finding a beat on the table. "Maybe this weekend. Work out some lyrics. I'm really feeling my vibe among these trees. I could create great things here."

I could hear the lyrics now in my head: "Give me that ass. Give me that ass. Where's that ass? Give me that ass." I bopped my head along to the beat she created. She'd be a billionaire.

"What are you doing?" Parker asked, with an amused expression on her face. "Are you chair dancing?"

Caught! I played it off like I was taking in the view. "Just absorbing nature in all of its finery."

She stared at me another beat. "Mmm-hmm. Sure, you are." I smiled back, and distantly realized I'd missed something Sheila had said.

"What's that?" I asked.

Sheila held out the bottle of wine. "I just asked if you wanted a top-off."

"I definitely do," I said, and thrust my glass forward. This trip was going to be so much easier with a little fortification to see me through. "Hit me."

The night consisted of dinner at the restaurant, during which I got to listen to Carissa ask the waitstaff for fifteen different things not on the menu and sulk each time they apologized for not being able to accommodate her request.

"I just feel that a five-star restaurant like this one should have sea urchin available. Am I wrong?" She peered angrily at our three faces. Sheila and I exchanged a private glance and allowed Parker to handle this one.

She addressed Carissa gently. "I'm not sure this is a five-star resort. We're staying in a cabin in the woods. They're doing the best they can."

"Fine. Whatever." She tossed back her bourbon on the rocks, probably still defeated that they didn't have the unique brand she'd asked for from a small farm in Kentucky she'd once visited. "You work in a bookstore," she said to me, minutes later. It wasn't a question.

"I do."

"I'm guessing my girl's books are tearing it up."

I smiled at Parker, her girl. "They sell really well. It was great she was able to come to town for a signing."

She nodded and sipped. "I'm sure you loved that."

I turned to Parker, who sat on my left, unsure if that was a pointed comment or not. "We grabbed a really messy burger and got to know each other."

Parker laughed. "Best burger ever. It's where we first became friends."

"Harry's, right? You need to take me to that place," Sheila said, and squeezed my hand on top of the table.

"I can do that." We shared a smile. Parker shoved lettuce around on her salad plate.

Later that night, after drinks and conversation around the table behind the cabin, Sheila and I crawled into the ridiculously comfortable four poster bed in our room. She held up her arm and I slid beneath it, sighing in exhaustion and relaxing against her. The drive had been long, and my tolerance level for Carissa, famous or not, had become nonexistent. After falling asleep at the table out back, she'd tugged on Parker and whispered something in her ear. Who whispers so noticeably in a group of four people?

"You seemed to be having a hard time tonight," Sheila said, and kissed the top of my head.

"No, I'm good." I looked up at her. "Let's just sleep, okay?"

"Okay."

I kissed her lips softly and she killed the bedside lamp. The ambient sounds from outside drifted into our room, underscoring my gradual relaxation. Crickets, wind rustling, an occasional owl hoot. I loved it. Wait. That was weird. Was the owl crying? My eyes opened and I listened. It did sound like crying…only in rhythm, and it wasn't an owl at all.

"Are you hearing what I'm hearing?" Sheila asked.

I raised up onto my elbows because oh, I definitely was. I looked at Sheila with wide eyes. The cries grew louder, longer, more obnoxious as the seconds ticked by. It wasn't sexy. They were constant and grating.

"That can't be Parker," Sheila whispered.

"It's not," I said. I remembered exactly what Parker sounded like in the throes. Quieter, measured, and a lot more sensual. I fell back onto the bed and hoped to God it would end soon. It didn't.

"Cutes, you're doing me. You're doing me."

I looked over at Sheila. "Cutes?" she asked.

I shrugged. "And isn't that second part kind of already understood?"

She nodded. "You'd think."

"You're doing me good," Carissa chanted in her obnoxiously loud sex voice. The seconds felt like hours. "Oh, Cutes. More of that. Fuck me more. You're doing me."

"She takes a long time to…get there," Sheila finally said. I nodded. That's when another chant started.

"Take me there. Take me there. Take me there." It was a repetition, which, I was going to hell for thinking this, reminded me a lot of "back of the club, back of the club, back of the club." I covered my ears but I could still hear her. Moaning, shrieking. The howling only grew louder as it went on. Either Parker was the best lover on the face of the planet, and I could admit that yes, she was pretty great, or Carissa was prone to wild theatrics. I covered my eyes next, trying desperately to erase the images that began to surface.

"Take me there, take me there, take me there," Carissa chanted loudly, followed by a long scream which might or might not have signaled that Carissa was being attacked and viciously murdered from the sound of it.

"Wow," Sheila said, after a beat of silence. "Think she was taken there?"

"I'm going to go with yes."

"Back to bed?" Sheila asked.

"Definitely." Another quick kiss. Sheila trailed her hand down my back briefly, and we were on our way to dreamland, enveloped in quiet.

Only, I didn't sleep at all that night. Imagining Parker with that woman, who was none of the things I wanted for Parker, made me cringe. I turned over and ordered myself to get those sounds out of my head. To not allow my friendship with Parker to be tarnished by her awful decision to partner with someone like Carissa. My heart ached regardless. I was a mess and didn't know why. Lost. Confused. Angry. All of it.

CHAPTER NINE

I tapped my foot as I perused the caddy of Keurig flavors stocked for us by the resort. French vanilla, salted caramel, cookie dough. I wasn't sure if this cabin was offering me coffee or a liquid pastry. I skipped over the lightweight stuff, located an extra-bold offering, and snatched up the K-Cup in victory.

"Morning, Hannah. How did you sleep?" I turned at the sound of Parker's voice. She touched my back lightly as she passed, grabbing a mug for herself. I bristled at the contact after what I'd heard the night before. I'd put a mental distance between us whether she deserved it or not. Without any sleep, my ability to cope was at an all-time low.

"I slept better than you did." I tried to say it with a sly smile, remembering that she was simply living her life, and I didn't have a say.

"Hmm. What does that mean?" She kicked a hip out against the counter and stared, waiting for me to explain.

I went for it. "Give it to me. Give it to me. Give it to me good," I said in a hushed but breathy impersonation of the performance I'd overheard.

She nodded but didn't seem terribly fazed. "Okay. Gotcha. I'm embarrassed that you heard that."

"The whole resort heard it. You guys had quite the time." My tone sounded clipped, and I cringed. That wasn't who I wanted to be, and that wasn't the message I wanted to send Parker. She owed me nothing. All I wanted was her friendship. I'd come to value it and depend on our phone calls to help center me in the world. Parker's entrance into my life had already changed it for the positive, so why was I giving her such a hard time?

"Then I'm doubly embarrassed."

"Don't be," I said, with a lift of my shoulder. "You do you. No reason to apologize." I was doing it again and couldn't seem to stop. I picked up my warm mug and headed to the couch. I could feel Parker's eyes on me.

"Are you okay?"

"I'm fine."

"Is this about us? Because we have a history?" She was referencing our one night together.

I smiled serenely. "Absolutely not. All in the past."

"Are you sure?"

"Yes. Ancient history." I conjured another smile. "Just tired. Late night all around, you know?" I punctuated my words with a bounce of my eyebrows, making the sexual insinuation clear, making me a complete ass for going there. Especially since the insinuation was a lie. In reality, Sheila and I hadn't had sex the night before. We'd cuddled for a bit before breaking off to our own sides of the bed. In fact, over the past few weeks, we'd become very chaste in general. Why was I projecting differently to Parker in some kind of one-upmanship? My relationship and sex life were not in competition with hers.

"Gotcha." Parker raised her mug as if in toast but didn't smile back. She picked up the newspaper that had been dropped on our doorstep that morning and went about reading it on the couch. I settled in across from her with a new suspense novel I'd bonded with at the store, even though I'd actually rather be catching up on Parker's backlist. I stole glances at her occasionally and noticed how she chewed on the inside of her lip as she read. She glanced up at one point and I casually looked away like a third grader. She smiled back into her paper and chewed on her lip some more.

"Well, don't party too hard, you guys," Carissa said loudly, behind us. I turned to see her standing there in a bright red bikini. "I'm hitting the fucking hot tub," she said proudly. "If there's breakfast I'll take some."

Parker and I glanced at each other.

"I can make breakfast," I said. "Fresh biscuits, and maybe this scramble I got the recipe for the other—"

"Sounds perf," Carissa said, and scampered to the back deck, popping on oversized headphones as she went. I ignored the boobs.

"Perf," I said, and nodded at Parker.

"Hannah, you don't have to make her breakfast. We can order something from the main kitchen, or she can have cereal."

I stood and headed to the open kitchen. "I don't mind. I promise. I like to cook."

She sighed. "Okay, then. I'll keep you company." I felt her following me as I made my way. "Plus, I have something for you." I could tell she was trying to put us back on track, and I was willing to go there with her. I didn't want a contentious weekend. Parker and I had always gotten along. It was time to reset the board.

I went about unloading the ingredients I'd brought with me. "A brand-new pony? Did you bring me a pony, Parker?" I fluttered my eyelashes.

She chuckled. "Close." She reached into her messenger bag that was hooked on the back of one of the chairs around the table and returned with a bound stack of pages. "My new one. I had a few hard copies bound before the official galleys hit. I made one for you, just as you asked."

I snatched it off the counter and practically hugged it to my chest, wondering just what kind of story she'd woven together this time. Who were the characters? Just how would they fall in love? How would I feel about them once our journey together was complete? And okay, the odd sexy scene or two also had me eager to turn a few pages. "I get my own advance copy? I feel like I've arrived," I said, with what felt like a twinkle in my eye.

"Oh, you definitely have. I don't do this. Do you understand? Ever." She pointed at the manuscript. "And don't share that with anyone. State secrets and all."

I passed her a look that said, "really?"

"I'm dead serious. Can you imagine the fallout if spoilers leaked out? The romance world as we know it could implode."

She was being playful and I liked it. There was an electricity bouncing between us that I'd experienced before. I both loved and hated that it was back. "I simply can't imagine it."

"If that thing shows up on the internet, you and I are going to have words."

"Words?" I gestured with the spatula. "Wow. Not *words*."

She laughed and took a step closer to me at the stove. "Serious ones."

I felt my height advantage via our proximity, which, by the way, left us a step closer to each other than was probably apropos. "Somehow, I'm not afraid."

"Yo, when are we eating? Soon?" Carissa yelled. She stood at the open sliding glass door, her boobs on full display in that dental floss of a top. I glimpsed all but her nipples, which I guessed was the whole point.

I glanced down at my ingredients and did a quick calculation. "Oh, uh, maybe fifteen minutes?"

She threw up a deuce sign and retreated to her hot tub, giant headphones back on her ears. I stared after her, mystified and frustrated. "So, what exactly brought you and Carissa Swain together? I'm still a little confused by the order of things."

"I told you the story at one point. We met at a party in New York. My friend had everyone over to a rooftop christening of his new apartment and Carissa was there with her promoter."

"I remember the logistics." I set down my spoon and began to kneed my biscuit dough. "I mean the other part. What bonds you together? It's a combination I wouldn't have predicted when I first met you."

"Are you jealous, Hannah?" She said it with a grin, but the fact that she was half-serious annoyed me. The fact that she was right annoyed me even more.

"God, no. Just answer the question. I'm curious. It's my nature. I'm like Nancy Drew."

Was it just me or did she deflate? "We have fun, and beyond that…I can relax. Not worry too much about things getting too heavy or dramatic. We can enjoy our relationship for what it is."

I opened my mouth to answer, to push back, to challenge her, because it sounded like Carissa might be in Parker's life because she felt light.

She changed the subject before I could do so. "What about you and Sheila? I'm also a little surprised by the matchup."

I gestured for the glass next to her to use as my circular mold, just as my mother had taught me, and she handed it over. "I don't know what you mean. We're incredibly well-suited. In so many ways."

She whistled.

"What?"

Parker leaned against the counter and folded her arms. I could smell her peaches and cream lotion, and my gaze wandered to the column of her neck. "Well, you're already a pretty conservative personality. I just imagined you with someone a little more...free, to pull the fun out of you."

I narrowed my gaze. "I think you just called me unfun, and I'm figuring out how I feel about that, leaning heavily toward mortally wounded."

She laughed. "It sounded that way. But no, no, no. You're a lot of fun, just at your own Hannah pace. You like to take things in, turn them over in your hands, and think about them until you're blue in the face."

She knew me so well after only a few months. "I've never been blue."

Parker sighed. "This isn't going well." She seemed to make a decision and straightened to her full height. "The tax woman is awesome. You guys are a nice couple. I should have led with that."

"She is. We are. Thank you. The pop star is...fine." It was all I could manage. Why couldn't I be more adult about this? What in the hell was wrong with me? The idea of those boobs in Parker's face last night made me start kneading my biscuit dough aggressively.

She pointed at what I was doing. "I can tell." She covered my hand with hers and stilled my next knead. "We're a good match and have a great time."

"I heard how *great* last night." I picked up a kitchen knife and began to stab the dough, which, let's be honest, is not productive to biscuit making. It felt amazing, though.

"Again, sorry about that. You can stop stabbing dough now."

I did. "Not a problem. Isn't that what life is all about? Having a great time? Fun, fun, fun, and nothing more? Who needs companionship, depth, or good conversation when there's a hot body in the room?" I smiled through it, though, and ordered myself to hold that damn smile for four whole seconds if it killed me. Hard to do when you couldn't even hold your own tongue.

"I'll let you finish here," she said quietly. I turned and watched her walk away, retreating to the deck and Carissa. My eyes fell to her backside, her legs, and how she filled out the white shorts she wore perfectly. She was a genetic lotto, coming with so many layers, all in one package. Good looks, sharp wit, kindness, and a strong intellect. Maybe that's why she left me so confused half the time. I slid the biscuits into the oven and blew a strand of hair from my eyes.

"You okay, Hannah?" Sheila asked, emerging from our room all showered and ready for the day. She looked pretty with her hair pulled back and her face fresh. I felt myself calm down.

"Yes. Sorry. In my own head."

"You sure?"

I nodded and swallowed. "Yes, I'm just having a weird morning. Now that you're here, I can rebound." I hoped to God I could.

❖

"Do you think this place has a chef they could send over?" Carissa asked, coming back inside.

I glanced at the clock. It was just past midnight. "I don't think so. If they did, they likely wouldn't be available right now."

"God," she said, practically stomping away. "I want those miniature corn dog things. With the good mustard." Apparently, Carissa didn't realize we hadn't submitted her rider before arriving at the resort. "Cutes, call them and see?"

Parker shrugged. "I don't think there's anyone to call. The information packet says the kitchen closes at midnight. It's not that big an operation, Ris." I internally cringed at the nickname. It spoke of intimacy, and I didn't like the thought of Parker getting close with this particular woman, who outside of her success and appearance, was entirely mean-spirited and immature.

"Perfect." Carissa sighed. "Get me another beer, then?" She leaned backward over the arm of the club chair, further showcasing her midriff and killer abs. Parker did as she was asked and carried another beer over to Carissa, who—let's be honest—had consumed more than I had been capable of keeping track of.

"I can cook something for her," I said quietly to Parker.

"You don't have to do that," Parker whispered back. "She's had a few and will probably crash soon."

"What about little corn dogs?" Carissa asked, clearly having overheard the offer. "With cheese inside. And extra flaky. Can you do flaky?" She laughed at the word for reasons I wasn't clear on.

I turned around, hands on my hips. "Not confident I brought the ingredients for cheese-infused, extra-flaky miniature corn dogs, but how about an omelet?"

"Biscuits?" she countered, popping up from her spot over the arm of that chair. Apparently, she'd liked the breakfast I'd made more than she'd let on.

"I can do more biscuits," I said, and went about pulling out the supplies.

"God, you make good biscuits, Hannah. I should bring you on tour with me just to do that. You'd be my biscuit maker."

I nodded. "Yep. That sounds…like something. Probably all I'm good for, right?"

"You know that's not true," Parker said.

"She doesn't," I said back quietly.

"What's going on?" Sheila asked, coming out of our room in a black tank top and yoga pants. She looked fantastic and I watched as Parker's gaze moved from Sheila to me. Yep. She'd noticed, too, and I wasn't sure she enjoyed it very much. There was something gratifying about that, after having watched Carissa parade around all day in washcloth-sized clothing. "Why are you cooking again?"

"Carissa is hungry and wants biscuits."

"She's drunk," Sheila whispered in my ear.

"Ya think?" I tossed the flour into the mixture. "It's okay. I really don't mind."

"Hannah," Carissa said, "do you have a crush on Parker?"

I exchanged an incredulous glance with Sheila and turned around to face Carissa, careful not to even look in Parker's direction. "I do not. No. Why do you ask?"

"Just a feeling I have that you like my girlfriend. You do, don't you?"

"Carissa," Parker said in warning, but the girl was too drunk at this point to care.

"It's okay if you do. She's fucking hot, but she's mine. As long as you get that, we're cool."

"Understood," I said, cheerfully, and turned to Sheila. "Any chance you can finish these biscuits? I need some air."

"Of course. You okay?" she asked quietly in my ear.

"Yes. Just need a break." I offered her hand a squeeze and reminded myself how lucky I was to have someone who had my back the way she did. I walked to the sliding glass door and exited onto the back deck. The cold air hit my cheeks, and that helped, because they burned with both embarrassment and indignation. How dare she? I'd been nothing but nice to Carissa, and to have her come at me with her wild theories about Parker left a mark. I gripped the wooden railing hard and shook my head.

"Hannah?" Parker. I closed my eyes in further defeat but didn't turn around. "She was just mouthing off. She does that when she drinks."

"I noticed."

"I'm really sorry. She was out of line."

Parker came to the railing and stood next to me. For a few moments, neither of us spoke. I stared out at the oaks, the lake, and the quiet world that came with it. In my head it was anything but quiet.

"You're not going to say anything?"

I turned to Parker for the first time since she'd joined me. "And what words should I use? Should I tell you that this weekend has been a nightmare? That there's been weird tension between us, and your girlfriend is entitled and spoiled and childish in a combination I've never quite experienced. Would you like for me to list all of the ways I feel like a lesser person since I've arrived? Which of those things would you like me to say right now, Parker? You can choose."

I don't know what I expected, unleashing on her like that, but it wasn't what I got.

Parker blinked several times. Then she nodded at whatever she was blinking about. "Okay. Got it. So, it's like that."

"I don't know what you mean." I let my head drop in defeat. This was going nowhere, and now she was defensive.

"I wanted to do something nice for us all, but I guess it didn't live up to the Hannah Shephard standard."

The tables were turning? Really? I couldn't believe it, but then I could, because we'd both been ready to boil over for the past twenty-four hours. The sound of a ticking clock had played steadily in my ear, growing louder as the weekend progressed. Now it was apparently go time.

I met her gaze evenly. "Standards? If you had standards of your own, this weekend wouldn't have been a problem."

She pulled her face back. "Is that another shot at Carissa? Wow, you really are jealous, aren't you?" The surprised look she sported showed off both dimples, and I hated her for it.

So, the gloves were off. I had a lot of unnamed feelings and they were rushing to the surface now. "I realize you'd like that, because I honestly believe it's your goal in life to make everyone worship and follow after you like your adoring readers do, but I'm afraid I won't be granting that request."

"I'm an egomaniac. Is that it?"

"That's what it's starting to feel like."

"If I'm an egomaniac, then you're a pretentious snob."

I applauded. "Good one."

She stared at me as if I had made zero sense. "I don't understand you. What is it you want from me? What have I done wrong?"

The door opened and I turned to see Carissa standing there, arms crossed, pout in place. "Cutes, let's go to bed and snuggle. I don't want to wait on biscuits. I don't think her girlfriend makes them the same anyway."

Parker turned back to me, met my gaze, and I knew the answer to her question.

"Not a damn thing."

CHAPTER TEN

The phone calls stopped. I should have expected that. It still didn't make the silence any easier. I missed my friend. That weekend getaway had been an undoing of us, Parker and me, in which we'd picked each other apart, all of it fueled by jealousy, longing, or whatever you wanted to call it. I hadn't been able to admit my feelings at the cabin, but a month later, as I sat in the silence of us, I could see them for what they were. Romantic.

After my fight with Parker, Sheila and I quietly packed and left early the next morning, saying only a brief thank you, all much earlier than I'd even planned. I just couldn't fully face Parker in the aftermath of our argument. I hated that we'd fought. I hated that I'd initiated it and carried much of the responsibility for the way the weekend ended. Parker had come to the deck to check on me that night, to make me feel better, and I'd lashed out. Whether it was out of insecurity or embarrassment didn't matter. How I'd treated her did.

I hadn't called her, and she hadn't called me, and the hole in my life was growing larger with each day that went by. I thought about her a lot. The twinkle she got in her green eyes when something amused her, but not enough for full-blown laughter. I adored the way her face transformed when she concentrated on a task. More than anything, I missed our talks. She'd been the ultimate cheerleader for me, and I'd done my best to cheer her on right back. Well, right until I didn't.

Parker's new manuscript sat on my kitchen table. I couldn't bring myself to open it, feeling like I didn't have permission. Shouldn't have, more like. Regardless of if I ever heard from Parker again, I knew what I had to do.

"So, it's over?" Sheila asked. "Is that what this means?"

I wasn't sure she'd see it as a true loss. We'd sailed through a romantic stretch of our relationship and landed smack on the barren island of friendship, which was where our relationship had remained for a while. Surely she'd felt it, too. We'd burned out before ever truly catching fire. It wasn't there between us. "I'm so sorry, but I think so. I enjoy your company so much."

"But there's no true spark."

"No," I said carefully.

She sighed and smoothed her hair, pulled back for work. We'd agreed to meet for coffee, ending us the same way we'd started. There was a melancholy fullness in that. "I knew we'd run a little cold lately, but was hoping we'd sort it out," Sheila said.

"I'm just not sure it's there for me in a romantic sense. Would you be willing to, maybe, work on being friends? We really get along well."

"I have a lot of friends," she said. "I was hoping you were more."

"Me too."

Sheila stood and held up her cappuccino. "In light of this new development, I guess I'll take this to go."

I stood, as well. "I'm really sorry, Sheila. I have some things I need to sort out in my head."

"And they all lead to Parker."

I felt my skin warm and I chewed the inside of my cheek uncomfortably. I didn't want to bring Parker into this, but Sheila had witnessed everything that had transpired at the cabin. Even if I'd been stupid, Sheila wasn't. "Some of them do. Yes. But I'm working on that."

She nodded, satisfied. I could tell she'd placed a barrier between us now. She looked at me differently. The familiarity had vanished so very quickly. "Give me some time, and maybe we'll see about that friendship." I appreciated the small smile she afforded me. Sheila was a good person. She just wasn't *my* person.

I drove home with an uncomfortable ache in my chest. I was alone again, and though that had always been just fine with me, something in the recent past had shifted my perception. There was a what-if factor that tugged and poked and kept me thinking. What if there was someone out there, who could make me feel the way I'd felt back in September? Special. Alive. Happy. What if life really could be different, changed for the better? The one what-if I held back from myself? What if Parker Bristow was that person?

I glanced at the phone sitting next to me on the passenger's seat. The one that hadn't rung in more than a month. The melancholy ache persisted. I drove on.

❖

"We're going to need a bigger children's nook," Luna whispered to me with a gleeful smile.

"This is not a bad problem," I said back.

We stood side by side, taking in this week's puppet show in which the Big Bad Wolf was threatening to blow down the house of straw. The space was overflowing with young children, which meant that the bookstore was bustling with parents. I had all hands on deck during the weekly puppet shows, which meant both Luna and Kurt were working the floor, as well as my new part-time employee, Justin, on the register. Justin, I'd found, was a poetry geek and would burst into impromptu verse whenever the mood moved him. That had worried me at first, but the customers seemed to enjoy his enthusiasm and lame attempt at rhyme, and that's what mattered most. He was also lanky, six foot three, and came with a rather impressive pompadour.

"My lady," Justin said, as I came behind the counter.

"Justin, you can just call me Hannah. I'll call you Justin. It can be a thing we do." Why could no one at this store use my actual name? I was beginning to wonder.

"Come back and see us next week," he said, as he handed a sack of books to a young woman.

I smiled at her, too.

He turned to me. "Whatever my lady would prefer. Lady Hannah it is."

I sighed, not actually minding his nicknames or the fun he'd brought to the store.

"Excuse me," another woman asked.

I turned to her. "Yes?"

"I'm looking for a book by Parker Bristow in which the guy goes off to war and doesn't know he's fathered a child."

I nodded. "*Traitorous Heart*," I supplied for her. "Follow me."
"Is it true that Bristow did a signing here?"
I nodded, feeling heavy and flat. "It is. She was in the store last August."
The woman shook her head in distress. "I can't believe I missed it. I only found this place when my book club started meeting here on Thursday nights. My own fault, I suppose. She's my favorite author. I can't get enough. It's crack, I say."
I grinned. "I love the club, and I'm so glad we're on your radar now." I paused and relented. "I like Parker Bristow's work as well. A lot."
"Any chance she'll be back?"
I wished I had better news for her. I swallowed. "I don't think so."
Two and half months now since the cabin, and not only had I not had the courage to call Parker, she'd not reached out either. As a result, I'd stepped back from all things Parker related to give my heart space to rebuild. I didn't seek out any of her funny tweets or mentions on the gossip websites. Her manuscript still sat untouched on my shelf. The mention of her name carried such power to affect me, however, and in a cruel twist of fate, hearing it on the regular was a function of my job.
"Well, that's too bad," the woman said, accepting the paperback copy of the book I'd located for her. I glanced away as Parker's photo flashed on the back.
I pointed at her copy. "Not to worry. This book will make up for it. If there's anything I can help you with, please let me know."
The conversation stuck with me, though. Later that night, as I put away the dishes to a little early Diana Krall, I stole glances at the manuscript. Tomato blinked at me knowingly. I tried to distract myself with my own slow-paced dance moves. I sashayed to the cabinet with the soup bowls and kicked my hips back and forth as I placed the dishes on the shelf. Bacon snaked his way around my ankles in a show of solidarity. That's right. We were grooving together. "Don't be jealous," I told Tomato. "You had your chance."
Ten minutes later, I'd lost the battle. With my feet pulled beneath me and a glass of Merlot on the end table, I set to reading. One page turned to ten, and ten turned to fifty. I was amazed at the words in front of me. This wasn't Parker's standard romance. She'd written, for

the first time, about two women. The firefighter had been a *girl*. The narrative was intriguing, the characters rich and textured. I flipped the pages as fast as I could tear through them, knowing full well I could always go back and reread later. The couple was apart, unjustly so, and I needed to see them fix the issues between them. Just as they'd come together, unable to resist the tension in the room, unable to keep their hands off each other, there was an irritating knock at my door. I dropped the manuscript onto my coffee table and scrambled to deal with Bo or my neighbor, Miranda, who often locked herself out of her own apartment.

"Hi," Parker said uneasily, as I swung open the door.

I stared, not quite sure if she was actually standing there in front of me or if I'd conjured up her image. "Um…"

"That's not exactly the welcome I was hoping for, but I get it."

"What are you doing here?" I asked. "I was just…" Apparently, I'd lost the ability to cap off a thought.

She tilted her head and smiled, and the world went still. "Can I come in and we can talk about it?"

I stepped back and allowed Parker, who carried a Chanel duffle bag, into my apartment. She dropped it and ran her hands down her jeans, as if to smooth them, only they didn't need smoothing. "I'm nervous. I don't usually get this nervous, but my heart is pounding."

I closed the door and followed her in. While I struggled to understand what brought her here, I tried to harness the bolt of energy her presence inspired. "Why don't you start by telling me what's going on."

She nodded. "*You're* going on."

A pause hit, and it felt like it lasted forever. I heard my own heart beating. I wish I'd turned on more lights than just the lamp on the table because there were shadows on her face that kept me from understanding how she was feeling.

"You're in my head a lot and I can't run in circles anymore, Hannah, trying to not think about you." She held out her arms and let them drop. "So, I'm here."

"You're here." I'd said nothing productive since she'd set foot in my apartment. That luxury was MIA. The very familiar zing that came with being in Parker's presence shot through me from my fingers and toes to my hairline and much lower.

She blinked. "I imagine you're still upset about our argument."

The words tumbled back to me then. "I'm not. I was childish, and emotional, and I took it out on you, who hadn't done anything wrong."

"It's okay," she said, quietly. "You can beat up on me anytime. It's so much better than silence."

I nodded. "I agree." Yet I still didn't fully understand the nature of her intentions. Was she planning on us repairing our friendship, or maybe she—

The thought came to a screeching halt when she walked toward me and, with determination, kissed me soundly. No, expertly. I felt my knees sag for a moment before I stood more fully to accept her kiss, to give back just as much. I wasn't sure what was happening, but everything in me wanted to go along for this ride. We were slow and then not. My hands held her face, our mouths danced sensually. That is, until my brain joined the party.

I pulled back. "Your girlfriend."

"Over. Six weeks ago." She searched my eyes.

"Six weeks?" I kissed her some more, not really able to do anything else. She smelled like peaches again. I loved peaches. Why would I want to do anything but kiss her?

"Yours?" she asked, stopping the kiss and pressing her forehead to mine. Our breathing sounded ragged and only heightened the urgency I felt to touch Parker, this time with knowledge of how I truly felt about her. "I shouldn't kiss you if you have a girlfriend. I should have asked first." Parker closed her eyes and waited for my answer.

"I haven't for a month."

"Oh, thank you, Jesus." She nodded and took my face in her hands for another kiss. We kissed so well together, making the process automatic, effortless. It reminded me how explosive we were. It hadn't been just the one night. Our chemistry was still intact. I wanted Parker. I wanted her hands on my body and wanted to explore hers just as much, but everything between us had been such a blur, a jumble of uncharacterized occurrences. I needed to understand.

"Wait," I said, reluctantly pulling my mouth from hers yet again. "We can't just leap in like this. Steps have been skipped. We're bad at steps."

She blinked. "Okay. No. We won't skip them, then."

I blinked. I mean, I expected a little bit of a protest. I walked a few feet away and stared at my kitchen, hands on top of my head, trying to focus. The space helped. I located my vocabulary, at least a portion of it. "You have an effect on me. You make me forget to think, and we need to do just that right now."

"Right. I get it. I just showed up here and kissed you—"

"With very little explanation, I might add." I held up a hand as she opened her mouth to speak. "But maybe I haven't been as communicative as I could have been either. Until recently, I'm not sure I would have been able to articulate what was going on in my head. I didn't get it myself."

She nodded. "And now you do?"

"I think so."

Parker looked around. I loved her big green, expressive eyes. "Do you have some water? Gatorade? Anything?"

I laughed, expecting something more serious to come out of her mouth.

"Sorry. Just feeling a little light-headed. All your fault." She gestured to the spot where we'd just been making out, which caused me to heat all over again.

I fanned myself on the way to my fridge and didn't care if she saw. I grabbed a bottle of water for Parker and refrained from placing a cool one against my own damn forehead and chest. I still felt the zing zigzagging all through my body like a pinball. What was it with her and the zing? When her hand brushed mine as I handed it to her, it quadrupled its pinball pace. Oh, what a tangled web this might be for me. I didn't care. I was embracing the web and the zing and planned to sort out that crazy metaphor knot at a date in the future that wasn't today.

"You were saying?" she asked as she took a seat on my couch and drank generously from the bottle, which, let's be honest, just exposed the elegant shape of her neck.

Something about having unofficial permission to look now added fuel to my previously tamped-down lust. I was a harlot. I sat in the chair next to the couch to be sure to keep a few feet of distance between us as I tried to explain. "I was grappling with some feelings I wasn't fully aware of when we saw each other last at the cabin."

"Feelings for me?" There was a sliver of hope behind her eyes that spoke of vulnerability.

My heart grew. I nodded. "I was angry at you for choosing someone like Carissa."

"I got that part. It was the feelings I wasn't sure of." She took another drink. More neck exposure.

I swallowed. "She was right. You were right. I *was* jealous and lashed out." A pause. Deep breath. "I wanted you for myself."

"God, Hannah, then why didn't you—"

"Why didn't *you*?"

"I didn't know how. I'm not as strong as you think I am." She ran a hand through the waves of her hair. "Now you answer."

"Because we live in different worlds. We still do. You'd be bored with my life."

"I'm terrified of it."

I quirked my head. I wasn't expecting that answer. When I studied her face, I saw that there were tears in her eyes. I'd never seen Parker cry, or get sentimental at all, for that matter, and wasn't prepared for how it affected me. "What are you terrified of?" I asked, softly. I wanted to take her in my arms and hold her until she felt safe and happy.

She held out her hand, gesturing for me to come sit next to her, and I did. "This. Feeling for someone what I already feel for you." A pause. "I'm going to confess something here." She took a deep breath. "I felt it that first day. Not only a physical connection, but this intense interest in who you are as a person. It's the reaction of someone that I write books about. I was caught off guard to experience it myself. I wanted to spend the next year just learning everything about you."

"And that was a bad thing?"

She quickly dabbed away a tear that I could tell mortified her. Her composure seemed to have returned. "It was awful because paralysis took over. Listen, I don't get mixed up with people long term. At least, I never have. I weave. I dodge. I move on." She stared at her hands. "I don't like that about myself, and I've tried to overcome it, but it's hard for me to attach to someone who…matters." She met my gaze, her implication clear.

Suddenly, it all started to make sense. "You took up with Carissa right after we were together in Mystic."

She met my gaze, shame radiating off her. "I don't believe that was a coincidence. She was fun, and exciting, and not at all someone who could hurt me or who I had any intense feelings for."

"Oh, Parker," I said, sympathetically. My heart hurt for her, and I hated seeing her look so sad. This wasn't at all the Parker I'd come to know. This person was cracked open, raw, and forthcoming, and I still wanted to protect her at all costs.

"I've missed you a lot since we've stopped our phone calls," she whispered. "Talking to you, hearing about each of your days meant so much to me. And you were always there for me right back. I talked through everything with you."

"I missed you, too." We stared at each other, trying to figure it all out.

"Hannah," she said. Her expression was nervous, hopeful, wistful. All of it. "We don't have to leap into bed."

I nodded because I wasn't after another hookup. "Okay."

"That's not what I'm asking for. I mean," she traced the tiny bit of collarbone exposed at my neckline, "I'm not saying I couldn't be persuaded." I placed my hand over hers, stopping that movement because in about 3.4 seconds, I wasn't going to have a say. She took the cue and sat back. "I'm here because I wanted to lay eyes on you. Talk to you. Be in the same room with you. Plain and simple. Nothing more."

"Well, let's do that. I think maybe things escalated between us... too quickly in Mystic."

"Probably so."

"Every bit as much my doing as yours."

She let her head drop back on to the couch, her curls fanned out. "But that night?" She shook her head and covered her eyes. "I've never had that before. I've never experienced anything like it."

I dropped my tone and leaned in. "Wasn't just me, then?"

She shook her head. "Ha. No. I've replayed it a lot, Hannah." She touched my chin. "Replayed you. I didn't sleep that night. I couldn't."

I smiled, and she reached out and gave my chin the smallest of shakes. Everything she did was sexy to me, and I was doing my best to not let my physical instinct take over. "But I scared you."

She nodded slowly. Her smile faltered and she blinked several times in succession, broadcasting how nervous the topic made her. "You still do. It was hard to make myself come here, as much as I wanted to."

I eased a strand of hair behind her ear, hoping to relax her. "Another reason to go slow."

She smiled. "How about I give you some space? Check into a hotel, and—"

"No way."

She laughed at that.

I pressed on. "We can go slow right here. You're staying with me." She seemed to like that. "All right. Then let's just relax tonight." "Relaxing is my favorite pastime." I sat back against the couch. I stretched out my arm, and she accepted the invitation by relaxing back against me. When her weight settled and the sweet, familiar scent of her hair hit, all the tension in my body released. In a manner I can't fully describe, I felt like I was right where I was supposed to be for the first time in a long while. Everything about the moment—the feel of her in my arms, the quiet of the apartment, even the wind whistling quietly outside—made me feel that for the first time in a long time, everything was in place. She reached up and squeezed my hand, signaling that she felt it, too. I handed her the remote control and watched as she surfed from channel to channel. An hour ago, I was wrapped up in Parker's latest novel, and now she was wrapped up in my arms. My heart was full.

"Do you think the *Family Feud* lies?" she asked sleepily an hour later, pointing at the TV. "I just can't imagine only twenty-four people saying that the bathroom was the reason they got up in the middle of the night. What are these other seventy-six people doing at two in the morning when they wake up? Hitting up dance parties? Their taxes? Are they baking pies? I call bullshit."

I squeezed her from behind with a chuckle, enjoying her game show outrage. "I think you might be putting too much thought into it. It's probably interns at Universal Studios conducting an on-the-sidewalk poll." That wasn't enough for her, and I laughed.

"I need to know. I'm not sure how I can move forward without understanding these seventy-six people and what their nightly rituals are."

She'd already retrieved her phone, and as she lay with her back against me, I watched as she fired off a tweet to her millions of followers demanding answers. I smiled because I knew whatever witty way she worded it would bring lots of attention to her *Family Feud* plight. All part of the job and persona she was incredibly good at.

Two episodes of *Family Feud* later and I struggled to keep my eyes open. Parker lay slack, which told me she was out. "Hey, there," I whispered in her ear. "Why don't we head to bed?"

She stirred, turned back, and blinked a few times, smiling at me when she came to. "I can just sleep on the couch. Kind of my tradition when I stop by."

"No way. Come with me. We'll just sleep. Totally PG." As she sat up, I turned off the lights in the living room, leaving the cats to their nightly games, picked up her bag, and offered her my hand. She sleepily accepted it, and I walked us into my room, reveling in the feel of her hand in mine. She slipped out of her clothes and into my bed wearing only her black bra and underwear, which I glimpsed before she disappeared beneath the covers. Gorgeous. It astounded me how much. When she unclasped the bra from beneath the sheet and dropped it to the floor, I went still.

"What are you trying to do to me? PG, remember?" I placed my palm on my forehead.

"Valid point." She sat up with the sheet across her breasts, which was every bit as sexy. "Maybe you have a shirt I can sleep in? I don't really travel with pajamas. In fact, I'm not a huge fan of pajamas at all."

I tried to bypass that piece of information, nodded, and pulled an old T-shirt from my dresser.

"Your ceiling is amazing," she said, staring up at the billowing fabric. "I could never leave this spot and be just fine. Hannah and her magnificent ceiling."

I watched Parker lying there in my bed, and felt the same way. I wanted her right there in that spot. My heart squeezed pleasantly. My body hummed for her.

Once I was ready for bed, a girl who *did* wear pajamas, shorts and camisole specifically, I slipped between the sheets next to Parker, who stared at me from her pillow, wearing my shirt. "I'm glad I'm here."

"Me too," I said with a smile.

"Can I give you a kiss good night? Is that too fast?"

I didn't answer her but instead leaned in, pressing my lips to hers, allowing them to linger. She sighed happily and closed her eyes. I hit the lights, very aware of her skin near mine, subtle heat emanating from her body. I was relaxed and turned the hell on in tandem.

"Come here," she whispered. "Let me play with your hair as you fall asleep."

I allowed Parker to hold me. Her fingertips grazed my scalp, lifting and dropping my hair slowly. I thought I'd died and gone to heaven. I don't remember drifting off, but it must have happened fairly quickly, safe and nestled against Parker. That night in her arms, even with the absence of any kind of sexual contact, was one of the most wonderful nights I've had.

To a certain extent, Parker reminded me of a flame—beautiful, hypnotic, but hard to capture, and capable of burning you if you tried. For that reason, I was every bit as afraid as she was. Underneath it all, I had a feeling we were worth it.

CHAPTER ELEVEN

"Can I help you find something?" I asked an elderly man I'd seen move up and down the aisles of the shop about six times now. He was really adorable in his tweed hat and glasses but seemed to be lost. "Hello, there. I pass by here some mornings on my walk, so I stopped in today."

"We're so happy you did," I said. I had a feeling this man needed his perfect match, and I was going to make sure that happened. "Is there a certain type of book you're looking for?"

He nodded, seemingly happy for assistance. "I need something specific. But I can't find the books on cooking desserts anywhere. I need to cook one, see?"

I grinned. "Follow me to the baking section." I glanced back. "What will you be baking?"

"I'd like to cook a cake with chocolate pieces in it for my next-door neighbor. She likes chocolate things, and well, I like her. I'm Wally, by the way. Wally Spooner."

My heart squeezed. "Then it's important we find you a good recipe, Wally." We pored through a few different books together and opted for one with simple instructions and some photos for guidance. There was a fairly straightforward recipe for vanilla cake with a ribbon of chocolate frosting through the center of it.

"Oh, I think Tillie is really going to love this, and if she does, I'll be in. She might even want to smooch."

"She might."

He paused and took off his cap in thought. "If she doesn't, I'll just have to be ready to accept that."

I nodded. "You seem to have examined this from all angles."

He gestured with his cap. "Matters of the heart are nothing to leave to chance. Gotta put some thought into it. I like Tillie. She deserves a cake, smooching or not."

"Good point." I nodded. "But I hope there's a smooch."

"From your lips." Then he smiled. "Or rather Tillie's." He chuckled at his own joke, and I couldn't help but laugh along with him because today was a good day, and he was a sweet-seeming man. Romance was in the air. Smooching was. Not only had I been charmed by the potential smooching, but as I walked back to the front of the store, I felt a pair of welcome eyes tracking me. I met Parker's gaze across the room and smiled. She'd wanted to come to work with me and said the backdrop of the books would inspire her writing. She sat behind the counter with her laptop open, typing and watching, typing and watching. To say I loved having her there was an understatement. When we got busy, she even jumped in to offer a hand.

"Can I help you with something, ma'am?" I turned when I heard Parker speaking to a customer and smothered a chuckle when I saw who it was. Oh, man. The woman from the book club, the very one who'd asked if Parker might ever return for a signing. I watched with interest.

The woman clutched two paperbacks to her chest as she peered up at Parker, who had a good four inches on her. The woman blinked, looked down at her books—which, joy of joys, seemed to be Parker's—and blinked again. Finally, she flipped one of the books over slowly to the author photo on the back and held it up to Parker's face to compare.

I decided to save her. "Hey, there," I said, casually, coming around the corner. "Turns out Parker Bristow did come back. She might even be willing to sign those books for you."

She looked at Parker, then me. "It's her?"

"It's her." I folded my arms and smiled at her very wide eyes.

"I'd definitely be willing to sign if you wanted me to," Parker said, and accepted the books from the woman, who then promptly returned to the shelves for more. When she was done cleaning me out, Parker set to signing the eight books the woman had thrust at her.

"Hi," she said to Parker, still a little mesmerized.

"Hi," Parker said, beaming.

The woman turned to me as I rang her up. "Is it because I asked?"
"It definitely helped," I lied. "We try and take all customer suggestions into consideration."
She looked around in amazement. "This is a really good store."
Parker leaned in as if divulging a secret. "My favorite one, in fact."
"I see why," the woman replied. She looked back to me. "But maybe a little more advertising next time. No one else seems to know."
I nodded vigorously. "Another great suggestion."
"Hannah and I are friends," Parker said, sending me a warm look, "and I'm a big supporter of her shop. Don't you just love it?"
"I do. So very much," the woman said. She watched as Parker signed her books with a big swooping "P." "I'm here twice a week these days, and telling all my friends about this place. I'll tell even more people after today. Just amazing to walk in here, and bam, what do you know? Parker freaking Bristow is sitting behind the counter ready to sign all your books." She leaned in. "I saw you on the lip sync TV show, and was so happy you beat that schmarmy talk show host."
"Me too. He was far too egotistical. I had a great time pretending to sing and dance." She handed the books back to the woman. "So glad we ran into each other."
"You have no idea how exciting this is for me. This store is the best." The woman bid us farewell and then left the store shaking her head, muttering in victory.
"Hey, Parker freaking Bristow?" I said. "I think you just made her week."
"How's yours going?" she asked, leaning her chin on her hand. "Because mine is the best in a really long time."
"Ahem," Luna said, rounding the corner to the break room. "Are you two flirting? I feel like you're flirting but would never dare presume to know the nature of your friendship."
"Oh, I don't know that I'd say that," I answered, conservatively. Luna knew we'd become friends, but I hadn't shared a ton of details beyond that. Bo was the only human who knew the entire story, at least from me. But Luna was excellent at filling in blanks, and I wasn't shocked she was doing so now.
"She may not be flirting, but I am," Parker said to her matter-of-factly. "I'm working really hard at it, too. Trying to give little seductive glances and say things that are sweet and playful, toss my hair in her

direction. Maybe if I keep doing those things, she'll notice me. What do you think my chances are?"

Luna nodded sagely and studied me. "She's looking fairly weak to me. I think you might be making progress."

"I've noticed you," I said to Parker as I began to close out the register. We were near to closing and I wanted to get a head start on the evening. After all, I had a reason to. When we'd gotten ready for the day that morning, Parker told me that she wasn't sure how long she'd be in town, which in my head meant I'd have her for at least a little while. No end date on the calendar.

"I don't have any media booked for a couple of weeks, so I thought I'd just take a step back. Get away from it all, so we can just…be. Is that okay?" she'd asked as I'd stirred my coffee before work that morning.

I took a moment to answer because she was wrapped in a towel when she asked, fresh from the shower with the tops of her breasts peeking out. I wasn't clear whether that was by design. I had my suspicions. Either way, it was highly effective and I would have signed over the title on my car had she asked.

"You can step back from it all here for as long as you like."

"You realize that's a dangerous statement. You might have an author permanently attached to your kitchen counter, sucking down your orange juice and rarely buying more and typing away the details of an imaginary world in your kitchen. It could be a lot. Are you prepared?"

I lowered my eyebrows. "Are you an orange juice sucker?"

"No. But what if I become one?"

"I think we can cross that bridge when we come to it, but I have to admit, it might get dicey. Can you go put on clothes now? That might be good." I still felt it was in our best interest to go slow, and her wardrobe wasn't helping my resolve, what little of it remained. This was torture, and another approach might be called for.

She glanced down in confusion and then blossomed into a proud smile. "You don't like what I'm wearing?"

"You know damned well I like what you're wearing." I sipped my coffee.

"I damn well do know," she said, and then walked back to the bedroom to finish getting ready. I made a point to stay out of there and give Parker her space, but my mind certainly went to town on the most amazing fantasy of me coming up behind her in the bathroom, unfastening that towel, pressing my lips to her shoulder, then her neck, while my hands explored the rest of her. She could consume all the damn orange juice she wanted, as far as I was concerned. I felt more alive than I'd felt since…well, the day we'd spent together in September. Everything since then had paled in comparison. I'd been chasing that feeling, addictive as it had been, trying to get back there, yet knowing Parker was the only route.

Now here we were, and I just wanted to leap with my eyes closed. So unlike me, yet so compelling. I'd tapped my cheek and whispered to myself, "Go slow. Just go slow."

"What do you fun-loving folks have planned for this Monday evening?" Luna grabbed a rag and some Windex and headed in the direction of the interior windows.

"Um…" I looked to Parker, as we had made no definite plans.

"I'm taking her to a fancy dinner," Parker said. "She might protest because she's practical, and it's what she does."

Luna nodded. "Hannah McSanta is very practical."

"Who's practical?" Bo asked from the door in her business suit, which meant another afternoon in court. "Hannah, right?"

I balked. "I feel like I have a reputation."

"Nooooo," Bo said, and then froze. "Don't move, but Parker Bristow is behind your counter."

I turned. "How the hell did that happen?"

Parker waved four fingers at my sister. "Hi, Bo. I'm visiting."

Bo looked from me to Parker and back. "Visiting in a good way, right?" She placed her attaché on the counter.

"It's feeling very good," Parker said. My only answer was to exchange a smile with my sister, who beamed at me. After really liking Parker at the signing, she'd continued to quietly root for us even when I'd insisted the possibility didn't exist. She seemed to celebrate this new development with a gleeful, told-you-so smile.

"I had a feeling I'd see you again," Bo told her.

"The day's been riddled with stolen glances," Luna said to Bo with smolder. "It's been very tawdry in here."

I pointed at Luna. "Well, they certainly don't look like that."

"Do so," Luna said, wiping down the windows. "I had to drop the thermostat in here. Twice."

Parker chuckled, seeming to enjoy the dramatic attention. While it was against my nature, I tried to lean into it. "I can't help it if I'm a little distracted. I'm…happy."

"Aww," Bo said, grabbing me in an upright headlock. "My stoic little sister just emoted."

"Stop that right now," I said, through laughter. "I don't even know what you're doing here."

"I always swing by after court. You're literally within walking distance. Plus, I thought you'd want the update."

I definitely did. I'd been following Bo's ongoing fight for her client against the deadbeat dad with interest. "What happened?"

"He's lost all rights to see the kiddo until he pays up, which he has yet to do."

I threw a fist in the air. After weeks and weeks of setbacks, it sounded like a victory for the single mom at last. "That's fantastic. Is she relieved?"

"You have no idea how much. She burst into tears after court was adjourned. The whole time I could feel the guy glaring at us, even though I refused to give him the satisfaction of looking his way. Let that eight-hundred-dollar suit go to waste."

"Give me his number. I can't stand him already," Parker said.

"He's pretty awful." Bo shook her head. "So many of them are. I've always struggled with why some of these parents can't put the needs of their children before their own needs. Don't even get me started on the domestic violence claims against him."

"We're living in an ego-driven society," Parker said.

I nodded. "But we need people like you to help stand up to them," I told my sister. "Dad would take you out for an ice cream."

"We could do that," Parker said, seeming to love the idea.

Bo shook her head. "No way. You two spend your time together. Alone. I'm not pushing you to settle down and get married this week, but at least talk about it for next." She said it with a playful wink, but I knew she was actually half serious.

"Well, dinner out I can manage," Parker said. She turned to me. "If you'd like to go on a date with me. I would hate to be presumptuous."

"Since when are you not?" I said back, with a smile. "And since when have I ever turned you down?"

Luna chuckled from her spot at the window. "This is getting good. The sparks are flying."

An hour later, with the shop closed for the night and the moon appearing over the river, I walked next to Parker along the streets of Providence. "Where are we headed?" I asked.

"Well, we have a reservation at Landon's." She smiled. "I read about it on Yelp. It's all the rage."

I laughed. "I know all about Landon's. It's really expensive, and I'm certainly not dressed for it." I glanced down at my jeans and black Henley.

"They don't care. You're beautiful. You walk in a room and people turn. How have you not noticed that?"

I shrugged off the comment. "Because when I'm with you, it's Parker Bristow they notice, and why wouldn't they? You have an amazing presence about you. It's one of the things I admire most."

"Thank you," she said quietly. She linked her arm through mine, which brought us close together as we walked. "Sometimes I have that thing where you feel like a fraud, and people just haven't discovered it yet."

I nodded. "Imposter syndrome."

"That's the one."

I watched her stare ahead of us as we walked, as if something clung to her uncomfortably. How crazy that someone as successful as Parker, who so many people loved and adored, thought of herself as anything less than worthy. Even in my small corner of the world, living my less glamorous life, I felt confident in myself and who I was. I wanted to break a piece off and hand it to Parker. I decided I would do what I could to help her see what I did.

"Did you notice your manuscript on my coffee table?"

She looked over at me. "I did catch that. You hadn't said anything about it, so I didn't either."

"I'd read close to half of it when you knocked on my door. I set the whole thing aside for a while when you and I stopped talking, but I couldn't stay away from it for too long."

She nodded and looked away. Another glimpse of her vulnerability. There was so much more of it there than I ever realized. "And?"

"I snuck out of bed this morning at six a.m. to finish reading it."

"You did not."

"Except I did."

She stopped walking altogether. "That's where you went? I thought maybe you'd had a freak-out moment and panicked that you'd let me into your home, or maybe you just needed some space to gather your thoughts."

I laughed. "Nope. None of those things. I had my thoughts. I just...needed so badly to find out what happened to Kelly and Erica. You're *that* good. You made me give up sleep, which is my favorite, and it was the most perfect ending ever. So sweet. So romantic. I can't stop thinking about them and the happy life they're going to lead. I'm sad I can't go with them on the journey."

She looked back at me, beaming. "Really? I've been so nervous about this one. I've never written two women, and I didn't know if my style would—"

"You nailed it. It was the most authentic, heartfelt romance novel I've ever read. This feels like a game changer." I wasn't exaggerating even a little bit. I didn't know if it was her knowledge of the way two women connect that elevated it above all the other wonderful reads of hers, but the emotion, the chemistry, the angst, it all came roaring off the page in an incredible unravel.

She let out a slow breath. "I can't tell you how relieved I am to hear that."

"I do have a question, though."

"Tell me."

"It doesn't have a title. What are you going to call it?"

She walked a few feet ahead of me. "*Back to September.*"

I stopped walking. Smiled. Caught up to her. "September, huh? Because you like to shop for school supplies?" I had noticed the tie-in, and how important the month was to the two main characters.

She nodded. "It was a key month for me, so it is for them, too."

"And don't think I didn't recognize that sex scene. The first one?"

She chuckled. "I wondered if you'd pick up on that. I tried to disguise it a little. Change up the location and the circumstances."

"I'm not sure you could ever disguise it enough," I said quietly. "I'd recognize even the most subtle of details from that night."

"Me too," she said, matching my tone and taking my hand as we continued walking. It was dark now, and we were along the Providence River. The lights from the nearby buildings reflected beautifully on the water's surface, making downtown feel like the most romantic spot on Earth with Parker's hand in mine. The weather was helpful, giving the night a warmish feel. Spring peeked out from its slumber.

"I hope you're hungry. I sure am."

I liked that about Parker, her unending appreciation for food. Hell, I liked watching Parker enjoy anything, myself included. "I barely had lunch," I pointed out. "So, this is a welcome idea."

We hung a left to Landon's, which I knew from photographs had large windows that looked over the river, and wondered if we would be lucky enough to be seated near one. To my surprise, the spacious dining room was empty. The lights were low, and there was a gentleman playing a grand piano in the center of the room. I looked at Parker, and the maître d', who smiled at us.

"Ms. Bristow?" he asked. This was a very popular restaurant, but one wouldn't know that from the scene in front of us.

"Yes, sir. Table for two, please."

He bowed to us. "Right this way."

I didn't quite understand what was happening, but I followed Parker to a table by the window with two beautiful candles and a white tablecloth. As soon as we sat down, a woman appeared with a bottle of wine and poured our glasses as if she'd been waiting. A shrimp appetizer was placed on our table by a gentleman in a suit. "You planned this?" I asked. Parker and I had always been burger and pizza kind of people when we were together, but this was a welcome surprise.

She grinned and sipped her wine. "I had some time while you were working today. You know, when I wasn't stealing glances of you in your element."

I looked around. "Where are all the people?"

"They had other plans." She set down her wineglass and I passed her a look. "Okay, fine. I rented the place out last minute."

"Parker Bristow."

"Yes?"

"You shouldn't have gone to all of this trouble."

"I wanted to. For you. How's the shrimp?"

I took a bite and my eyes slammed closed at the culinary wonder. "This is the best. This shrimp wins. Is it single?"

Parker passed me a narrow look. "Stop lusting after the shrimp when I'm sitting right here."

"Oh, right. You're here, too," I winked at her and squeezed her knee under the table. "You'll do."

"If you're going to keep touching me, you're going to have a very amorous houseguest on your hands." She sighed. "I feel like we've taken it slow enough, don't you? Probably we're through the slow part and can skate easily into the unbridled sex beneath a canopied ceiling. If only we knew where one lived."

"I can't sleep with you yet. I don't even know your middle name."

She covered her eyes. "It's Eleanor. How about now?"

Spinach salads arrived, and the server poured warm dressing from a little dressing boat right in front of us, halting our conversation. This salad had bleu cheese and bacon, not that I love bacon or anything. I certainly didn't name my cat after it. "Thank you," I told our server. "This looks amazing."

Parker had already taken two bites, and I took a moment to watch the show. She pulled the fork slowly from her mouth and savored the flavors in a way that, dare I say, felt downright sexual. I adjusted in my chair. "Why do you have to be so attractive when you eat? The slow decree is in danger when you do that."

She met my gaze. "If anything that I'm doing is making you want me in the slightest, then please tell me exactly what it is so I can do it more."

I moved my fork in a circle at her. "That would be self-sabotage. I want to get to know you better. Uncover all the Parker Bristow hopes and dreams, rather than just rip your clothes off. That should say a lot to you."

"It says you have way more restraint than I do as I look across the table at a woman who has me entirely captivated. In clothes and out of them. I think of little else."

Everything slowed down. Her words landed and spread out. A prickle of importance moved up my spine as I slowly began to understand that I mattered to her the way she mattered to me. She'd told me as much simply by showing up, yet, hearing confirmation from her now brought a rush of warmth. "I think about you, too, Parker. A lot. What do you think it is?"

She sat back in her chair. "I wish I knew. The phone calls really resonated with me. I'd gotten to know you over the couple of in-person dates we had, but talking to you every single day was another level. I learned little things." She held out her wineglass and studied the ceiling as she explained. "You put pepper in every single thing you cook."

"It would be wrong not to." I sat back. "I think pepper notices when salt gets all the attention. It's misguided empathy, I'm aware, but I don't see me changing."

"I wouldn't want you to. Who would look out for the pepper?"

"Exactly. I'd say I'm quirky and cute, but really this is more about the fact that I'm neurotic."

She laughed and tickled the top of my hand. I felt the rest of me break into goose bumps. "You are very neurotic. You've organized your break-room snacks into food groups."

"Other people don't do that?"

Parker shook her head. "Not so much."

The entrees arrived not long after. Parker had ordered several in advance for our table, unsure what I would prefer most. I surveyed the spread. Steak, scallops, lobster, French green beans, spiral mac and cheese. "You didn't have to do all of this. I'm easy."

"We go back to burgers tomorrow. For today, I wanted to do something special."

That's how I felt: special. The way Parker looked at me, the time she took to listen to everything I said, and her careful attention made me feel like I truly mattered. When that attention was directed at me, I felt like the luckiest woman alive. I hoped I could do the same for her.

"Thank you," I said, quietly, and briefly touched my hand to my heart so she knew that the effort she'd gone to had resonated.

"Does this mean I'll get lucky later?" she asked, with a playful smile. "I'm just kidding, by the way."

"Does this all go away if I said no?"

"It does not."

"Let's play it by ear."

She sat up straighter. "You know how to get a girl's attention."

"Ahem. That would be you, slipping beneath my sheets topless last night." The server set down a fresh basket of warm bread and raised his eyebrows. "Sorry," I whispered to him. He smiled and took his leave.

"I like sleeping topless. But will happily wear that worn-in shirt of yours anytime. I love wearing your clothes. Maybe one night you can take it off me."

I exhaled slowly, as racy images flew through my mind. She

winked. Not many people could pull off winking, but Parker came with a built-in sophistication that allowed for it. "Are you having R-rated thoughts right now?"

I scoffed and ate a macaroni spiral that had been likely kissed by angels. But that wasn't the kind of kissing I had on my mind. I wanted to kiss her everywhere, every inch. I wanted her mouth to do wondrous things to me the way it had in her hotel room. In return, I wanted to make her cry out with pleasure. "No."

"X-rated? Really, Hannah, we're in pubic. I need you to behave."

I shook my head, not playing her game because I was already turned on and barely able to maintain my resolve, or my posture, for that matter. Why had going slow been a good idea? "I'm merely enjoying my macaroni."

"Oh. Well, then carry on."

I did. She did. I missed the topless talk. The sexy talk. "You can flirt if you want to."

She grinned. "That would be okay with you?"

I felt her bare foot move up my calf from under the table. Such a simple, fairly innocuous action sure pulled results on my end of the table. I met her gaze and realized I wasn't alone. "Yeah, we may not make it too slow. I'm just preparing you now."

She shrugged. Her features told me she was concentrating all of her energy on me. "I wasn't attached to the idea."

I wouldn't say we raced through the meal, but it wasn't what I would call leisurely. The temperature in the room certainly rose steadily the longer we sat there, and my skin was feeling incredibly sensitive. The anticipation overwhelmed every part of me, and as we walked hand in hand along the river, Parker stopped us.

"What?" I asked, meeting her gaze. The lampposts not far away offered just enough light for me to catch the green of her eyes.

"I'm just…happy."

I didn't answer her and I also didn't hesitate. I went onto my tiptoes, because she wore heels, tilted my head, wrapped my arms around her neck, and met her lips with mine. I'd never kissed anybody on the streets of Providence where I lived, and doing so now sent my heart soaring. I was living out my own romance novel, feeling things I'd never felt for a man or woman, and never wanting to stop.

"Take me home," I said quietly, against her lips, "right now."

CHAPTER TWELVE

I let us into the apartment and walked into the quiet space. There was one lamp glowing from the living area, but the rest of the room was dark and still. The cats had tucked themselves away somewhere. I heard the door close behind me, and when I turned back, Parker was leaning against it, watching me. She hadn't moved. I hadn't. Yet the connection between us stretched all the way across the room like a tether.

I crooked my finger at her because the seconds I wasn't touching her or being touched were excruciatingly long. She walked to me slowly. Her hands went to my waist, she pressed her lips to my neck, and all I heard was my own soft, gratifying moan as my body went slack in her arms. She kissed my neck, my collarbone, the underside of my chin until she caught my lips with hers. We didn't work up to anything. We were there. Wild, free, and uninhibited. I slid my fingers into her hair as we kissed. I explored her mouth with my tongue and walked her the short distance to the wall. With her back up against it, I pulled my mouth from hers, slipped my hands beneath the hem of her black shirt, and let my fingers skate from her stomach to her ribs. I flattened my palms against her skin and she smiled at me. When I caressed both breasts through her bra, the smile faded, and her eyes darkened.

"They're so sensitive to you," she whispered and closed her eyes as I freed them from the cups. I rolled her nipples between my thumb and forefingers. "Yes, like that," she said, and hissed in a breath. "More, please." Her shirt hit the floor. It was in my way. The bra joined it seconds later, also my doing. I was drunk on desire. A gorgeous, topless woman waited for me to lower my lips to her breasts. I stole a quick kiss first, letting our lips cling for a moment, and then lifted one breast to my mouth, swirling the nipple, grazing it with my teeth. She whimpered, her hands behind my neck, in my hair. I showed the same attention to the other breast, realizing I could spend all night on them. They were just as amazing as I remembered, just as full, just as round, and incredibly responsive. I sucked and licked and took my sweet time doing it.

"Hannah. Please."

I heard the request and was right there with her. I unbuttoned her pants and ran a finger along the waistband of her bikini underwear beneath. Light pink. I exhaled slowly as the throbbing between my legs doubled.

"Touch me," she said.

I slid her pants to the floor and she stepped out of them. I trailed a finger down the front of her underwear and lightly teased the spot between her legs. Her eyes closed and she sagged against the wall. I palmed both breasts and found her lips for a scorching kiss to tide us over.

"Let's go find that canopied ceiling you were looking for," I whispered in her ear. She nodded and allowed herself to be led by the hand the short distance down the hallway. The lights were off, and that was fine with me. I'd always been a lights off type of person. Not Parker. She used the dimmer on the wall to bring the lights to half.

"I want to see you tonight," she said simply.

I couldn't argue. Taking in the visual of her climbing onto my bed barely dressed won the argument for her handily. She knelt on the edge of the bed and undressed me slowly. I watched her eyes, her facial expressions as each new part of me was revealed to her for the second time. I joined her there and we were off. She positioned herself on top and rocked her hips into mine. I wanted to say I lasted, but dinner had me too far gone. When she reached between us and slid inside, I took off like a shooting star. I clung to her as I came, as my body responded to hers. I rode her hand until the last of the aftershocks faded. Every second of that payoff had been worth the buildup. Parker lived up to every memory I had of her, and more.

She was touching herself alongside me as she looked at my body. And when I turned to her with desire behind my eyes, she replaced her hand with mine between her legs. The gasp she let out was feminine and primal. I circled my thumb intricately and watched her face as her breathing turned rhythmic. When she came that first time, I watched her body stiffen and arch in the most beautiful display I'd ever seen. Five minutes later when she climaxed a second time beneath my mouth, she said my name, in a moment I would treasure forever.

I'd never fit so perfectly with another human. As we lay together in the very late hours, it was as if I could anticipate how she'd move or turn and compensate. She did the same for me.

We were an honest to goodness pair.

Happiness thrummed in every part of my being.

CHAPTER THIRTEEN

Very quickly into her stay, Parker made herself at home in my place. She helped herself to food, did the dishes, even picked up groceries for us when I was at work. Nothing about her presence felt like a houseguest or someone I had to take care of. She liked writing each day at my kitchen table, and when I came home in the evening from the shop, she often met me with a kiss and a glass of wine. Our rhythm was easy, and in Parker, I found my safe place to fall.

"I miss my mom," I told her one evening, as we sat on the couch. I'd relaxed against her while we read books. A thriller for me, complete with a serial killer and a pile of victims, and a Judith McNaught regency romance for her.

She set her book down and wrapped her arms around me. "When did you see her last?"

"It's been almost a year. We talk on the phone once a week, but it's not the same, you know? I miss her hugs."

She nodded. "What about this summer? Didn't you mention taking some time off?"

"I could take a trip to Florida. Maybe you could come, too?" I turned around so I could see her face better and found her smiling at me.

"Meeting the parents is serious."

"Um, so is reading books on the couch together. Do you think I do this with just anyone?" I turned in her arms, and she slid under me so I was more firmly on top. "Books, Parker. This is big."

She reached up and touched my lips. "I love reading books with you, even if yours are scary books instead of sexy ones. Kiss me."

I did.

"Again?"

"Hmmm. You think I should?" I leaned down until my lips were a breath from hers. She angled her mouth and nodded almost imperceptibly as her breath tickled. She tasted like heaven, and I lost myself in her almost immediately. As we kissed, our tongues entered the mix, and before I knew it her legs parted for me and my hips nestled between them, a position I'd come to adore. We made out like high school kids, turning each other on as we pressed against each other fully clothed. I wanted all of her, naked and beneath me, on the verge. "This is a really nice night," I breathed, at the same time realizing how wet my underwear was.

"I know what might make it nicer," she said and then hissed as I pressed my hips firmly against her. She tossed her head back on the couch pillow and I kissed her exposed neck.

"What's that?" I asked.

"If you took me right here on this couch." Though I'd quickly decided that was exactly what I was doing, hearing those words out loud did decadent things to me and made me want to do even more to her. I sat up, straddling her, and caught the waistband of the black leggings she wore, lifted myself, and slid them down her smooth legs. She wasn't wearing underwear, and I swallowed. Parker, I'd found, only wore underwear sometimes, and it was always a reveal to find out just when. She quickly freed herself of the tank top that said Trust Fall across the center, and I blinked at her gorgeous breasts. My hands touched them first, covering each breast with my palms, prompting her to moan quietly and close her eyes. I ground into her with my hips and caught her nipples with my fingers, squeezing slightly, twisting, watching her react. I knew her body well, but not well enough yet. I needed to know what drove her crazy and what made her ache. I eased myself down the couch so I lay alongside her and touched her intimately, allowing my hand to play between her legs. The rocking of her hips begged me for more, and I'd get there. I listened to her sounds, surprised by the quick breaths. "I'm so close," she said, arching her back and pressing into my hand. So fast? I slid inside in one motion, which practically sent her off the couch. She cried out and shattered in a glorious revel. I cradled her breast as she rode out the orgasm, still inside her and loving it.

"Oh my God, I feel like you had a manual," she said, and tossed her arm over her eyes. I traced a circle around her nipple. Kissed it. "I came so fast that time."

"That *was* fast, but incredibly beautiful," I said. I lightly trailed my hand down her body, amazed that she shared it with me. "Arresting even."

"Arresting? No one has ever called me arresting before."

I kissed her. "You are. You're arresting, and delectable, and I'm going to be honest, possibly habit forming."

She turned onto her side to face me. "You might have to explain that one."

"I could get used to this."

She touched my lips. "Do." She shook her head.

"What?" I asked, touching her hair. I adored the waves.

"You have the most perfect lips, the kind you see in a drawing. Have you noticed how much I like to touch them?"

I rolled them in, aware of the scrutiny. "Now I'm aware of them, and it's weird."

"That makes two of us, because I'm constantly aware of them." Naked on my couch, she glanced over her shoulder at the hallway. "I could make love to you beneath a billowed ceiling now. Many times."

My body stood at attention. "How can I say no to Parker freaking Bristow and a fluffy ceiling?"

She stood and walked naked and assertive toward my bedroom. I bit my lip at the glorious sight. I loved it when she walked around naked like that.

"Coming?" she asked sweetly over her shoulder.

She didn't have to ask me twice.

❖

Three mornings later, I decided to do what I should have been doing for years, which is share the responsibility of opening the store with the employees I'd grown to trust. I'd go in an hour later than usual, allowing Kurt to open up and hoping he'd say a proper hello to the store and the books the way I usually did.

The longer morning allowed me the opportunity to stretch a little, have a cup of coffee and enjoy the sunshine on the balcony of my apartment with Parker before we each started work for the day.

"What's a ten-letter word for vanilla sex?" she said as much to herself as to me. One thing I'd learned about Parker was that she used crossword puzzles in the morning to warm up the words portion of her brain for writing.

"Let's go with missionary, Alex."

She used the pencil to point at herself. "Parker."

"*Jeopardy.*"

"You're mixing games."

I smiled at her wearing my T-shirt, a tradition now, and lounging with her legs crossed and resting on the railing across from us. "I'm the neurotic one. We should be embracing my stepping outside the box."

"Good point, Alex." Parker beamed and sipped her coffee.

The sun was shining. We'd had early morning sex. The coffee was perfectly brewed. Did life get any better than this?

"Bad news. I'm gonna need to head to LA tomorrow." Parker held up her phone. "My publicist managed to book a last-minute guest spot on that Jackson Jupiter radio show that's so hot right now. They want me to come up with a top ten list for to-dos this summer."

"Oh." I deflated. "As in…"

"I don't know. Create seashell-covered love letters. Become a sand mermaid. But funnier. I'll need to hit some comedy." She glanced around in thought. "I need to start brainstorming. This will also be great promo for the book." She was up and moving around the apartment in project mode, and I felt the most wonderful few weeks start to morph away into a series of filed memories. "Hannah?"

I looked back at her as she stood in the doorway. Bare legs and my baby blue T-shirt. "Yep?"

"Are you okay?"

I nodded. "I'll miss you. I'll miss this."

She came back, knelt in front of my chair, and tucked a strand of hair behind my ear. "We'll have so many more mornings like this. You know that, right?"

"I hope so." But a kernel of doubt grew and moved uncomfortably in my midsection.

She stood and pulled me up with her. With two hands on my waist, she kissed me. "Hannah and Parker on a balcony in Providence."

I smiled. "That's us."

"And no one can ever touch that. You're my safe place. My home."
She paused. "Can you come with me?"

"To LA?" I actually considered it until the realities of small business ownership came crashing back down. "I can't just leave at the drop of a hat. There's so much to have in place. The schedule, for one, and—"

"Okay, okay. No need to raise your blood pressure." She laughed. "Another time. I'd just love it if you were there with me. I feel like I can take on the world when we're together. Crazy?"

"No. It's been really nice having you here." I tucked my face into her neck and inhaled her as her hair tickled my forehead.

"Hannah," she whispered and kissed my cheek. "I really needed this time. Needed you."

I smiled as the sentimentality rose in the form of a lump in my throat. This wasn't good-bye, I told myself. Parker just had to get back to work. "We both did."

Our last night together came and went. We didn't go out for any more fancy dinners. I made grilled cheeses after work and we ate them together on the floor as we told each other about our days.

"I turned in the title to my publisher. They're completely on board."

"They are? That's amazing. I love that title, and I'm looking forward to reading the book again. It's honestly your best work."

"I have to say that you were right. Once I started writing a couple that I identify with more, it was as if the emotion, their connection just fell out of me in a tumble in the most satisfying writing experience of my life."

I paused with cheese strung from my sandwich to my mouth. She laughed. "Oh, that's a photo right there." With lightning speed, she snapped a shot with her phone.

I balked. "That can't have been attractive. Why do you hang out with me?"

"It's the cutest photo ever, and your good looks shine through even a mouthful of food." She turned her phone around and showed me the perfectly composed shot. "I'm framing this one." She winked and stole a pickle off my plate.

"My food is rarely safe around you, I'm finding."

"Pay no attention to that," she said, and grabbed another.

We read books and drank wine together as evening became night. Just before bed, Parker rubbed my feet and my shoulders in a heavenly massage. "Don't let anyone else do this while I'm gone."

I smiled against my pillow. "I don't think it would have the same effect." I lifted my shoulders in response to the shiver that hit. I relished the feeling and leaned into it.

She turned me onto my side and trailed a finger down my neck. "Describe it to me?"

"Wanting. You make me want." Oh, and I did, too. So many decadent things. But not just that.

"Right now?" Her eyes darkened and she pressed closer to me. "You want me right now?"

I nodded. "Now."

"Sold."

CHAPTER FOURTEEN

I missed Parker. How could I not? She'd sparked my life into color, giving me such a wonderful reason to look forward to each new day. Not that life hadn't been fulfilling before, but sharing it with somebody made all the difference. I understood what all the hype was about now, and the romance novels we'd all joked about? Those kinds of relationships could exist in the real world. I believed that now. They weren't common, and they came around once in a great while, but they existed. Now with Parker gone, the hole in my life was especially noticeable, and what was more, it became astoundingly clear that it wasn't just another person who could fill it. There was no one else. Only Parker.

Currently in Venice. There's a man in front of me in line for coffee wearing sunglasses on his face and also on his head. Save me. I smiled at the text.

It was morning on a Tuesday, and the shop was just starting to find its stride. A few customers had come and gone, and a few more trickled in. Parker had been in LA for a couple of weeks now. After her spot on the radio show, another opportunity had popped up for her to do a short guest spot, playing herself, on a new sitcom for NBC. Too good an opportunity to pass up. She'd head back to New York after they shot the episode, making me wonder when the next time I'd see her would be. We'd moved the date about three times now when her schedule continued to shift.

Well, it is Venice, I typed back, happy to hear from her, just as Wally puttered his way into the store. I waved heartily and he waved back. "How'd it go?" I asked, when he walked closer. "Did Tillie like the cake?"

He shook his head. "I burned it to hell. Bottom stuck to the pan like you wouldn't believe. Made me shake my fist to high heaven and ask why me?"

"Oh. I'm sorry."

"That's okay. Tillie said it was the thought that counted, and we ate just the top part on her front porch just before it got dark out last Monday. I like to be home before dark if I can work it out."

"Well, it sounds like a nice time, then. How are things now?" I wasn't about to ask if he'd received the kiss he'd been hoping for. Correction, smooch.

"We're going out for blue plate specials tomorrow night, and I'm here to read up on stars and planets. Tillie likes them a lot, and I can't look like a dodo even though I am."

"Astronomy books can be found on the fifth aisle down on the left."

"Thank you, Hannah. If things go well, I'll lean in for a short smooch once I walk her to the door. Hers is blue and very pretty. Tillie has great taste."

"Of course she does. She's going out for blue plate specials with you, isn't she?"

He blushed and shrugged sheepishly. "Oh, well, I hadn't thought of that. She's a really nice lady, though. Had seconds of my cake even though it wasn't very good because I might have left out the sugar. That says a lot about her character, wouldn't you suppose?"

"It does." I nodded. "That says a lot."

"Yes, ma'am. Fifth aisle, you say? I'll find the moon and stars stuff there?"

"You got it, Wally."

As he set out to find his book, my phone buzzed again from its spot on the counter. Parker. *There's a cat wearing pajamas on my cup. Not a drill.* She included a photo and I smiled. A second photo arrived of a lipstick print after she kissed the side of the cup. *For you.*

I smiled and imagined Bacon in a striped pair, pretty confident he'd be down, but knowing full well that Tomato would tell me to go to hell if I showed up with any type of clothing for her. *He knows how to relax in style*, I typed back. *And I'll take that kiss anytime you're offering one.*

Now you're in for it, she wrote back.

I smiled, imagining her day, but it didn't last. When Parker and I were together, it oftentimes felt like I was the center of her world. Yet when we were apart, it felt like she slowly drifted from me. Text messages that used to be frequent came a couple of times a day. We talked on the phone at night, but then it became not every night. Her fast-paced world was her comfort zone, and when she got back into it, I wondered where her head went. My insecurities flared, because why wouldn't they? I was just regular Hannah from Providence, and she was famous, exciting Parker Bristow who traveled all over meeting famous people like Carissa Swain with the boobs. When she was away, did she think about me in the same way she did when we were together? Did she banish me from her thoughts and place me on a shelf until she was brave enough to take me back out again? There were times I felt like her soft place to fall, her break from the world before she was ready to head back into it. I shook my head and ordered my brain to stop analyzing everything.

She was busy.

That was all.

To cheer myself up, and not miss Parker and her smile, I took out my laptop and went about crunching the numbers for this month. I caught Kurt throwing glances my way, no doubt wondering what I was discovering. Were we doing better, and if so, by how much?

"Did you know Mars is red? Actually red, not just made up by a storybook." Wally approached the counter and slid his purchase, a child's picture book on the solar system, across the surface to me.

I smothered a grin. "I'd heard that before, but it really puts it in perspective to see it for yourself, doesn't it?"

"I bet those spacemen are red, too. I always believed in aliens. Just hope they don't come to eat us for breakfast until I'm long gone."

I rang up his purchase and accepted his Visa. "Let's hope that if there are inhabitants on Mars, they're kind."

"Nah," Wally said. "Makes the story more fun if they're mean. Bye, Hannah. See you soon."

"Bye, Wally. Be good out there."

He glanced back. Gave it some thought. "Nah."

I chuckled and went back to the books. Before I knew it, the day had passed me by. I had my answer, though. "We brought in twenty-six percent more this month than this time last year," I said to Luna, who'd come in midday.

"You're glowing," she said, pointing. "Your entire aura has lit up, which means this is a big day for you."

"It feels like a big day. Did you hear what I just said?"

"We made money."

I exhaled slowly and smiled. "We made money. More than I had hoped. Things are looking really good for this place."

She nodded, absorbing the news. "We have a future. The store is gonna pull through." She placed a hand over her heart and then pointed at me in determination. "I'm picking up restaurant food for dinner on my way home. Decided! Now that I know my job is secure, I can afford a Harry's burger, right? My spirit guides want me to be happy."

I handed her a twenty from the register because I was big-time and making it rain now. "On me. Let's give your spirit guides the night off. Get two."

Luna held up the twenty. "This is a big day indeed. Your aura doesn't lie! You have plans tonight, Hannah? Your aura thinks you should."

"Didn't know it was so opinionated, but yes. Meeting Bo at the courthouse and we're gonna grab a bite."

"Oh, tell Bo hi for me. I haven't seen her in days."

"That's because she's been locked in her office, preparing for that appeal. The loser dad won't back down and found some sort of technicality to bring before the judge. She finds out today if the decision will be upheld or reversed."

"Justice will prevail," Luna proclaimed loudly, pulling a startled and then supportive look from a customer. "Don't you think?" she asked the man, who nodded. They fist-bumped. Part of the Luna charm.

A few hours later, Bo stepped out of her car in the parking garage and waved as I pulled in. We'd agreed to hop into one car, and since I worked so close, picking her up seemed easiest. I rolled down my window. "That looks like the best damn attorney in Rhode Island."

She made a show of glancing behind her. "Oh, you mean me," she stated with a laugh, and slid into my car. "Today, I will take that dazzling compliment because I earned it." She had her red hair piled on top of her head today in a professional-looking jumble. I knew I wouldn't want to mess with her, looking like a million bucks in the courtroom. I was continuously proud of my sister.

"How'd it go?" I asked as she slid into the passenger's seat and right out of her heels. I don't know how she made it around life in those things.

"Well"—she slapped her hands down onto her knees—"the new judge was sympathetic to the dad's desire to be a better father but ruled in our favor once again."

I grinned. "Even more reason to go out for dinner. I'm buying. My store is making money now, and I want to show off my millions."

Bo pointed through at the road as we exited the garage. "Drive on, moneymaker."

The Chinese place we loved brought the three orders of pork dumplings, and as always, our server checked in to be sure we wanted *three* in addition to the two hot and sour soups, spring rolls, and pineapple fried rice they'd already set down.

"Yes, we're very hungry," I assured her. "Three orders."

Our server held up the number three because it really was a lot of food for two.

I winced.

Bo nodded.

"Yes. And can we possibly trouble you for extra dumpling sauce?"

The server nodded skeptically and excused herself, but I knew we'd inhale those dumplings Bo and Hannah style, and she'd see we didn't mess around with the silly concept of wasting food. Now that we were alone and face-to-face, I couldn't help but notice that Bo, who I knew as well as I knew myself, was extra fidgety tonight.

Before I could ask what gives, she leapt in first. "How's Parker these days? Will we see her soon?"

"You know," I said, scratching the back of my neck, "I'm not sure. Hopefully."

"What does that mean?" She quirked her head.

"It's strange. We spent close to a month here, and I've never connected so well with another person. We rarely got on each other's nerves."

"Amazing in its own right."

"Right? Our conversations were always interesting, we were considerate of each other, and the physical was…" My cheeks heated and I let the sentence finish itself as I glanced around the room. "My God," I mouthed, to punctuate.

"I see nothing wrong with any of that. In fact, it sounds awesome." She paused and sat back in her chair. "Why do I feel like the other shoe is about to drop? What's the problem?"

"I'm not saying there's a shoe." I sipped my wine.

Bo looked at me.

I looked at her. "There might be a shoe."

She poured more wine as more of a gesture than a necessity. "Spill your guts. I'll need to know about any and all flying footwear. As the older sister, it's my job."

I sighed. "Is it too perfect? That's a concern I have."

"Well, that's dumb. How can anything be too perfect? Embrace it."

"And our lives are not exactly compatible. She travels all over. Her home base is New York, until it's not, and I'm married to Providence. I can't pick up the store and work from the road, flit to LA and then back again easily."

"True. But you have more flexibility than you're utilizing. You have two fantastic employees, and you could hire more to cover yourself if you were to travel here and there."

"I can't afford to do that."

"Parker can afford it."

"No. I don't want Parker's money. I want to take care of myself."

She squinted. "Well, I'm not sure that's how a serious relationship works."

I sighed and went for it. "I think she's keeping me at arm's length now that she's gone." There. I'd said the thing that was eating away at me and keeping me up at night. "I can't relax because of it, and it's stressful as hell."

"Why would she do that?"

"She's confessed to me once that I'm a terrifying concept for her. I think she's not used to anyone in her life with staying power. In fact, I think she's preferred it that way."

"In the past."

"Yeah, but what if it's not just her past? Maybe this isn't for her.

What if I'm giving everything to this woman, who I can honestly say I'm falling in love with, and at the end of the day, she's not emotionally available?"

Bo nodded sagely. "It's not unheard of, unfortunately." She leaned in. "But Parker? From what I've seen, is over the moon for you. You should see the look she gets in her eye when you so much as walk by."

"I know. Until she's back into her life and over the moon for everything else she has going on. I hear from her less and less lately. It's…telling."

She took a bite of a dumpling and gave it some thought. "Is it still good between you two when you do?"

I nodded. "We pick right back up again, but, Bo? I don't want to be the woman who just sits around and waits until Parker decides she's ready for me again. If I'm going to be with someone, I want it to be an equal partnership, you know?"

"And you want to be with Parker?"

My heart thudded away. "Very much." I took a moment, realizing how much I had at stake. I was in deep. "Too much."

She reached across the table and covered my hand with hers. "Then don't you give up. You fight for her."

"That's my plan. What we have is too good not to." I smiled at the amazing food on my plate, nervous now that I'd voiced my concerns out loud. Something about sending them into the universe made it all seem exceptionally real. "What about your world, Bo? You seem…out of sorts."

"I had court today," she said, gesturing with her chopsticks. "I'm always extra keyed up after going to battle."

"Nope. Uh-uh." I folded my arms. "More than that. What gives?"

She met my eyes and looked away. "No idea what you mean."

I dropped my head and stared at her. She was too preoccupied with her own plate. "You're lying to me. I know this because you fixate on unimportant objects in the room when you lie, and that fried rice is not all that riveting right now. Pony up the details, Bo."

She shifted her lips to the side. "I've gotten myself involved with someone, and it's messing with my head."

"Now, this I can identify with," I said with a smile. Bo didn't get tangled up with romance too much, simply because she was a no-nonsense girl with a career that took up most of her time. She vicariously lived the life of a heroine through romance novels, and films, and TV shows, always vowing she'd get to it soon enough. It seemed like maybe soon enough was now here. "Who is he?"

"You're going to shake your head at me."

"Well, it's my job, so let's get to it."

"I've fallen for a client, and it's a whole conflict of interest thing, and I'm awful for doing it." Her always present composure came tumbling down, her vulnerability on full display.

"You're not awful, first of all. Is there a law against seeing a client?"

"The laws are pretty watered down, but when there's a divorce and custody in question? It shouldn't happen."

"Oh, this is one of your divorces? How long has he been divorced?"

She opened her mouth and closed it. "It's more the custody case I've been telling you about?"

"The one with the jerk dad? I don't get it. He's an asshole, first of all, and he's not even your client."

She paused, and I struggled to piece together what I was missing. Because Bo would never date a guy like that. She wouldn't. She would rather— "Oh my God, you're dating the single mother? You're dating a woman?" I realized I had said that really loud. Perhaps I yelled it. The swiveled heads and Bo's wide eyes indicated that yes. Yes, I had.

She held up a hand to get me under control, and I drank heartily from my glass of water to busy my mouth. "I didn't plan on any of this, and I certainly didn't see it coming, but she sparked something in me."

I nodded. "But the woman thing?"

"Is very unexpected. I get that. It was for me, too. It was for *her*."

"But?"

My sister broke into a small smile that instantly reached her eyes. Her hand fluttered to her cheek as the smile grew. "The past few weeks, I feel like my feet haven't touched the ground."

Hearing that from Bo was everything. "Awww. Bo." I blinked happily.

"But that doesn't mean there aren't obstacles. I'd have to step back from representing her."

"But you can do that."

She nodded. "It makes me nervous. There's a child involved, and

I've been the one fighting for him every step of the way. But it does seem like most of the litigation is behind us."

"See?" I stole another dumpling from the platter. "The timing is playing out nicely." I shook my head. "There's just nothing about you that ever said you'd be interested in dating women. I'm so impressed right now."

"You weren't impressed before?"

"You're always impressive. I'm just extra taken by your ability to continue to surprise me." I shook my finger at her. "You're tricky, Bo. I like that. What's her name?"

"Amy. She's thirty, and blond, and the kindest person I've met. She likes a lot of the same things I like, including making fun of boy bands, and any and all pasta."

"All important things. You've landed a good one." I dropped my voice. "Sex? Have you had sex with her?"

She blinked at her plate. "No. Not yet."

"There's nothing to be nervous about."

She winced. "Isn't there? What if I'm not good at it? With a woman, I mean."

"You'll get the hang of it. Just need a little practice." I smiled as warmly as I could to reassure her. "Outside of that? You know what you like, right? Start there."

She seemed to take to the advice. "I can't believe I told someone. That it's out in the open now." She was smiling again.

"How does it feel?"

"Absolutely amazing. I've never been so excited by someone before, and I truly saw a future I wanted to pursue."

"I think we've earned a little more wine, don't you?"

Bo held out her glass for me to pour. "Lay it on me."

"I can't believe I have to share the whole 'dates women' thing with you now. Is nothing sacred, Bo?"

"Is this going to be like the straightener in high school? Where you remind me for years that it was yours first?"

I grinned. "I think it's going to be a lot like that. Now, drink your wine and tell me more about Amy, so we can be old friends as soon as I meet her."

CHAPTER FIFTEEN

"Good morning, books," I whispered reverently and flipped on the lights that spring morning. I took a deep inhale of the distinct aroma of so many pages in one room. *Back to September* would be out in ten days, and I was excited for Parker and all this would mean for her career. It was a big step. Not only that, but I took pride in having maybe been an influencing factor.

"You were more than just an influence," Parker told me on the phone late last night. It had been three and half weeks since I'd laid eyes on her, and I felt the strain. "Without you, there would be no book. Or there'd just be another, very similar book to the others I've written."

"Then I'm extra moved. What are you wearing?"

Parker chuckled. "A T-shirt and purple underwear. I forgot pants."

"Purple, huh? That's a really good look." I blinked happily as I imagined it.

"Oh, yeah? My favorite look of yours is you topless at the mirror in the morning. You run your hands through your hair to give it a fluff. I know you're about to hop in the shower and it takes everything I have not to drag you back to bed. I have no idea why bookstores have to open on time."

"Topless, huh? Now I'm feeling objectified and sexy. More of that."

"There's tons more where that came from. Trust me. I've never been so attracted to another human being before."

"What?" I shook my head. "Really? You've never told me this before."

MELISSA BRAYDEN

"Well, Hannah, I have to hold a few things back or I'd be an open book. A little mystery is fun."

I hesitated. "Sometimes I worry you hold a lot back."

"Okay." She paused on the line. "Tell me about that."

Did I really want to go here? We hadn't had an actual disagreement, other than who was going to do the dishes, since the cabin. I pushed forward, though, because what I was feeling was valid and the circumstances were real. "I suppose I thought we'd see each other, talk to each other, more than we have been."

"I know, and I'm so sorry about that. Things have been so fast-paced lately and I'm trying to balance my writing time with the PR appearances, and I guess I'm not doing such a great job."

I nodded. "I haven't heard from you in three days. Even when we were just friends, we talked each night."

She went quiet. "Yeah." Another pause. "My head's been a little…"

"A little what? You can just say it, Parker. Lay it out there."

I could tell how hard this was for her, but pushing was the only way to get an honest answer. "Scattered."

It wasn't enough information for me. "Do you think you're running again? We know you did that once before. Is it happening again?"

I heard her blow out a slow breath. "I'm not going to let it, Hannah."

"Will you tell me what it is that you feel when you're afraid?" I walked from one spot in my kitchen to another, the movement keeping me focused, clear, and courageous. I needed courage for this conversation, because it felt like there was so very much at risk.

"That I'm too close, that I'm putting all my eggs in a basket that might get smashed to pieces once you get to know me and decide that I'm not all that special."

"Baby." I couldn't believe she'd even think such a thing. I'd seen Parker at her most glamorous and I'd seen her at her most mundane. "That's not going to happen. I've never met anyone I thought was more special than you."

She sniffed, and I wondered if she was crying. Parker tended to default to strength, so she might not have wanted me to realize.

"I don't know why I get this way. It's not how I want to operate."

• 156 •

I nodded, as if she could see me, and absently gave Tomato a rub as I passed her sitting on the back of the armchair. "Do you think there's a reason?" It was a very personal question, but after all we'd shared, I felt empowered to ask.

Another pause. "My therapist does."

I didn't want to push, so I stayed silent, giving her space to say more, hoping that she would.

"Not the best childhood. Here we go."

I imagined her fluffing her curls as she did absently when she was about to launch into a story.

"I was removed from my parents' care when I was eight."

My mouth fell open and I was thankful she wasn't there to see. "Oh, Parker. I'm so sorry."

"It's okay. They weren't the best people. Completely ill-equipped and uninterested in having a child. Addiction was more their jam, and from what I was told, the man I believed was my father may not have been. They're currently both in jail, my mom for robbery and my father on assault charges, which was not at all a surprise, let me tell you."

I felt nauseous.

"It was traumatic, though. Losing my home, my family."

"Of course it was."

"I moved in with my aunt, who was a lot older than my mom. It was the first time in my life I'd felt...I don't know...safe. Happy. Her name was Lydia, and she took care of me, made dinner at night, and kissed me before bed. She, unfortunately, had a debilitating stroke, so I became her caretaker when I was twelve. She died when I was fourteen. But wait, there's more." She said it as if impersonating an infomercial announcement, probably to lighten the mood.

I couldn't imagine even the first part of that story, the second knocked the wind out of me, and the fact that there was a third had me gripping the countertop for her.

"I moved in with my best friend Daniela's family. They agreed to take me in when I was pretty much on my own in the world. The thing was, though, that I tried to make them my family, and her parents did everything in the world to make sure I remained just a friend of Daniela's. It took me a while to get the message. They'd done their part and put a roof over my head and even took me shopping when I needed school supplies or clothes. But when they went to visit relatives? I was left behind. When there was a soccer match? It was Daniela they cheered for, not me."

"That's awful."

"It really wasn't, but I was a teenager at that point, and made a lot of decisions about life and people and my place in this world. Probably screwed me up, doing that."

"Sounds like self-protection to me." So much made sense now. So much. "A lot of people let you down, Parker."

"Not intentionally."

"Doesn't matter when it's burned into you like that."

"Yeah." She sounded sad, and I wanted to wrap her up in my arms and never let her go, show her that it was okay to get used to someone, that I wasn't going anywhere.

"You still sure you want me around after hearing about all that baggage?" She chuckled sardonically.

"When can I see you again?" I asked, needing to more than ever now.

A moment passed. "How about this weekend?"

I grinned. "Yeah? I'd love that."

Her tone took an energetic upshift. "Perfect. I'll fly to you or you can fly to me. You decide."

I'd already put a few systems in place that would give me the ability to take time away from work more often, should I need to, anticipating that it might useful, given Parker's schedule. "I'll fly to LA."

"Hannah, I'm going to see you, and speak to you, and laugh with you, and eat messy food with you in just four short days."

It felt like a gigantic weight had been lifted off my chest. "Is that all? I was thinking of more." I was flirting and enjoying it. "I have additional plans beyond your agenda. I should probably confess that now."

"Oh, really." She drew that last word out playfully. "You can't see me, but I'm fanning myself like a teen at a boy band concert."

"Interesting. I didn't know I had quite that effect. What I do know is that I plan to put my hands on you." God, I missed this woman. Her smile, her humor, her scent. All of it. Lying in bed, my face nestled into her neck was one of my favorite places to be.

"You're killing me, right now," Parker said.

"In a sexy way?"

"In a very sexy way. If you think I don't have plans to get you naked and beneath me, you're very wrong." She was using what I had come to call her quiet/sexy voice and I loved it. "Why aren't we in the same room together? This purple lace underwear wants you to slide it down my legs."

I swallowed. "You wouldn't have to ask."

"That's what I love about you in bed. You always anticipate what I want before I even know I want it. And damnit, talking about this is doing a lot to me."

"Are you wet right now?" I was surprised at myself. Was this phone sex? Or at least phone sex foreplay? I'd never engaged in that before. It was very un-Hannah-like, but I couldn't help myself with Parker. She brought it out in me.

"I am. Just hearing your voice does that to me. It's always been that way."

I withheld a gasp. "Another new piece of information. Even when we weren't together?"

"Are you kidding? Yes. After our first night, everything about you got me going. The cabin? Which I thought would be good for helping me out of that mode?"

"Yeah?"

"Only solidified that it was impossible. I don't know why I fought so hard. I had no chance."

"I happen to think there's something to that. Maybe we were meant to have a few hiccups in the early stages."

"Hannah, I will hiccup with you anytime. On a boat. With a goat."

I laughed. "Back at you. On the lam. With a ram." I felt my confidence, everything I thought I'd known about Parker and myself, come rushing back. We were really good together. Yes, we'd hit a rough patch lately, but we'd talked it out. Parker had taken a leap and confided in me about her early struggles.

❖

Three days later, I watched as all of Los Angeles flew past the window of the cab I'd grabbed at the airport. Parker didn't have her own place in LA but instead rented what she called a small bungalow in a trendier area of Hollywood called Franklin Village, close to all sorts of restaurants and shops.

I had been in Los Angeles a total of ninety-seven minutes, and I was already fascinated by the fast pace of it all. Never had I seen so much traffic. Never had I seen so many beautiful people. Never had I seen so many skateboarders, rollerbladers, and joggers on the sidewalk of a residential street.

"Here you go," my cab driver said, and paused at the curb next to a cute red house with three steps up to a small front porch. I paid for my ride and pulled my suitcase up the walkway, taking a deep breath. I was nervous. Whether it was because I felt out of my element or just excited to see Parker was hard to say.

She swung open the door before I even had a chance to make it to the porch. This wasn't the first time she'd been watching for me as I arrived. Remembering how she'd burst out of the cabin in greeting, as well, I had to admit that I liked the early greeting a lot.

"Hi, beautiful," Parker said with a wide grin. She was barefoot and wore shorts and a soft looking-baby blue T-shirt that made her look extra cuddly. Her hair was down and the curls were more like subtle waves today. Her eyes were bright and happy. She was everything.

"Hi back." I paused for a moment so I could take her in, like a cool breeze on a hot day. She scurried down the stairs and took me in her arms and held me close. I didn't want to let go once I was in her arms, and apparently Parker didn't either because we stood like that, locked in an embrace, for a long time. I was hit with the scent of peaches that was so very Parker. I nearly choked up with happiness.

"You have no idea how much I've missed you," she said quietly. "I'm so happy you're here."

I took a step back and my gaze dropped to her lips just as she moved to kiss me.

"Hi," she whispered again.

"Hi."

"Let's go inside. I already have a glass of wine poured for you."

"Bless you." I watched as she took my bag, and followed her into the house that was incredibly charming inside. Hardwood floors, lots of natural light, and an open one-story layout. "I love it here."

Parker smiled. "Me too. I've actually considered making an offer, but I'm just not here enough for it to make sense financially."

"Third houses, man. Gotta make sure they're worthwhile."

"For you," she said, and handed me a glass of white wine.

"Thank you. This is much needed. You should know— Oh, wow," I murmured as her lips descended on my neck from behind. I sagged against her, melting like butter at her touch. Her hands encircled me and landed on my breasts, and I found myself pulled into the vortex that had always been Parker and me and our off-the-charts chemistry.

"I have friends coming over, but we have a few minutes."

I turned, faced her, and caught her mouth for a kiss. "Let's use the few minutes."

"We've always been resourceful."

"We should keep our reputation intact." Another kiss. And then we were on, stumbling toward any kind of surface and taking our clothes off as we walked. There was a desk pushed up against the wall before reaching the sitting area. We backed up into it, and as Parker pressed closer, I slid on top of the desk's surface, wrapping my legs around Parker's waist, surprising even myself at my sexual freedom.

"I've missed you," she said, as she unbuttoned my jeans. The doorbell chimed at that exact moment.

We stared at each other. She glanced over her shoulder to the door. "Shit."

"Friends?"

"Untimely ones. Since when does seven actually mean seven?"

"I think most of the time," I told her. Someone knocked on the door. "I think they really, really want in," I said in a whisper.

"I'm going to let them in, but I need you to understand that I'm not going to be able to think about much beyond you on this desk. Are we clear?"

I nodded. "Desk. Me. Crystal clear."

"God, Hannah," she said, with a head shake.

I put myself back together again and she pointed at me as she headed to the door.

"To be continued."

We exchanged a smile that said we were truly happy to see each other, and she disappeared to play hostess. I heard chatting in the entryway and felt nervous about meeting Parker's friends. Let's be honest, the only person I'd met from her life was Carissa, the beyond-spoiled pop star, but when the woman came around the corner into the room, she came with a much more down-to-earth vibe.

"Hi, you must be the famous Hannah I've heard so much about. I'm Marley, the longtime confidante and sometimes wine drinking buddy," she said, extending her hand. The woman had short blond hair, kind eyes, and a flowy shirt. All three things I liked.

"So great to meet you," I said, accepting the handshake. I wish I could have said I'd heard so much about her, but in keeping me at arm's length, Parker had also apparently held back details of her own life. I hoped we'd move past that now that we were communicating more.

"Marley and I met at a writer's retreat."

"I'm a recovering writer," she said matter-of-factly. "Much happier as an editor these days, doing shorter pieces for *Working Women*."

"She's selling herself short, because she has two near best sellers on her backlist."

"Notice this one just said the word 'near.' I now leave the world-conquering via book to Parker and stick to lifestyle pieces for myself."

"Well, I happen to love *Working Women*." I had a subscription, in fact, but I didn't want to gush too much.

"Enough about us," Marley said, clapping. She turned to me. "What do you think of LA? I'm home-based here, so it's nice when the New Yorker has a gig that brings her west."

"I'm a definite nomad these days," Parker said, and ushered us to the kitchen, where she began putting out snacks. Celery, hummus, tiny sandwiches she'd cut into cute triangles. I'd gotten a taste of her domestic side in Providence, and it always made me smile at the effort she put in to try and make everyone feel comfortable.

I brought my wineglass to my lips and sipped while Marley poured herself a glass. They had a nice ease about them, which told me their friendship was not new. "I like Los Angeles so far. The sunshine and the weather are both perks, but I must admit, I've only been here for a few hours. The traffic is…something."

"And it never changes." Marley pulled a folder from her bag and dropped it onto Parker's kitchen counter. "Before I forget. The story for next week's deadline." Marley turned to me. "I've written up a piece about Parker Bristow's jaw-dropping turn to lesbian romance."

I grinned. "I think it's her best yet."

"I do, too. I haven't stopped fanning myself since I got my advance copy." She fanned right then to demonstrate.

I stared at the folder, eager to read the story but not wanting to intrude. I felt Parker watching me.

"Go ahead," she said.

I passed her a questioning glance and she nodded, providing me the permission I needed. I took the folder and sat at her kitchen table as Marley and Parker chatted about mutual friends. The story took a get-to-know-the-woman-behind-the-books approach, and Marley described her friend, her home, and their chat together, in detail. She asked Parker about the decision she'd made with the new release, and though Parker laughed it off, she went on to say that a very special woman in her life influenced the decision, and the heat raced to my cheeks.

"Does that mean you're seeing someone?" Marley asked, within the context of the interview.

Parker's answer was a perfect balance. "While I'd rather not discuss my personal life, out of respect for the other individual involved, I will say that I'm the happiest I've ever been in my life."

I smiled at the pages in my hand. Behind me I heard a flurry of voices, which told me more people had arrived. Before leaving the table to meet them, I held the story in my hands as a mixture of love and affirmation came over me.

This was real, what Parker and I had. The caliber of our connection and what I was already feeling for her was nothing I'd ever imagined for myself. Not because I didn't want it, but because I wasn't sure it existed. Tears threatened when I realized that, though there were still hiccups to come, I was moving toward the kind of love people only read about, talked about, or longed for. The fact that the reality was so readily in my grasp left me floored.

"Hannah?" Parker asked quietly. The voices had dissipated. "My friends Alec and Jimmy stopped by. I moved everyone out back. You okay?"

I stood and blinked at her. "I am. More than okay. What you said in the piece," I touched my heart, "means a lot."

"All true," she said, kissed my cheek, and gave my hair a stroke. "That's why I went MIA on you, Hannah. It's felt *too* wonderful. I freaked out."

I squeezed her hand and stared into those green eyes. "I'm not going anywhere. Know that."

"I do now. Just keep telling me, okay?"

"I can do that."

She smiled. "Want to meet some more of my friends?"

The smile that faltered a little when she asked told me that she was nervous and that this meeting of her worlds was important to her. It all made so much more sense now. She'd invited over the people who mattered to her specifically for me to meet them. This was her way of letting the curtain down and introducing me to the aspects of her life, the people in it, that truly mattered.

As the evening went on, I met not just Jimmy and Alec and Marley but Parker's editor, Leigh, who happened to be in town, as well as her workout partner on the West Coast, Wink. The group seemed relatively familiar with each other, with the exception of Wink, who only stayed for a drink or two, and all seemed incredibly receptive and warm to getting to know me, which in turn, helped dispel some of my own nerves.

"The thing about Parker," Jimmy explained to the group, as we sat around the pool. It was dark out and we all had glasses of wine. A couple in for me, and I'd loosened up quite a bit, loving the group assembled. They were chatty, polite and fun. "Is that she is blissfully unaware of her capability to land a quality partner, and you, Hannah, are the first one I can happily say a resounding yes to."

Parker shook her head. "I should never give him wine." She placed a platter of chicken kebabs that she and Alec had grilled together on the table with a stack of plates.

"Well, it means a lot to me that you approve," I said, and clinked my glass to his. He and Alec were a couple, I'd learned over the course of the evening, and spent a good part of the evening saying sweet things to each other when they thought no one else was listening. Exactly the kind of personal and loving relationship I'd want for myself.

"I'm not kidding," Jimmy said. "That last one was all about service. What could she have brought to her, how much of it could she get, and what time would it be here? No respect."

"We don't need to talk about the past," Parker said, and slid him a stop-that smile.

"It's okay," I said to Parker over my shoulder. I turned back to Jimmy. "We've met. It didn't go well."

"Then you realize why we're so happy to meet *you*," Leigh said, a bit more gently than Jimmy.

"You guys," Parker said, with a shake of her head. "It was a huge mistake, and I see the error of my ways." She sat down next to me and let her feet dangle in the water alongside mine. She smiled at me as the others chattered, and I enjoyed the private moment. Her hand rested on the side of the pool next to mine, touching it slightly, inspiring tingles and goose bumps down my arms.

"What it really comes down to," Marley said to me from across the pool, "is that Parker likes to keep her orbit small."

Parker nodded. "Okay. I can agree with that. But can I ask why it's suddenly become analyze Parker hour?"

"Because it's the most interesting topic," Jimmy filled in. "For example, why do you drink grape-flavored drinks like you're seven? I muse a lot."

I grinned at her. "I do still have a six-pack of grape soda from your last visit."

She held out a hand. "And you're welcome."

There was a collective laugh.

"So, do you two have any plans?" Leigh asked. "Anything exciting coming up?"

Parker took my hand. "I want to get through the PR for this book and then spend some time with Hannah before the next tour which, if I have anything to say about it, will be shorter."

I raised my hand. "Well, I know one bookseller who wouldn't mind you coming in for a signing."

That earned a collective "aww" from the group. What could I say? We were adorable.

Two hours later, everyone was gone and I helped Parker stack the dishes in the sink. "So, what did you think of those characters?" Parker asked.

"They're fantastic. You have assembled a great group of friends."

"I'm glad you think so."

"And I'm honored to have been brought into your inner circle." I met her gaze and squeezed her arm so she knew that it meant something to me. Parker was taking baby steps toward allowing me in fully, and I wanted to be sure I encouraged her. "Pass the scrubber?"

She smiled and handed over the brush. "I like watching you do things. You always put your own personal Hannah spin on them," she said. "Even though it's rude to allow my guest to help with the chores that should be mine."

I used the scrubber to point at her. "I'm not your guest, I'm your girlfriend." It was the first time either of us had said it out loud, but after tonight, I really felt like I was. I watched her blink several times, and wondered how that word would affect her. She took the scrubber, placed it along the sink, and took my hand.

"Where are we going?"

"To bed," Parker said, matter-of-factly, flipping off lights as we went. "I want to make love to my girlfriend."

And I had no objection to her plan whatsoever.

We went slower that night than we'd ever gone. Her fingers across my skin lingered reverently, her gaze moved across my body with such adoration. Don't get me wrong, we were still hot as hell, and I came harder that night than I ever have in my life, a testament to the fact that slow can be really, really good.

The next morning, I woke up in her arms, nestled in and interested in going exactly nowhere. "Do we have anywhere to be this morning?" I asked, sleepily.

"Hmm. I have a Q and A at noon, but it's for a radio show in Portland, so I'll do it from the house. Should only take half an hour." She kissed my cheek, and I relaxed against her body. "You were so hot last night. I sound like a pubescent boy, using that word, but it's true. Hot."

I grinned as the naked memories flashed through my mind. We had been so in sync. "I was not. You were."

I felt her shake her head. "I don't think you have any idea how sexy you are or the things you do to me. Things no one has been able to."

I pushed myself up so I could see her. The sun streamed through the window, filling it with natural light. I could hear a lawn mower a few houses down. The world was awake, and we were tucked away. I loved it. "Like what?" I watched the slight blush blossom.

"Get me there, for one. You have, every single time without fail."

I frowned. "Get you there. What does that mean?" I had a feeling, but I needed her to say it.

"I'm not always able to…climax during sex. I've enjoyed it regardless, but that one element tends to elude me. With you it's very, very different."

I let the information settle, as I had it on good authority that she'd had two orgasms the night before. "I don't understand. You just… didn't before?"

She stared up at her ceiling. "It's not that I never had. Just…very rarely. I got good at faking it, and that is not something that I'm proud of."

I settled next to her with my head resting on the inside of my arm. "So, with Carissa…" I internally winced when I remembered what I'd overheard. I'd made a point to wash it from my memory until this moment.

"Yeah. That was a no go from the start." She covered her eyes. "When I look back on what I was doing with her…" Parker shook her head. "I was lost, and scared, and freaked the hell out by what I'd stumbled onto with you."

"And now?"

"Now I'm here. I'm going for it. And I'm very happy." Parker ran a hand down my body. "I've missed waking up next to you."

I watched as she circled my nipple with her forefinger, and the results shot lower. I hissed in a breath.

"Tell me something you're afraid of."

I blinked. It was an odd and heady combination to be asked such a personal question while being touched so intimately. For reasons I wasn't yet acquainted with, it increased the intensity of my physical experience. "I'm afraid of what happens when something scares you again."

She nodded. Her eyes carried understanding. Her hand slipped lower, tickling the outsides of my thighs, then the tops.

"I worry about the shop, about keeping it afloat and successful. I don't want our new endeavors to get stale."

"Mmm-hmm. What else?" She eased my legs apart and gently trailed her fingers along the insides of my thighs. It made me crave more.

"What if I'm a disappointment in the end? That scares me. To you, to Bo, my parents?" I'd pulled my underwear back on before sleeping last night because it was a thing with me, but Parker had no problem moving the rectangle of fabric to the side.

"You could never disappoint anyone, Hannah. You're too smart, too kind. Know that."

I waited for her to touch me, quivering with anticipation. My gaze never left hers. "I'm scared that I'm already in love with you and you won't let yourself love me back."

"Too late," she said. She leaned down across my body and kissed me softly as my world and its amazing potential sparked into color, just as her fingers pressed intimately against me.

"Sweet Lord," I murmured.

She stroked me once, twice.

I whimpered and rocked my hips, lost in a dizzy haze of desire. A fourth time, a fifth. Sensation rushed toward me. A sixth. I shattered. Pleasure hit hard and fast, and I saw light behind my eyes. I clutched Parker's arms. I was out of control and didn't care, flying high on the momentum she'd inspired in me.

As I returned to Earth a bit at a time, I opened my mouth to speak and then closed it.

Parker tucked a strand of what had to be sex hair behind my ear. "What, baby?"

"I lose myself with you. I feel alive, and my inhibitions"—I shook my head—"are strangely just...gone."

"If that's what it looks like when you lose yourself, then we should make sure you lose yourself as often as possible. I'll be project leader. Do you know how hard it is for me to say the words 'I love you'? I've never said them to anyone."

"It's okay, though. It might be a situation where you need time first, to feel—"

"Hannah, I love you."

"Oh." A flood of warmth hit and I felt myself inflate like a carefree balloon. She'd said it first. Never in my smallest of hopes did I think that would happen, given what we'd been through, what I now knew.

"I love you, too." I reached over and cradled her cheek, feeling it with every ounce of my being. I loved Parker, and I was in this thing with her for the long haul. "I know that I don't have all of the answers. I know we're still figuring this out as we go, but I want this. I want us.

I can be patient with you and help if you're struggling. I just need you to tell me is all."

She smiled through the tears that glistened. "I want us, too. In spite of all my baggage, and I admit it's a lot, that's the one thing I know beyond all else. This matters to me, Hannah. You do. I want so badly to not screw it up."

"Then we won't."

I didn't want to leave this warm bed, tucked away from the world with Parker. So I didn't. We talked, and snuggled, and snoozed a little more, enjoying the Saturday properly. Hours later, I plugged in my blow-dryer as Parker headed for the shower. She stopped behind me, rested her chin on my shoulder from behind. "Hey, Hannah?"

"Yes?" I asked, wet hair and all.

"I love you."

There was no greater sound.

CHAPTER SIXTEEN

Heading back to reality after our whirlwind weekend in LA was harder than even I would have expected. I was thrilled to see the store and wanted to wrap it in a warm hug after being away for two days, but the wonderful moments Parker and I had spent together lingered in my mind, the feel of her against me, the sound of her laugh, and her very opinionated take on game shows, which she still refused to watch like a normal human. I smiled as I restocked the latest Groffman, remembering our call that morning before work.

"Good morning, beautiful," Parker had said as I clicked onto the call.

"Well, this is a nice surprise." I shifted the phone to my other ear as I walked to work. "I thought I wouldn't hear from you this morning."

"I only have a moment, but I wanted to hear your voice before the shoot. It gives me confidence." She was doing a photo shoot that morning to accompany Marley's piece in *Working Women*. "I'm in the makeup chair, have curlers in my hair, and would frighten away the faint of heart."

"Luckily, my heart is anything but faint. It's feeling rather robust lately."

"Happy to hear that. Okay, I gotta run. Be ready to tell all about your day tonight. I want all the details."

"Deal."

"I hope you have the best Wednesday. I love you."

"I love you, too," I told her, smiling into the phone like a preteen. "Go be pretty for your shoot. Toss those curls around luxuriously."

"Ma'am, where are the sexy books?" I stuttered for a moment at

the question, catapulted back to the here and now of A Likely Story and
the rather studious-looking woman peering across the counter at me.

"I'm sorry. I was somewhere else. Can you ask your question
again?"

"Of course I can. I'm looking for the hot stuff, the sexy books?
Please direct me."

I tried to decode the request. "Romance novels, maybe?"

"Yeah, but the especially hot ones. Not sweet stuff. I want the
goods." She pushed her glasses up onto her nose and blinked at me,
and I wondered if this was a nun on the lam. She certainly looked the
part, and nothing resembling someone with a strong need for erotic
content. It just went to show me that not everyone's perfect match is
immediately evident and that it takes a little chatter to get to the heart
of what a person wants in a book.

"Follow me. I know of some rather steamy novels you might want
to take a look at."

"If they have shower sex, I'm in."

"Shower sex. Got it. Hey, Luna?" I asked, as I passed her finishing
up with a customer. Having read more in the erotic section than I had,
she might have more success. "Could you perhaps assist in a very
specific content request?"

"More shower sex?" she asked, pointing at the woman. "Or are we
looking for something new?"

Well, well. Apparently, she was a repeat customer.

"You know what I like," she said to Luna and followed on her
heels. "Let's mix it up."

"I dig it."

I smiled as the two made their way down the aisle, and returned to
the front of the store, checking the clock on the wall as I went. I would
knock off an hour early to swap out Bo's car for mine at the courthouse.
We'd traded. She'd been generous enough to let me borrow her SUV
for transporting books to the children's book fair downtown and then
head back to the shop for a late dinner with Luna to talk possible
evening events beyond just the book club. I knew she was percolating
with ideas, and it was about time I harnessed my team for the skills they
brought to the table. Luna was my idea girl.

"We still on for burgers at Harry's?" I asked. Luna would close
tonight and then meet me there. I'd chat with Parker after, when I

got home. She'd mentioned something about maybe flying out the following weekend, and I was hoping to work out the details to arrange more time off. I'd hired two more part-time employees to fill in gaps, and so far, it'd been a big help in terms of flexibility. With the shop making more money, why not?

"Yes, the signs are all steering me to Harry's. In fact, they're telling me, strangely, that we should go now." She shrugged. "Not sure why."

"Because they have the best burgers ever and you're beyond hungry?"

"Could be."

"See you in an hour?"

She smiled. "Okay, but you're buying."

I held up a finger. "The store is buying. We're about to storm the book world as we know it, and that makes this meeting of the minds a business expense. Though I do plan to get the scoop on how things are progressing with your Madame Pencil."

Luna made the same face she made when I asked her to sweep the break room. "It's a whole thing."

I made a yikes face and got out of there. As I made my way to Bo's parking garage, it occurred to me that if she was free, I could always invite her out with us. She wouldn't mind shop talk, and it'd be nice to catch up, see how she was doing. I pulled her car into the spot in the garage next to mine and kept the spare key with me, knowing she had her own. Given that it was in the midst of what I knew were back-to-back court appearances, it was probably smarter to text rather than call. I pulled my phone from my back pocket, already imagining that I'd order the Harry's Double Wide and splurge a little. Footsteps loud and behind me pulled my focus. Someone was apparently in a hurry.

"What's up, bitch?" a gruff voice said. I turned just in time to see a black pipelike object raised above my face; when it came down with force, everything moved slowly. I was falling and so confused about why. I'd been struck, but I'd yet to feel any pain. There was a man above me. I blinked but couldn't see him clearly because there was water in my eyes. No. That was blood. He raised the object again and I watched as it came down, too confused, too stunned to speak. I opened my mouth to try just as it smashed into my midsection. I doubled over onto my side.

He hit my back next. I screamed this time.

My voice worked, at last. It was an awful sound, but it wouldn't be nearly as awful as the pain when it finally hit. I heard voices. Maybe someone would help me. The footsteps retreated. I tried to lift my head to look, to see his face, but that wasn't working. My body wouldn't obey.

He's wearing a ball cap. He's wearing a ball cap.

And then I managed to say the words in the midst of my groaning. Nothing looked normal, not the cars, not the concrete pillars, not the orangish lights that lit the garage. What had I been doing here? My eyes closed. I couldn't remember. Next, there was a man. He was leaning over me, speaking. He had a woman with him. I couldn't understand their words. "He's wearing a ball cap," I said. Red-hot pain started strangely in my fingertips and radiated inward. I shook, trying to fight it off.

"Don't move," the woman said.

Where were her words? Could she help me? Would she? I needed help. Someone should tell Parker. And Bo. They should know. The water fell into my eyes again. "Ball cap," I managed to say. The orangish lightbulb above me grew smaller and smaller. Wait. Where was it going? Where was I going?

❖

I blinked. That hurt a lot. I tried it again to worse results. I winced in reaction, and that caused me to swallow what felt like razor blades.

"Hi, there," I heard a kind voice say. I turned my head to follow the sound and saw a warm smile, and kind eyes looking back at me. The woman was wearing scrubs and was doing something to the IV stand next to me. "You sustained a few injuries, and you're in the hospital. Can you tell me your name?"

"Hannah Shephard." My voice didn't sound so much like mine. Raspier. I glanced at the cup and Styrofoam pitcher on the tray next to me.

"Good. Let me get that for you." She poured me a cool cup with ice chips and I took a drink, savoring the refreshment. The water felt amazing on my throat and eased my dry mouth. "I'm Joanne, and I'll be your nurse until seven p.m. How are you feeling?"

"When is this?"

She paused a moment to decode the question. "Oh, it's Thursday afternoon."

"Thursday." My mind stuttered to catch up. I remembered the events leading up to this in flashes. The parking garage. The footsteps. I'd been planning to meet Luna at Harry's. Did Luna know? Who had attacked me and why? My head hurt too much to push. My body, however, felt especially heavy and numb. I had a feeling I should be grateful for that. "Am I on painkillers?"

She nodded. "A steady drip. Let me tell your sister you're awake. She's at the nurses' station filling out some paperwork for billing."

I was grateful for the generous insurance plan I'd gone with, even if it had been the more expensive option. I'd need it now.

"Oh, my goodness, there you are," Bo said, rushing into the room. Her hair hadn't been brushed and her eyes were shockingly red. She'd been crying. A lot. Right on cue, she welled up again.

"I'm okay," I raced to say. I couldn't stand to see my sister so distraught. My instinct to ease that stress in any way I could took hold.

"You're not okay. I'm so sorry, Hannah. This wasn't fair at all, and I hope you'll forgive me. I can't stand that this happened to you."

"Why would I need to—I'm sorry. I'm not following." I sighed, and blinked several times, wondering why the pain meds didn't touch this killer headache. I was also exceptionally tired. Was that normal?

"The attack was meant for me, Hannah." Bo shook her head sorrowfully. "The loser ex-husband. Remember him?"

I did remember. I'd been mistaken for Bo? "He thought I was you?"

She nodded and squeezed my hand, which had a giant, ugly-looking bruise that crawled up my arm. I remembered holding it in front of me in defense. "You were in my car, and because of the dim lighting of the garage, the asshole didn't catch his own mistake."

I nodded. "It was the husband." It made sense. I stared down at my body, which felt a little disconnected. Pain meds were wondrous things. "What are my injuries?"

Bo and Joanne exchanged a glance, and Joanne took the lead. "Concussion, two broken ribs and two fractured. Facial laceration. Some internal bleeding that we're treating intravenously."

"Wow."

"Yeah," Bo said. "Mom and Dad are on the way. They had trouble finding a flight."

I looked around the room for my phone. Parker probably wondered what happened to me last night for our call. I needed to let her know.

"I heard she's awake." I turned at the sound of the voice I knew so well. Parker stood in the doorway. "Hey, there."

"Oh my God. You're here?"

She nodded. "I'm here." She hadn't come farther into the room, though. She also seemed to be clutching the doorframe, which was puzzling. She finally came half the distance toward me. "How are you feeling? Are you in pain?" Concern marred her features.

"I have a headache." I held out my hand to her, and she took it, coming to my bedside, scanning my face.

"I came as soon as Bo called me."

"Aw, you didn't have to do that."

She nodded. "I did. I needed to see for myself that you were okay." She shook her head and looked from me to Bo. "Leave me alone with that bastard for an hour. That's all I want."

Bo nodded her understanding. "He was arrested this morning and is denying everything, of course, but we have him on camera entering the garage and walking in your direction, leaving in his own car a short time later." She shook his head. "He's a bad father and a bad person. Now he's even a bad criminal."

"Could be worse." I attempted a smile. "I could be him." I looked to Parker, who attempted to smile with me but never quite made it there. She'd been rocked by this. I could see it.

"Don't you worry for a second. They're going to prosecute his ass, and he will do time for this. I guarantee it. In fact, I'll make sure of it."

For the next hour, Bo vacillated between anguish and anger, chattering on about justice and her guilt in alternating soliloquys. I let her talk, as she seemed to need it. Parker, on the other hand, sat next to me in a chair and said very little. She nodded at Bo as she spoke and passed me the occasional loving look. But I felt myself start to drift, no longer able to keep my eyes open and feeling the next dose of pain medication pulling me under. I remember sending an encouraging smile Parker's way just as I fell into slumber.

When I awoke next, it was dimmer in the room. Through the window I could see that night had fallen, and now my mother stood next to my bed. I blinked. "Mama, is that you?"

"Hi, sweetheart," she said, and leaned down and placed a kiss gently on my forehead, careful to mind the bandage covering the stitches. "I can't believe this has happened to you. We're gonna get you fixed right up, okay?" Another kiss, and a stroke of my hair. "I don't want you to have to worry about anything. I'll be here as long as you need me. I'll sell books, or make you dinner, or both!"

"So will I," Bo said, from across the room.

"I have to get back in a few days, but I will leave this lovely woman behind for you," my stepdad said with a wink.

I absently thought that it might be crowded with my mom and Parker battling it out for nursemaid duties, but we'd make it work. "It's so good to see you both," I said, looking from my mom to my dad. "Sorry I'm not livelier, but you don't have to stay, Mom."

My mom put her hands on her hips in that overly expressive excuse-me-missy stance I remembered from childhood. "Well, that's just silly. There is no world in which my daughter is in the hospital and I'm not here to help. What are you thinking?"

"My apologies." I gestured toward myself. "Head injury and all. Did you two meet Parker yet?"

"No, not yet. Will she be by later?" my mother asked.

"I would think so. Yes? I haven't seen her in a couple hours." I looked around my mother to Bo, who smiled at me conservatively. My father picked up the conversation to tell me how important it was for me to advocate for myself and what I needed when in the hospital, but it was Bo I couldn't take my eyes off. Something was off. My stomach clenched uncomfortably. Once my parents excused themselves to grab a quick bite in the hospital cafeteria, I turned to her.

"Where's Parker? Is she feeling okay?" I needed to see Parker's face, have her there with me. Maybe she needed to steal a few minutes and catch up on sleep. If that was the case, I could certainly wait. "Did someone give her the keys to my apartment? I should have mine with me, and we could hand them off to her."

"She's gone, Hannah." My sister said the words as if she were breaking difficult news to someone, which didn't make a ton of sense.

Sadness bled through in the way Bo looked at me, yet I couldn't quite make it all compute. I'd just seen Parker that afternoon. She'd sat next to my bed, and held my hand, and made me feel cared for and loved.

"Oh." A pause. "She had to be somewhere for work, I'm guessing." Typical. Her schedule had been packed lately. I carried such hope when I said the words, yet the reality of the situation was already starting to settle over me like a vise I couldn't wriggle free from. I adjusted myself in bed, absorbing the physical pain that so easily matched what I was already beginning to feel on the inside.

Bo shook her head. "She bailed. Some sort of emotional meltdown that I couldn't talk her down from. I'm so sorry, Hannah. This isn't something you should have to deal with right now." She came to stand next to me, and I could fully see the anguish on her face as she told me the worst news I could ever remember receiving. "I don't know how to explain it other than she freaked out, couldn't handle the gravity of what happened. She said to tell you that she was sorry. She thought she could do this, but she wasn't strong enough." Bo shook her head in judgment. "She apologized about eight times and left."

"She wasn't strong enough," I repeated flatly. My brain couldn't seem to absorb the meaning behind the words. The woman I loved had just walked out on me at my most vulnerable, without so much as saying good-bye. My heart ripped open. I was angry, hurt, and sad, and yet I still missed her and longed for her. How could all of those things exist in one moment?

Parker was gone.

I stared at a piece of thread that broke free from the seam on the sheet that covered my battered body, ran my thumb across it as I realized how different the world already felt. I'd always known Parker carried a good share of fear when it came to us, but I never imagined she'd run from me, especially when I needed her so much. I nodded and let go of the thread between my fingers, understanding that I would need to get myself back on my feet on my own. Without her. Everything, in fact, would now be without Parker. It didn't seem possible.

"Hannah." Bo just said the one word, but it communicated so much more than just sympathy. My sister's eyes shimmered for me. In the midst of my internal and external trauma, Bo was my rock. She was there with me, for me, and I could count on her. And you know what? Being able to count on somebody felt like everything.

So Parker couldn't handle our relationship. I nodded as the tears hit the blanket tucked around my midsection. That was fine. Fucking fine. My life before Parker had been good, and it would be good again. Wouldn't it?

"Please don't cry," Bo said. "You don't deserve what she just pulled. Or this," she said, gesturing to the bed. She sat down next to me, appearing frustrated. "You're too good a person for any of this, and it sucks. I just want to do something about it, trade places with you."

"Thanks, Bo." Silence hit, and I felt a wall of emotion headed my way. Daunted by what was about to hit, I turned to her. "Do you think I could have a moment to myself?"

"Are you sure?" She watched me, questioning if she should honor this request.

Too late. The words wouldn't come anymore. I nodded instead, holding everything back with all I had left in me. I would not crumble in front of my sister. I'd stay strong for a few moments longer.

"All right." Bo shifted her weight. "I'll check on Mom and Dad."

I held my smile in spite of the pooling tears that had already betrayed me.

Bo looked at me hard. "She's not the one, Hannah. You deserve so much more. You need to listen to me on this. This is *her* loss."

Another nod. I didn't have a visual of the door from my spot in bed, but as I heard it click into place and close behind Bo, I let my head fall back onto the pillow. I stared up at the barren hospital ceiling, feeling like the worst kind of unwanted. I hadn't been enough to combat Parker's fear. *We* hadn't been, and that sliced at me seven different ways.

Just me now, I told myself.

Don't look back.

CHAPTER SEVENTEEN

L et me get that for you," Kurt said, and dashed to my side to retrieve a copy of *Nicholas Nickleby* from the top shelf of the literature section. "You can't be just reaching for stuff." He gestured to my midsection about eight times. "You're hurt. You have to let us help you. I demand it, actually. It's a condition of my continued employment."

His indignation warmed my heart. I appreciated the concern but was honestly okay. "I'm not hurt anymore, actually. I'm well into recovery and doing great." I'd been out of the hospital for a month now, and though this was my first week back at work full-time, I'd made great progress. The ribs had been the trickiest, and anytime I'd forgotten to take care of them, they reminded me with painful gusto. The facial laceration and bruising had taken a while to recede, and there was still an angry pink outline on my forehead, but it faded a little more each day. The scarring should be minimal, and I was grateful. Apparently, the best plastic surgeon in the state had handled my stitches personally.

"Still not gonna let you overdo," Kurt said, shaking his finger at me. "Please don't argue, okay?"

"When did you become a finger shaker?" I stared at him.

"Since you went and scared me to death."

The look on Kurt's earnest face said he meant it. The attack had been difficult not only on me but for so many of the people in my life. Kurt, especially, had taken it hard. He was an independent soul, who surrounded himself with only a select few who he truly considered family. I'd always believed he'd had a big heart, and he reserved it for all of those close to him.

"You stay safe from now on, or I'm just gonna...I don't even know." He stared at the books, unable to meet my eyes, shaking his head. "Nothing more can happen to you," he mumbled quietly, his fist clenched at his side.

I nodded and gave his arm a squeeze. "It's a deal. I'll be the safest."

"And you should know that every time I opened the shop, every morning, I said the thing you say. Good morning to the books. I want you to know that I did that."

"That means a lot, Kurt."

He nodded a few more times and finally glanced my way. He was still nervous around me. That would pass, and things would return to normal. "Better get back to work. We have that group of women who wear the red hats coming for their meeting."

"That's right." I clapped once. "I'll start the coffee. Will you assemble the chairs at the back?"

"On it."

I headed off to work my coffee magic, taking a deep inhale of the books as I passed and relishing being back where I belonged. Routine would help. Although my body was healing nicely, my heart hadn't fared as well, and I wondered when, and if, I'd feel whole again. If I hadn't had my body to worry about, I'm not sure what would have happened to me. Instead, I'd thrown every ounce of energy into regaining my strength, even when that meant forcing myself to rest. In those moments when I felt like bursting into tears, I'd engage my mother or Bo, my alternating caretakers, in frivolous conversation about the cats, or a TV show, or the crossword puzzle I was struggling with. I ruthlessly policed my brain and refused to reminisce because if I did, I felt the loss of my relationship with Parker too intensely. Not that any of it stopped me from missing her, from thinking *Hey, I need to tell Parker that funny thing Bo said*, or making plans for us that weekend, or picking up my phone to see if she'd messaged before I'd remember... Mornings were the worst. I'd mentally reach for her only to be reminded, once again, that she was gone.

I'd been home from the hospital for about five days when a letter arrived. I recognized Parker's handwriting on the outside of the envelope. I'd let it sit on my nightstand for several days before eventually finding the mental fortitude to open it.

Dear Hannah,

I'm not sure you'll ever read this letter. If you do, I'll count myself lucky. I'm writing to say this: With everything I have in me, I'm sorry. So sorry. I can't fully describe what happened to me over those two days, but I panicked, and it was crippling.

Leaving you there in the hospital is easily the biggest regret of my life. All I've ever wanted was to make you happy, and it seems I'm wildly unequipped. You likely don't want to see me or talk to me, and if I were you, I would feel the same. I hate myself and what I've done to you, to us, and am not sure I'll ever find a way to forgive myself. You deserve better, Hannah. So much better. If you want to talk, I'm here. I miss you. I love you. I was wrong. I will spend the rest of my life living with all three of those things.

Parker

It had been hard to breathe after reading those words. For close to an hour, I didn't move from where I sat on the edge of my bed. The force with which I held the stationery caused it to crumple in several spots. It was after midnight, and my mother had turned in for the night in the guest room, leaving me alone with thoughts of Parker and me, and us together. The same thoughts I'd had under strict lock and key came spilling out in an avalanche, banging into me from all sides.

The takeaway? Parker loved me. But somehow, I already knew that was still the case. Love wasn't the problem. Trust was. How could two people build any kind of life or future together without the basic foundation of trust? And in Parker? I had none. She'd left me at my most helpless, hadn't been there for me when I needed her, and in the end, I would have no reason to expect anything different when the chips were down. I refused to set myself up for more heartbreak, no matter how much I wanted to believe that we could work. Believe the pattern, not the promises. That's what my mother used to always say.

In the end, I hadn't answered the letter, and Parker hadn't contacted me again. The hardest part? Trying to get over someone in the public eye. I'd seen on Buzzfeed that Parker had canceled her book tour. I tried not to let it bother me or catapult me into action—namely convincing her that this was the best damn book she'd ever written, and she needed to get it into the hands of the people. That wasn't my role anymore, as hard as that was to accept. During a weaker moment, I'd pulled up her Twitter feed to see that she'd not tweeted anything since the week of my hospitalization. She'd gone effectively off the grid in every sense of the word. I refused to concern myself, helped along by the resentment I now dragged behind me like a bag of bricks.

I needed to let go of Parker Bristow, and I was. Slowly but surely.

After preparing my best brew for the ladies of the Red Hat Society that afternoon, I returned to the retail floor with the large urn of coffee, only to have Kurt race over and take it out of my hands. Okay, that one I was grateful for, because God, my ribs felt like they'd entered the fires of hell.

"Will you stop that, you crazy, aggressive boss lady?" Kurt speak for "I care about you and don't want you hurt."

"Thanks, Kurt." I straightened and exhaled, taking note of just how busy the store was. Almost double from what I would expect on a weekday, midafternoon. In addition to all of our new programs, initiatives, and marketing efforts, my public circumstances had thrust the store into the spotlight. The local news stations had taken a solid interest in the story of the bookstore owner who'd been attacked, mistaken for her attorney sister in the parking garage of the courthouse. They'd all run reports, and follow-up reports, and even feature stories. The results, while positive for A Likely Story's visibility, still left me feeling weird about my own spotlight. In the end, if my personal struggle connected people to their perfect books, then that was a silver lining I could focus on.

"Hannah, there you are." It was Wally, and he came into the shop in a hurry. He'd left me a get-well card made out of a file folder once he saw the shop on the news. I hadn't seen him in person since before the ordeal, and my spirits soared upon his arrival.

"Hi, Wally. It's good to see your face."

"Yours, too." He dropped his hands, which had been clasped together, in relief. "Thank goodness it's not that beat up. I was worried."

I smiled. "Very sweet of you. So was the card."

He waved me off. "No big deal. I make those a lot." He seemed to refocus and unbuttoned his maroon cardigan as he did so. "That creep has taken a deal."

I wasn't following. "What do you mean?"

"The creep," he reiterated. "The one who messed you up really bad. He's taken a deal from the other side."

"The prosecutors," I said. It all made sense. They'd offered the loser dad, who I had come to know was named Raymond Martindale—yes, that smarmy a name—a plea deal. Essentially, less time for sparing me the trauma of testifying. Bo had been furiously concerned about post-traumatic stress disorder. Luckily, other than an occasional nightmare, I'd fared rather well on that front. Yet the idea of facing my attacker in court was perhaps more daunting than I was willing to admit, even to myself. I'd encouraged the plea deal, when consulted, and had been assured that he would most certainly serve time in prison. "It's a good thing, Wally. Means it can all be over, and we can get on with our lives."

He nodded. Was it me or was his hair especially coifed? I smothered a smile.

"Just know that if I ever see him, I'll punch his lights out for you, old man or not. I used to box in my twenties. Maybe I should take it up again." He demonstrated a rather slow bob and weave.

"Thanks, Wally. You're a good guy. Speaking of, how are you and Tillie?"

"Going steady." He rocked forward onto the balls of his feet and back again. "I'm her certified boyfriend."

"Wow. That's the big time." But in my head, I'd said it less than enthusiastically. Even hearing about Wally and Tillie, the sweet couple I adored a month ago, now brought on a hit of bitterness. Apparently, I now belonged to the love sucks club.

"Oh, I know it. I don't take it lightly either. I continue the courting every single day. It's what you do."

"Well, I wish you happy courting, Wally. I better get back to work."

I could feel him staring after me. I'd never ended one of our conversations before and felt bad about that.

"You all right, Hannah?"

I turned back from where I'd landed behind the checkout counter. "I am. Just a little tired."

"Understandable." He offered me a gentlemanly bow. "Just wanted to bring the news I saw on the boob tube."

"And I appreciate it."

He left, and I sat alone with my thoughts. Ruminating on Raymond Martindale and my lifelong connection to him. Wishing I had someone, perhaps someone in particular, to talk it all through with. Still, I dragged that bag of bricks and vanquished the unhelpful longing from my mind.

❖

I loved my sister, but I sure saw her a lot. I'd swung open my apartment door to head out for a smoothie, only to find Bo poised and ready to knock, two smoothies on a tray in the other hand.

"How in the world?" I asked, pointing at the tray as she breezed past me. "I was just heading out for one."

She shook her head, red hair swaying. "I have no idea how I would know that your new, very rigid routine has you leaving your place at eight p.m. every single night to secure yourself a mango-strawberry smoothie from the place on the corner. I mean, how would I know that? I'd have to hang out with you a lot, or something."

"You just called me boring to my face. I've been dragged."

"Nah. Let's go with predictable and sad. Rolls off the tongue better." She handed me my smoothie and sucked on her own, which looked to be blueberry.

Bo visited more than ever once our mother headed back to Florida two weeks back. She still carried concern for my well-being and guilt for her part in what had happened, which I'd told her countless times was silly. She hadn't whacked me with a tire iron. Yet I made sure to give her the love and attention she needed, as she'd done so much for me.

"How's Amy?" I'd still yet to meet the woman in Bo's life, and now everything surrounding that meeting felt infinitely heavier given the recent events. It still wasn't clear if Bo's relationship with Amy had contributed to the attack, and Martindale wasn't talking. But if he'd known, it surely fueled his already angry fire.

"She's hanging in there. Still asking daily how you are. Her appetite is coming back, which allows me to breathe a little easier."

"Tell her that I'm doing just fine."

"I will." Bo paused and set her smoothie on the counter. "Are you, though?"

"Yes. You haven't noticed?" I was shocked she was asking because I'd been proud of my progress. My mobility was increasing daily, and now that Martindale had been sentenced to seven years—and would likely serve at least two or three—I had peace of mind and no longer wondered what was lurking beyond each corner. It was a process, but I was getting there. How could Bo have missed this? Boring? Sure. Stagnant? Nope.

"I noticed this," Bo said, indicating her own body. "But I'm more concerned with where your head is. Your heart. You've been so quiet lately—that is, until you launch into a full-on monologue or conversation about the weather forecast out of nowhere, which has me freaked the hell out." Aha. So, Bo had picked up on my "start a conversation" tactic. Might have to rework that one. She was more observant than I gave her credit for.

I decided to level with my sister. "I'm getting better, but there are parts of me that are taking longer to heal." I sighed and geared up to lay it all out there. "I was in love, Bo. I've never been in love before. It's a lot to undo. Maybe you're finding out a little bit about that yourself now."

She nodded. "I really am. It helps me understand what you must be going through so much more vividly. I can't even imagine if Amy was there one day and gone the next. I'd come out of my skull."

I pointed at her. The familiar pain hit, and my chest ached. "Nailed it. It's awful, but I'm not going to quit life. I'll survive this." I did my best to sound breezy and unaffected, finding that helped me buy into the idea myself, at least in the moment. Fake it until you make it was a good and real thing. As the new tool in my arsenal of self-preservation, I trotted it out a lot. When it wore off, my heart hurt. Yeah, that part hadn't changed.

Bo took a step toward me. "You will survive this. What's more? You're going to find someone who is one hundred percent by your side. Just wait."

I laughed. "No."

"What do you mean, no? You're young. Think about it, Hannah. This could be the exciting part. You know what you want now, and you have your whole life ahead of you to find it."

"Doesn't matter. I was all right originally, before ever meeting Parker." God, it pained me even to say her name. "My life wasn't glamorous, or exciting, or even overly social, but it was mine. Comfortable. I read my books, fed my cats, went to work, and enjoyed my quiet evenings at home. As a bonus, I have you and a few friends to keep me company. *That's* what I need again. This love stuff?" I lifted a shoulder. "Let's leave it for the romance novels. There's a reason they live in the fiction section."

"Ouch. Hannah, that is incredibly dark. Don't let one woman destroy you and your whole outlook on love."

Oh, but she had. Beautifully. Fantastically.

I set my smoothie on the counter next to Bo's. While I searched for the words to drive home my point, I studied the swirly marble pattern beneath my fingertips. "When you fall in love, it changes you. I didn't know that before. It's this all-encompassing connection to another person that leaves you open to whatever they decide to do to you or throw your way. Who knew that we gave each other such power?" I shook my head. "It's great for some people, but I'm not sure I'm one of them." What I didn't say out loud was that feeling the way I did now—hurt, battered, and lost—allowed me to understand why Parker ran the hell the other way. I now had a reference point for the heartbreak she worked so hard to avoid. "Maybe Parker had the right idea after all." My trailing bag of bricks became a little lighter once I'd made that connection.

Bo frowned. "I don't think she does. I think that's called laying up. That's what you're saying you're going to do."

"And what's wrong with that? I find it rather refreshing." I picked up my smoothie and drew from the straw to punctuate my point, then held my cup in the air. "Refreshing has its perks."

Bo blinked and looked like she'd had just about enough of me, and I didn't blame her. Here she was, newly in love and exploring a side of herself she hadn't even known existed, and I was waxing poetic about how love should be turned out and slaughtered. It probably wasn't a good look. "Well, on that uplifting note, I'll head out. Your smoothie has been delivered, and I've seen your face. Two of my goals."

"And a third?"

"Not quite landed." She grimaced.

I followed her to the door. "It's not your fault. I probably have a few more weeks of tears on my pillow, and then I'll be back and stronger than ever." Surely it wasn't as simple as all that, but again, faking it helped.

Unexpectedly, Bo turned around and pulled me into a tight hug. "You're going to be okay, Hannah. You are."

That did it. Double-crossing tears sprang, and I held the hug longer than I wanted to, simply to try and get them under control before my sister could see them. No dice.

"I will be," I croaked. "Time." I ducked my face and headed back to the living room, leaving Bo to see herself out. In my weakened emotional state, I did something stupid. I googled Parker's name, scanning a headline that indicated she was still MIA. I closed my laptop, taking control once again. As I drifted off that night, I couldn't help but wonder, though. Where had Parker gone?

CHAPTER EIGHTEEN

Time is an interesting thing. On one hand, the days felt long. They wore on me and beat me down. On the other, the pages of the calendar flipped as if on fast forward, with one month giving way to the next until I found myself back to September once again. It was a difficult month for me, admittedly. But I'd found a decent enough rhythm for my life and clung to it like a life raft. I'd returned to the stasis that was Hannah Shephard before that book display of Parker's ever arrived in my store.

Bo and Amy had turned into the picture-perfect couple. My heart soared for my sister's happiness, even though their couplehood was, at times, hard to watch. I recognized the little things they did, the looks they stole, the light touches of their hands at dinner that communicated a discreet intimacy. They were attentive to one another and laughed a lot, sometimes at things that seemed specific to them. I missed those things, and yet I shied away from them at the same time.

As I walked to work that early fall morning, I stopped at a stand and purchased a handful of miniature pumpkins and squash. It was getting chilly out these days, and I wore my turquoise corduroy jacket and enjoyed shoving my hands into the soft pockets. Surely we could set up a seasonal autumn display on the counter with my new purchases. I'd look to Luna for that with her flair for the creative. The morning felt promising, and I clung to that hope.

"Good morning, books," I whispered, took a long moment, and then brought the shop to life with a flick of the light switch. The store felt extra alive today, and maybe that was because we were in the midst of the biggest release week of the month and could expect an uptick in customer traffic as a result. The books knew when important days hit.

Behind the counter, I found several While You Were Out memos from my part-timer, Justin, from before closing the day prior. One message from the late afternoon and another from a couple hours later. *Call Sue Harstead. Wants you to speak on panel at some event.* Interesting. And then, *Sue Harstead again. Anxious to speak with you about that one panel thing.*

I had no idea what panel Sue Harstead was interested in me speaking on, or why Justin didn't ask, but as a small business owner, I'd learned the importance of seizing every opportunity. I dialed the supplied number and waited. Sue was with me in a matter of moments.

"Hannah, I'm so glad you called back. Yes, ma'am, indeed." Definite Southern twang happening. "I'm one of the organizers of the National Booksellers Association, and we saw a story on you and your shop on the news."

I flinched. "Oh. Yes, there have been a handful."

"Well, we are all just so sorry about all of your troubles. Yes, we are. Are you feeling better?"

I wasn't sure where this was going. "Yes, much."

"Well, faburific. Just a wonderful store you have there. So full of life."

I grinned at the compliment. I couldn't help it.

"I was hopeful you'd speak on a panel at our national conference next month titled 'Big Guy vs. Little Guy,' about the independent bookstore's plight to stay ahead of the big box chains. We'd love to have your voice be a part of the conversation and hear about A Likely Story and how you do it. The panel will be a combination of booksellers, consumers, and industry folks. What do you say?"

I was flattered. Of course I knew about the conference and had hoped to attend one day. No one had really noticed me much within the larger bookselling world, and while it felt strange that my less than fortunate circumstances had been the reason for the spotlight, I had to be practical and make lemonade out of the lemons. "I think I can make that work," I said, now full-on beaming.

"Well, that's wonderful. I'm pleased as punch over here. I'll email you the details and get you all set up for a great conference."

I rattled off my contact information and quickly looked at booking travel to Portland, Oregon, a place I'd never been and was now excited to visit. Maybe a break from the grind would be nice. I'd been lost in a world of the store and my routine, two things that had served me well and acted as the most helpful form of blinders to the rest of the world. However, they did make life rather predictable. Maybe a conference like this one would be good for me.

Sue's email arrived as she promised, and I was excited to see I'd be on the panel alongside Monica DeGraff, an author whose books I'd stocked many times over. The other panelists were fellow booksellers and a distributor. I made a mental note to read a few Monica DeGraff books in the next three weeks. I'd want to be knowledgeable. I'd also take a look at her sales figures for good measure.

A week later and my trip was set. I hoped to visit a couple of the vineyards in the area in my quest to learn more about wine. Plus, there was that really famous bookstore in Portland, Powell's, and Voodoo Doughnuts, where I could apparently purchase a donut smothered in peanut butter and Oreos. Who could resist such a combo? Yes, sir, this was going to be a fantastic trip. I was already counting the days until this new adventure.

❖

Portland, Oregon, had the highest number of strip clubs in the nation. Not that I'd planned to hit any up, but as I made my way to the conference hotel in my Uber, I passed a few of the more prominent ones and grinned at the claim to fame.

The scenery changed as we coasted into the neighborhood that would be home to the conference and that, in my brief assessment, could be classified as hipster light. Lots of coffee shops, smoothie bars, and craft beer locales flew past. The hotel came into view, and I took a deep breath, feeling the first flutters of nerves. I wasn't used to speaking in front of an audience, but I was determined to conquer that fear and meet it head-on.

The lobby of the hotel was bustling with conference attendees and I smiled as I passed each one, a potential new friend. Two hours later, I'd checked into my room, grabbed a quick lunch, and eagerly written notes while sitting in on a session about YA novels and their effect on the youth of America.

Luckily, my panel would take place that afternoon, the first day of the conference. I could get it out of the way and enjoy the next couple of days, fully relaxed. I chose to think of the conference as not just work but a miniature vacation for myself. After Martindale broke my ribs and Parker broke my heart, I had earned a little recreational time.

Now I just had to get past this speaking engagement…

❖

I shook hands with Sue, a smiley woman with extra-tall blond hair, just what I would have pictured. "I'm happier than a tick to meet you," Sue said, and one-upped my handshake, kissing my cheek with a smack. "You are a looker, too. The men at this conference better look out. I don't see a ring."

I didn't inform her that there likely would never be one and instead thanked her and took a chair at the center of the table, facing the audience.

"Hi, I'm Dean," a middle-aged man said, and took the chair next to mine. "Peter Pan Books in Santa Fe."

I grinned. "Hannah from A Likely Story in Providence."

"Beautiful city," he said politely. His mustache was certainly festive and far reaching. I wondered how much time he spent twirling it each morning to achieve the effect. Then I wondered if it ever interfered with sight lines because when you think about it—

"Dean, Hannah," Sue said. "Not sure if you heard, but Monica DeGraff had to bow out."

"Oh. Okay." I deflated like a bouncy house on a rainy day. I had managed to read two of Monica's books in advance of the conference, and she was a truly great writer. I had been looking forward to her portion of the discussion.

Sue gestured to the aisle. "Not to worry. I've called in a blockbuster replacement."

I turned and blinked. The world tilted, and my breath caught. Parker paused at the base of the stairs that ascended to the panel table, seemingly frozen in place, her gaze locked on mine. For one intense moment, neither of us moved. Everything around me seemed to be happening in slow motion. When my brain began to process again, it registered that the blood had drained from Parker's face. That told me she hadn't known I'd be here today. Her deer-in-headlights expression said as much.

"Parker Bristow, hello there. I'm Sue, and I'll be moderating our discussion. We're so glad you could join us today and with so little notice. Yes, ma'am. Pleased as punch." In the midst of my downshift, I noticed people in the audience begin to hold their cell phones in the air to take photos, forever documenting the moment I was sideswiped in front of a crowd.

Parker selected the chair two down, even though the chair next to me was open. I was grateful. I didn't want to make chitchat in front of a group of strangers in such a charged moment. I'm not sure I could have survived it. I hadn't heard from Parker since her letter. In fact, very few had. She'd gone off the grid until that moment. Didn't mean she didn't still smell of peaches, even two chairs down. The familiar scent had me grappling, trying to remember my trajectory and what I was in the room to do. *Think about books. Think about books. That's what you're here to talk about.*

She met my gaze. "I didn't know," she mouthed, with an apologetic shrug.

I nodded.

A fourth panelist arrived, Nancy somebody from some kind of book store. My very numb brain didn't retain the information. She sat right between us, severing our connection. But I could still look around Nancy to see Parker sitting there in person, and did, as Nancy chattered on about her travel nightmare. The last panelist, the one from the distribution company, settled into her seat, and we were off. The questions sounded like nonsense to me at first. In the midst of my shock, words weren't coming with their full meanings attached. The burden was on me, however, as I had been given the questions in advance.

"What do you think about that, Hannah? Has A Likely Story experienced the same kind of problem?"

Oh, no. This was bad. Sue blinked at me, and all I could think about was that the skinny microphone she spoke into reminded me of Bob Barker and *The Price Is Right* reruns. Plinko had been my favorite game. Why couldn't I think clearly? Who cared about Plinko, for God's sake? I was about to make a fool of myself, and Parker was sitting two people down from me. I blinked back at Sue, who seemed to blink back in concern.

"I've actually been to A likely Story, last year for a signing." Someone was answering the question. It wasn't me, though. It was Parker. "I can tell you from firsthand experience, it's a fantastic space, and while I don't know about Hannah's relationship with *her neighboring businesses*, I can imagine that in that neighborhood, they likely know each other and can cross promote."

That's what the question had been about, cross promotion with local businesses. I picked up Parker's gentle cue. She'd emphasized the points I needed to speak on like an arrow sign. "Yes, that's true. We're in downtown Providence, just a couple blocks off the popular shopping areas, which helps. There's a hair salon on the corner of our block that has been great with allowing us to advertise events like signings, and book club meetings, and our children's puppet shows, which have been a great source for generating word-of-mouth business. In return, we carry their business cards, flyers, and any discount promotions at our checkout stand. I'd like to get that going with a few more of the businesses nearby, actually."

"I'd like to hear more about the puppet shows," Dean with the mustache said. It pulled a chuckle from the audience, and we were off and running. The initial question helped pull me into the flow of conversation, and though I was still reeling, I was able to pay attention and contribute to what I hoped ended up being a lively discussion. I learned a few things and even had a little bit of fun.

"Hannah, dear girl, you were wonderful, just as I knew you would be." Sue pulled me into a big hug. We were old friends now, Sue and I.

"I can't thank you enough for having me. This was really great."

"I hope you'll join us for another one next year. I'll give ya a call."

"Oh, wow. I'd love that."

I turned to gather my belongings as Sue moved on to the other panelists. I could still hear her booming Southern proclamations from down the row. "Parker Bristow, you are a hero to swoop in and take that empty seat. We were thrilled to score you."

"It just all seemed to align," Parker said simply. "My agent called, and I was able to make the flight."

"Well, I won't keep you. Seems you have your fan club gathering."

Sue was correct. Parker had a throng of conference attendees lined up just below the makeshift stage, waiting for her. I took a deep breath and reminded myself that I'd done well. I'd survived our unexpected meeting, was still breathing and even smiling at the small number of people who approached me after the discussion. To my right, I saw a multitude of flashes from cell phone cameras. Of course they wanted her photo. They always did, and I, for one, couldn't blame them.

I scrapped the rest of my planned afternoon and hid out in my room. Ironically, I found a *Price Is Right* marathon on the Game Show Network and let the upbeat familiarity of the show calm me down. Honestly, it'd been months since I'd had this strong a reaction to anything related to Parker and me, and I knew from experience that I would be just fine if I took some time to work through it. So I watched another episode and another, feeling more at ease by the moment.

That night, I had a reservation at the quaint wine bar across the street and hoped to try some of the local varietals. I'd made a ridiculous list based on my research before the trip, embracing my inner nerd. When I arrived at the cute bar, I was seated at a small table along the wall. The wine bar, the Chalk and Slate, was small but posh. I selected a glass of the Tangle Valley Pinot Noir from the menu, placed my order with the server, and smiled at the very laid-back music coming from the speakers in the back. The room was half full, though I imagined it would start to fill up as the night went on. Beautiful-looking cheese and charcuterie platters flew past for a table down farther in and to my left. I sat taller to steal a glimpse of the creatively arranged assortment when I caught sight of her hair. Good God. Really? No mistaking it. That was Parker at the table of women, sipping a glass of red. I even recognized the rose lip print from the many glasses we'd gone through at my apartment. She must have felt my gaze, because the next moment, she turned, and we connected. Damn it. Her lips parted, and she flipped back to her tablemates and said something quietly.

My stomach muscles clenched uncomfortably, and I ordered my gaze to remain on my wine. I swirled it and studied the legs, which were plentiful and indicated a strong alcohol content.

Seconds later, she stood in front of my table. "Twice in one day."

I raised my gaze and met those beautiful green eyes. "Right? What in the world?" I asked, making the choice to remain friendly and lighthearted. No reason not to.

"I have no idea. It just keeps happening. I had nothing to do with these reservations. My publisher. If it seems like I'm stalking you, I promise that's not the case."

I nodded. "Not a big deal. Enjoy your night." What a breezy statement. I was proud of myself. If we were going to get through the rest of the weekend, that's what I had to do. Take control, remain unaffected. Damn, it felt good. *The Price Is Right* and wine had saved me.

Parker nodded. "You too." She took a step in the direction of her own table, then hesitated and gestured between us. "Weird question. Do you want to maybe join us, or…"

"No. I'm good, really. No reason we both can't enjoy a little wine." I left off the word *separately*, but it was implied. The server arrived just in time, and I lifted my newly delivered glass of Cabernet to illustrate my own enjoyment.

She eyed the glass and then me, as if trying to maneuver this very unexpected and complicated interaction. "Right. Well, I'll let you get back to it."

"Thanks, Parker." Hearing her name leave my lips felt so familiar. I moved myself out of the musing promptly. Not a good place to dwell. What was nicer? The Cab. Incredibly full and fruity. I felt myself relax after just three quick sips. A glass later, my cheese plate arrived, and I lifted a sliver of sharp cheddar. Parker's table had grown louder. Lots of laughter emanated from that direction, which meant the wine was flowing more freely. It made it harder for me to ignore them the way I'd hoped. Their presence chipped away at my attention. I stole an occasional glance. Finally, I noticed Parker was doing the same. Each time we made brief eye contact, the tension in the room doubled, until it seemed ridiculous to pretend it wasn't happening. We affected each other in a major way. We always had. At least I knew who I was dealing with now and could behave accordingly. When the group settled their tab and chatted their way to the door, I nodded at Parker, who smiled conservatively back. God, she was possibly more beautiful than the last time I'd seen her. Definitely the most beautiful person I'd ever seen. I had a flash of her sitting next to me along the water in Mystic, wearing that newsboy cap I'd purchased for her. My heart ached. I ordered another glass and refused to watch the group say their good-byes. Instead, I studied the menu as if it were the diagram to saving my life.

When I looked up, confident they'd gone, I saw that Parker had taken a seat at the bar across from my table, facing away from me. I swallowed. What was I supposed to do with that? I ignored her. When the wine arrived, I sipped and surveyed the room. I watched as a man approached her and spoke quietly. She said something politely back, and he bowed his head and left. He'd been hitting on her. Of course he had, he'd be ridiculous not to.

Maybe it was the wine, or the knowledge that we had two full days ahead of us that we could make awkward or not, but when she glanced my way, I purposefully caught her eye and inclined my head. I had no idea what I was doing. This was the equivalent of flying blind, but I'd extended the invite and couldn't take it back now.

Parker hesitated, until she finally gave in and made her way to my table. "I don't want to sit if you don't want me to." She said it more forcefully than I would have predicted.

"Please," I said, and indicated the chair across from me. Silence. Awesome. I picked up my cue. "We're both adults. I figure we can agree that things between us don't have to be awkward this weekend. But with you sitting over there and me over here, in the same room… it's weird. I don't know what to do with weird, except try to force things to feel…less weird. You know?"

That pulled a tiny smile. She'd always been a fan of my neuroticism and overthinking. "In total agreement. I just want you to be comfortable, Hannah. I'll do whatever you need me to."

"I appreciate that." I sipped my wine and gestured for her to sit.

She did. "I can also hop a damn plane and leave if that's better." Her eyes carried remorse and what looked like concern. For me. She cared about my well-being, something I'd actively wondered about in those moments right before I fell asleep, when my mind was vulnerable and unguarded.

"No, I don't think plane-hopping will be necessary. We'll be fine." I inclined my head to the side. "And thank you for saving me on the panel today."

"Least I could do."

"Right?" We laughed quietly. What a surreal moment it was, Parker and I, laughing about our painful past.

"Want me to head back to the bar now?"

I closed one eye and considered the offer. "Nah. I'm just going to finish this glass and go. If you sit there, you'll just get hit on twenty more times."

Her soft gaze landed on mine. "I'm not going to turn down the opportunity to sit with you a little longer." She took a breath, as if gathering herself. "But I do have to tell you in person that I won't ever forgive myself." She stared at her lap. "Know that."

I nodded. Not sure what else to say. "We don't have to talk about it. In fact, let's not."

"Okay." A pause hit. "You look great. Healthy. Do you feel all right?"

"Good as new. Have you tried the Tangle Valley Pinot?" She followed my lead out of that minefield.

"I haven't, but my glass is low. You recommend?"

"I do."

She picked up the long menu card and pointed at something she must have noticed earlier. "They have truffle mac and cheese, you know. I'm surprised, given your affinity, that you weren't all over it."

"Wasn't in the mood. But I'm guessing you devoured their little sliders, given your love affair with burgers. I mean, it's no Double Wide from Harry's."

She shook her head and the light in her eyes dimmed. "Didn't feel right." It seemed we shared the sentiment. No matter which way we turned, there were reminders. Instead, we sipped from our glasses and listened to the music, which was light and pleasant instrumental jazz.

"Wasn't sure I'd ever see you again," I said, finally. I was surprised to hear myself go there, and ran a finger along the edge of my glass, knowing it was the wine that had fortified me.

"I had no plans to bother you. I knew I should stay away." She glanced behind her to the bar. "I should have left with the women from the agency. Spared you this moment."

"But you didn't."

She shook her head as if trying to figure it out. "I needed to see for myself that you're okay, and as much as I tried to walk out of this bar, something wouldn't let me."

I understood what she meant. "I don't want to get back together, Parker. That's not really an option for me."

"I don't want to get back together either. In fact, I'm staying away from relationships altogether. New goal. Write about them instead. You?"

"Just worrying about me right now. Not dating. Didn't serve me well."

She sat taller and leaned closer as if on a mission. "No, no, no. Don't let my issues ruin your chances at happiness. Do not." She said the words with such determination that I felt them all over. I'd seen her fired up before, but this felt different. Vital.

I shrugged. "I feel like you maybe have the right idea after all." She was nearly finished with her wine. I was close. I decided I should pay the bill and put an end to this precarious meeting. "Where have you been?" I was shocked at the words as they left my lips.

She took on a faraway look. It lasted for longer than felt comfortable. Finally, she turned her face slowly back to mine. "I was in Providence for most of the time. Then I headed back to Austin, to the place I have there. I just needed some time away. Sat outside and watched the lake, hating myself a whole lot."

I heard the entirety of what she said but was focused in on that first part. It didn't make sense. "Why would you be in Providence?"

She sighed and touched the top of her glass. It seemed easier for her to look anywhere but at me. "I never left. At least not for a while after your accident."

No. Uh-uh. "How is that possible? Bo said you panicked and got the hell out of there. You were gone."

I watched as a battle seemed to play out on her face. Finally, she seemed to make a decision and sat back in her chair. "After I left the hospital, I packed in a flurry and drove straight to the airport. But from there, I was useless. I couldn't leave. I tried to get on the plane. Hell, I booked three different flights." She took a deep breath. "I just couldn't do it. There was no way for me to leave."

I reached for my wine and took a large gulp. "What did you do?"

"Checked into a hotel." She touched her hair. "Hung out on the first floor of the hospital most days until you were discharged."

I nearly came out of my seat. "Why didn't you come up?"

She shook her head slowly. "There was no way I could face you after that. I was ashamed, and you deserved better. But I had to be there as long as you were."

I scanned the rest of the bar as if a portion of it might offer some insight into what I was attempting to digest. "You realize this is staggering for me to hear, right?"

Parker swallowed, and I wasn't sure, but I thought I glimpsed tears gathering. "Yeah, I imagine it would be."

"No one saw you there."

"I didn't want them to. Plus, they were always with you. I stayed in the faraway portions of the waiting area like a lunatic. I needed to be there in case anything happened. I know it sounds crazy, but I needed to stay close to you."

I wasn't sure how to process any of this. In fact, I wasn't sure I needed to. Did this change anything? No. In the scheme of things, she'd still abandoned me. Kind of.

"I was a basket case. Trust me, you wouldn't have wanted me crying all over your fresh sheets."

God, I didn't like hearing that. As much as Parker had hurt me, I couldn't stand the thought of her so sad and hating herself. What did that say? It had been five months. Was I approaching forgiveness? Did this new development help usher that along? It meant that she had cared. "I don't want to get back together," I said flatly.

She flinched almost imperceptibly. The words had hurt her, but she didn't seem shocked. "No, I would imagine not. I don't blame you."

I softened. "You're not a bad person."

"I'm not a great person, or I would have put your needs before my own."

"Don't think I haven't thought of that." I took another sip and turned the stem between my thumb and two fingers.

"Another round?" our server asked. "You mentioned the local wines. We have a wonderful Zin from a boutique winery not far from here."

I was on the fence, and feeling the effects of the wine quite a bit. I glanced at Parker.

"Why the hell not?" she said, with a wan smile. Her nothing-to-lose-now attitude made me feel like I was looking in a mirror. Because honestly? All was already lost, and the wine eased that burn. She and I were on the same page, so why not get a little drunk and dull the effects of this whole crazy day?

"Tell me about Bacon." Her eyes shone brightly with affection, and she leaned forward. "Is he still infatuated with the television?"

"The cat's lost his mind lately." I widened my eyes. "He's obsessed with the ceiling fan, the television, and stalking Tomato. She, on the other hand, is on a revenge mission, pouncing on him from under the bed each night as he passes by."

She grinned as if seeing it play out in her mind. "I miss them. Now that I'm not traveling so much anymore, I'm thinking of getting a pet. Maybe a dog."

"No traveling? How come?"

She sighed wearily. "I'm not sure I have to go at it as hard anymore. It wasn't making me happy." This did not sound like the Parker I knew, all ambition, all the time. "Sometimes when you take a step back from your life and take stock, you make some key discoveries. I like to write. I like to play around on social media. Both have served me well, and both can be done from one location."

"I suppose that's true. Hard to imagine you not on the go." I accepted my final glass from our server.

"Well, it's happening. I stayed in Austin for weeks just to get my head together after you were home safe for a while. It was a helpful time." The smallest of smiles appeared and I could tell something important happened there in Austin. Maybe she caught her breath. Maybe she relaxed for the first time in a while. Who knew? "It was helpful in more ways than you know. I let my publisher know I'm staying put except for the very important stuff. I let my agent know there'll be less Hollywood nonsense on my agenda. Everyone's in the loop."

"I'm happy for you, Parker. You seem to be in a better spot."

"Well, I wouldn't go that far." The smile faded. Her gaze held mine for a moment before she glanced away. When she returned her attention to me, the Parker Bristow exterior was in place, the one that communicated all the confidence and charisma in the world. The very exterior I now knew wasn't the real Parker. I knew the real her. She felt different tonight, though. Grounded. Focused. I wasn't sure what to do with that. "I've made mistakes," the more self-assured version said. "I can't go back and fix them. But I can make damn sure I learn and do better from here on out. I want to make the world a happier place, and I'm not sure I've done that lately."

"You can be that person, Parker." *You just weren't that person for me*, I amended in my head.

"I will be one day. I'm going to make sure of that."

I smiled. When Parker set out to do something, she generally succeeded. The wine had me feeling warm and relaxed. I hadn't stood up since I'd arrived, and I wondered now how that might go. God, I hadn't meant to consume as much as I slowly had over the course of the couple hours I'd been there, but I wasn't sure I would have made it through this Parker-filled day without a buffer. She had the longest eyelashes, I thought, as she watched a couple be seated at a nearby table.

"What are you shaking your head at?" Parker asked.

Oh, yeah. The wine was taking over, because I hadn't realized I had been. "You're very pretty. That's all."

She blinked at me. She was tipsy, but maybe not as far gone. "After everything I've put you through, you're still able to say kind things to me. You should be yelling expletives and tossing this wine in my face, Hannah."

"I'd be happy to toss a glass. Imagine the headlines. 'Wayward brunette douses beloved author with happy juice.'" I laughed, and it sounded too loud.

"Maybe you should have been the writer," Parker said, with a chuckle. "And remember when you said I was pretty earlier? No one holds a candle to the way you look tonight. I have no right to say that, but I feel like you should know."

"Thanks." Why were my cheeks burning? I ordered them to stop. It didn't work. Damn cheeks don't listen when you tell them things. I wondered if the warmth showed, and covered one of them by resting it on my palm.

"You're even cuter when you blush." Question answered. "And I will stop comments of that nature now," Parker said, and killed the rest of her wine. "Because I have a very decided buzz happening and my mouth loses its filter. I apologize."

"Old habits." Yep. Just like the one I'd fallen back into within the last fifteen minutes, watching the way Parker handled her glass, took in the room, and sipped her wine. Each little action fascinated me the same way it always had. I loved her hands. As I watched them now, I carnally remembered how very much, and that was dangerous territory. I should flip that line of thinking the hell around. But it was Pandora's box, and it was open now. Lost, I bathed in thoughts and memories and sensations and scents.

"We should maybe head back," Parker said. "I'll buy. Least I can do for ambushing your conference."

"It really is." I felt Parker all over and did what I could not to give myself away, forcing a smile. "Plus, you have the big bucks, and I'm a starving indie bookseller."

She eyed me with amusement. "I feel like you're doing okay."

"I don't have Bristow money, damnit." I stood, and right on cue, the room tilted. Yep, maybe a glass too many. Or two.

"And now you have your drunk face. I've seen it before."

"You have not," I said, managing another grin that I hoped sold the fact that I wasn't drunk when, listen, oh my God, I so was.

"Are you kidding? There was that time we got into the debate about whether that news anchor had gotten Botox and you called her a little news minx with the subtle slur of the 's,' and we laughed."

"Oh. Right. I'd forgotten." I hadn't. I remembered each and every moment we'd shared.

"We love you, Parker!" a woman said. She belonged to a group of women who'd been sitting at the back of the restaurant. They all waved excitedly as they passed us for the door. Likely, conference attendees.

"I have every book you've written," another woman within the group said. "Especially the gay one. Love it. September is my new favorite month." She shot a fist in the air.

"Thanks, everyone. I appreciate it," Parker said back.

"Everybody loves Parker Bristow," I mumbled, shaking my head.

She signed the charge slip and closed the leather folio. "Yet she's better off alone. Ironic, isn't it?" Parker was tipsy, too. I could see it in the wistfulness of her expression. "Let's get out of here. I'll walk you back. Make sure you don't slam into parked cars."

"Deal."

The short walk back to the hotel was mostly silent. Parker steadied me a few times, which I appreciated. Yet the feel of her hands on my shoulders made me tingle, and I missed feeling tingly. You could really wage an argument about why it was nice to find ways to accommodate a good tingle across your skin. Heartbreak aside, I watched her as we walked, stealing glances at her whenever she wasn't looking. I'd always liked the way she looked beneath the streetlights. As we'd walked along the water in downtown Providence the night she'd surprised me with dinner, I'd made a point to memorize her image. The lights had acted as the most beautiful halo for someone who had always stolen my breath to begin with. The crisp autumn air wasn't helping me focus on much but her tonight. She was easily the most confusing figure I'd ever met.

The whoosh of cool air as we entered the hotel signaled the end of the evening for me. I'd made it out unscathed, a little rattled by some new information but still with my emotions under control. As much as this day had been a roller coaster, I planned to count that as a win.

"I'm this way," I said, indicating the bay of elevators to my left. The hotel was massive, with multiple towers and elevator bays in addition to those in the main section.

"Me too," she said quietly. Of course she was. What were the odds? I held the waiting elevator door open, and Parker stepped inside. Just the two of us. She selected the twenty-ninth floor, and I the fourteenth.

Alone now in the elevator, I glanced over at Parker. She turned and looked right back at me, and something in my chest shifted. I swear I didn't want to do it, but in that moment, nothing could stop me. I refused to think about tomorrow or the day after when I kissed her. I thought about my lips pressed to hers and the intoxicating sensations I craved and missed. I took what I wanted and, for once, didn't dwell on the consequences, even if they risked my own damn heart. Powerless and a little drunk, I stepped back from the kiss. We stared at each other. Her lips were swollen and sexy as hell as she blinked at me, mystified. I didn't blame her. I didn't understand it myself. The elevator opened to the fourteenth floor. Mine. If there was ever a literal sliding doors moment in my life, this was it.

"This one's me." I crossed the threshold to my floor. Parker hadn't moved. She offered me a small smile that could have meant good night, or thank you for not murdering me, or anything in between. As the elevator doors began to close, she stepped forward, her foot stopping their progress. Yeah, I was in trouble.

"Hannah." It was one word, but in it I heard everything she was feeling. Desire. Concern. Trepidation. Need. I shut all of that out. Emotions and feelings had nothing to do with what I was searching for tonight.

"I don't care about any of it right now," I declared, as if Parker were in my head and knew the battle I waged. I reached for her, an invitation. She stepped out of the elevator, paused, and then crushed her lips to mine, the hesitation gone. The rest of the world faded right along with it. Also gone? My masterful ability to think, reason, or protect myself—snatched away by the dizzying effects of alcohol and Parker. I wanted her body pressed to mine. I wanted her naked beneath me.

I wanted to make her come and watch as pleasure shook her to her core. We could put our connection back on the shelf later. Nothing had to change in the long run. I was perfectly safe. I shut the alarm bells off and savored the feel of her warm mouth on mine, because in that instant, it was my whole world.

We were in a public space, but you'd never know it. We kissed like teenagers unable to keep their hands off each other as we moved down the hallway. Mine were beneath her shirt, touching the heated skin at the small of her back, as our mouths battled for control. I didn't mind losing tonight, at least temporarily.

She pushed me against the wall between two doors. I let her. Her eyes, as they raked down my body and back up again, carried enough heat to set the building on fire. As they settled on the cleavage peeking out from my shirt, I felt my nipples harden. I was also incredibly wet.

We needed my room, and fast.

The key was a problem. With her hands on my hips from behind, I fumbled with the card. I was shaking, I realized. That was the problem. Parker took it from me and successfully let us into my room.

The lamp was on in the small sitting area and I turned it off, having it my way this time. The city lights bled in through the window as I removed nearly each piece of her clothing in a flurry of kissing, touching, and stroking.

Releasing her breasts from her bra remained one of my favorite actions in all of my life. I caught them in my hands as her black bra fell to the floor. It was my turn to back her up against the wall, using her breasts to do it. I'd turned the tables and was vaguely aware that I only wore my bra and underwear. She'd somehow managed to free me of the rest of my clothing. Parker liked me in lingerie. It wasn't my sexiest combo, navy on navy, but it would do. She, on the other hand, had only her bikinis on, pink silk.

"Your fucking body, Hannah," Parker whispered, running a hand down my side, prompting goose bumps. I stepped back to let her see me better. She blinked and bit the inside of her bottom lip.

"Yours," I said back. I stepped into her again, needing to feel her skin on mine. While I kissed her neck, I rocked my hips against her, pulling the best sounds. The little gasps, moans, and whimpers fueled my fire, encouraging me. I knew intimately what each one meant.

"More," she said in a strangled voice.

I reached between us and snaked a hand up the inside of her thigh, prompting her to close her eyes. She was trembling. It was the anticipation. I knew her body well and had memorized all of her signals. I eased my hand up to her stomach and then dipped my fingers into her underwear, holding her firmly around the waist with my other arm.

"God, I can't—" she stuttered, when my fingers brushed softly against her, causing her to jerk.

I pulled them away and studied her face.

"Hannah, please."

She sounded desperate and I liked that. "Do you want me to touch you?" I asked, and kissed her neck slowly, as if I had all the time in the world. I leaned down and pulled a nipple into my mouth and bit down softly, savoring.

I could feel her nod, and when I looked up, her eyes were still closed. "Yes."

I slid one finger inside, and she hissed in a breath, rocking her hips in an attempt to speed up the pace, searching for release. I let my thumb graze her most sensitive spot. Another time.

"Yes, like that. Please."

I took my time. One pass, then another. Her sounds were linked to my thumb's placement, and I could predict their steady beat. I added a second finger, a third, and let her ride, setting her own pace. I matched it.

"You're driving me out of my mind," Parker said, breathless. "I can't take it."

I couldn't take how beautiful she looked, how sexy. I loved the way her breasts bounced, but I needed to see more of her. I dropped to my knees and pulled her bikinis down her legs and went to work with my mouth, holding her hips in place. My pace wasn't measured this time. I devoured her. She sagged against the wall and threaded her fingers through my hair. She tasted like everything I remembered and craved. I nibbled and sucked and put my tongue to work until her hips moved furiously and she clenched around my fingers with a burst of a cry. Pleased, I stood as she clung to me. I felt the tears pool in my eyes as I held her. This was just sex; why was I allowing myself to feel? Her lips were on the underside of my jaw, my neck. She cradled my breasts through my bra and instinctually, I took a step away. "I can't."

She raised her gaze to mine, held our connection, searching my features for answers. Finally, understanding, she nodded. "Okay. It's okay."

I was capable of taking but couldn't quite manage the giving, because giving myself to her again was too terrifying a concept. I couldn't trust what I would feel, and what she would eventually do, and the best thing was just to not. Plain and simple.

"I'm sorry." My gaze settled on the floor. "I'm the one who started this and now…"

"You don't have anything to apologize for," Parker said intently. Her expression was carefully guarded and she eased a strand of blond hair behind her ear. "I'll go." She moved about the room, reassembling her outfit in silence. With the wine buzz fading, and the lust factor now dialed to dull, I felt the tug of *what the hell did I just do?* I'd spent months banishing Parker from my thoughts and feelings, and yet I'd just invited her into my room and had my way with her in a drunken weak moment. Not my wisest decision, and the ache in the center of my chest reminded me.

Parker must have seen me retreat into my thoughts. She paused and inclined her head to the side, her eyes gentle. "You can't get mixed up with me again, okay? I can't let you. You're too important."

I balked. "Who says I'm getting mixed up in anything? I'm not. Tonight was…tonight."

"All right." I watched her pull her shirt back over her head and push her bra into her bag. Now fully dressed, she turned back to me. "If you think I wouldn't leap at the chance to go back and do it all again the right way, you're wrong. I'd give anything for that, because I ruined the best damn thing that has, and will, ever happen to me."

"You did, and it's awful." It felt cruel to agree with her when she seemed so vulnerable, but I still carried that little bag of bricks. It wasn't entirely gone, and I couldn't pretend it was. I was still so very angry at Parker, but did I also still love her? God, it simply didn't matter anymore.

"Just so you know?" Parker touched her chest. "I'm not going to let myself hurt you ever again."

"Good."

She nodded. "Tonight was a misstep. I'm sorry."

It made no sense that she was apologizing. I'd kissed *her* in the elevator, yet the remorse behind her eyes hung heavy and large. She'd taken on every inch of responsibility for all that had transpired between us, and the effect it seemed to have on her surprised and saddened me.

Parker paused at the door and stared back at me with warmth, and something more. Reverence? She was memorizing me, I realized. I memorized her right back. This would be the last time. It had to be, as it hadn't been a good idea to begin with. I hadn't made a lot of mistakes in my life, but sex with Parker Bristow after she'd broken my heart was probably one of them.

"I guess I'll see you around the conference?" She offered a small but sad smile.

I hated that we'd come to this, after all we'd been through, all we'd shared. But it was for the best. I nodded. "Yeah, I bet so."

"Can you remember one thing for me?"

"What's that?" I asked.

"There was no way I could get on that plane. I loved you too damn much. I still do." She didn't wait for a reply. She softly closed the door and left me standing in my darkened hotel room, hollow, alone, and confused.

❖

The final day of the conference, I made sure to bury myself in activities. Meetings, workshops, panel discussions, followed by a perusal of the trade show. Everywhere I went, I kept an eye out for Parker. Not because I wanted to be sure to avoid her, but because against my own logic, I wanted to catch a glimpse of her, even if just from afar. Just one.

The day was nearly over, and I'd rebooked myself on a flight out that night rather than waiting until morning. My travel plans would now allow me to open the store the next morning, which was important to me. As I rolled my bag through the lobby of the hotel and headed to the taxi line, there she was. The woman who'd occupied my thoughts nonstop for the past forty-eight hours.

"Parker," I called across the lobby.

She turned and broke into a soft smile when she saw me. Her eyes shone brightly as she approached, wearing an all-white pantsuit that made her look like she owned the world. I saw she had a signing shortly in the grand salon. Any other time and I would have been drooling at the image of her walking toward me, looking the way she did. Today it only sent a pang of regret. I crossed to meet her.

"I just wanted to tell you that I'm headed home now."

"Oh," she said. Her disappointment was clear, and the sparkle left her eyes. "Well. I hope it's an easy trip. I'm sure those rascals will be happy to see you. Grab Bacon by the ear for me. He knows that means playtime."

"I will." A pause. "Before I leave, do you mind signing this?" I pulled out my copy of *Back to September* and held it out to her. It was still, in my opinion, a masterpiece of the genre, and I planned to add it to my personal bookshelf once I got home.

She stared at the book for a moment, as if stunned to see it. She glanced up at me. "Are you sure you want me to...?"

I nodded. "Please."

She accepted the copy of the book I'd purchased at the trade show earlier that day and flipped to the title page. I didn't watch her sign, and when she handed the book back, I slipped it into my bag for another time.

"Thank you," I said sincerely.

"Of course. Anything you ever need. Just ask."

"I'll remember that." It felt like something to say in the midst of another good-bye. I longed to be strong and unaffected in the face of everything I'd gone through with Parker, but the truth was that all I wanted in that moment was to pull her into my arms and tell her it was going to be okay, that we both were. I guess that's what happens when you care about someone—love rises to the top above everything else.

"Good-bye, Hannah. Safe travels." She stepped forward and pulled me into an unexpected embrace. Once I was in her arms, I felt the world around me melt away. All our problems seemed to matter less when Parker held me, and the complications reminded me of annoying gnats at an otherwise wonderful picnic. She released me, and reality intruded. They weren't just annoying gnats. Our problems were so much more than that, and I wouldn't allow myself to forget.

"Write some good books for the world," I told her.

Parker offered what I read as a sad smile. "I'll do my best." She touched her heart. "It's been a battle."

I nodded, understanding all too well. What a pair we were. "Good-bye, Parker."

"Good-bye, Hannah."

I walked away and refused to look back. By the time I arrived at the circular drive in front of the hotel, the tears gathered. We'd not had a proper good-bye when it had ended between us, and it felt like we were, at long last, doing that now. The finality resonated to the tune of a deep ache right in the center of my chest. I looked back at the hotel and ruminated on the very unexpected weekend full of ups and downs.

"Headed to the airport?" the valet asked.

"Yes, sir. I'm on my way home. Back to real life." A final glance at the hotel. I fantasized about heading back inside, taking Parker by the hand, telling her I forgave her and that maybe we could find a way back from this. After all, she hadn't gotten on the plane in Providence, a testament to her feelings for me. If we truly loved each other, maybe there was some measure we could take to safeguard against her fears and mine.

"Ma'am, your car," the valet said, and opened the door to the cab. The fantasy moved into a possible reality. I could walk right back in there.

We could maybe make it work.

Somehow.

"Thank you." I handed him the folded bills from my pocket and slid into the cab.

"Nice day we're having," the driver said.

"It is."

Eyes forward. Eyes forward.

As the car pulled into the flow of traffic, I pulled the signed copy of the book from my bag and read the inscription.

September will always mean you. I love you, Hannah. Now and for always.

—Parker

I hugged the open book to my chest as the hot tears slid down my face.

CHAPTER NINETEEN

Amy swung open the door to her beautiful one-story home in Acre Wood Park, a small subdivision south of downtown Providence. I'd agreed to babysit her son, Nash, while Bo and Amy had a little one-on-one time that night, which might have been code for sex, but honestly, I wasn't going to force it out of my sister. I knew their relationship had been physical but not intimate. Who knew? Maybe tonight was the night.

"Hannah, hi!" Amy said, beaming. She looked beautiful in a long-sleeved black knit dress and heels. Her golden hair held a soft curl, and she wore the most beautiful silver hoop earrings. Bo was going to lose her breath. "Your sister is running late. Her two p.m. hearing apparently kept getting pushed back."

"Oh, that's okay. I don't mind waiting."

She beamed. For someone with a very heavy recent past, she always managed to appear upbeat and chipper. I liked that about her. "I hoped you'd say that. Wine?"

"I rarely say no to such an offer."

I followed her down the short hallway to her kitchen, remembering that this was the same home that my attacker had once inhabited. It was a surreal component to my getting to know Amy, who I'd found to be nothing but warm and kindhearted. Nash, Amy's six-year-old, who I'd met once before, offered me a wave from the couch before turning his attention back to the gaming console in his hands. Amy waved him off. "He's allowed ninety minutes of screen time a day, and he's on his last thirty."

"Aha. Soaking it up."

"Exactly." She handed me a glass of red from the bottle she'd already opened and left breathing on the wet bar. "How was your conference? Bo said it was kind of a big deal."

"Interesting. That's a good word for it. But I was happy to have been asked to speak. That was certainly new." I stared at the glass in my hand and remembered how the wine from the week before had inspired a series of events that had me unsteady in my heart and head all over again. In all honesty, I should have handed the damned devil's liquid back to Amy and sworn off it forever.

"Tell me about it?" Amy said, and inclined her head to the side. "What made it interesting? You sounded dubious."

Amy wasn't just warm, she was intuitive. She and I didn't know each other that well, but the way she said the words, so calmly, without an iota of judgment, made me feel that I could easily talk to her. I sighed. "Parker was there. Wasn't expecting that."

"Oh," she said, with a knowing grimace. "My ex was notorious for showing up at places he knew I'd be. Do you think that's what happened?"

From what I understood, Amy's ex-husband had been not only a cheat but violent toward her as well. Made sense when I considered what he'd tried to do to Bo. "I don't think she meant to crash my conference. No. She seemed pretty embarrassed by the coincidence, honestly, and she's an honest person."

"Well, that's something. From what I understand, you two were pretty serious before you were hurt."

I saw the guilt gather behind her stare, and I covered her hand with mine to let her know that I didn't assign any responsibility to her, something I'd told her more than once already. "We were, but she left me there in the hospital and walked away from us."

"Oh."

"Well, I guess she didn't technically leave me in the hospital. I found out this weekend that she stowed away downstairs."

Amy inclined her head. "Wait. So she was there and never said anything?"

"Exactly. She was in town for weeks, and I never knew." I still couldn't quite believe it. "She was too scared and ashamed."

"Wow." Amy shook her head. "Does that change anything for you, knowing that she didn't jet in the same manner you thought she had?

I'm trying to imagine if I was in your shoes and how that might affect me."

I leaned against the counter and asked myself the question honestly. "It feels different, knowing the truth, yes. But the end result is still the same, you know?"

"Does it have to be?" Amy waved her hand. "Not that it should be any different. I'm just thinking out loud." She straightened. "Did you ever call her? Reach out to her after she panicked at the hospital?"

I shook my head. "I was too shocked, too angry." Yet now it seemed like the most basic thing in the world to have done. Maybe Parker, who had a history of loss, just needed some words of reassurance. I wondered now what might have happened if I'd offered some.

"Bo said Parker had a rough time of it when she was younger." Amy sighed. "I know it's awful that she wasn't by your side, but I bet it helps to understand that it wasn't you she was running from."

"It felt like it."

Amy nodded, looking thoughtful. "If I had to guess, and that's all this is, I imagine she was running from what she was feeling, the magnitude, and the concept of how she could ever be whole again if she lost you." She nodded. "In a lot of ways, that speaks highly of her capacity to love you, Hannah. That, and the fact that she couldn't fully go."

"I guess so. But what does that matter if there's no trust?"

"That's the tricky part. No relationship is perfect, but if it's a once-in-a-lifetime romance, you tinker. You work at it." She looked over her shoulder at Nash, who seemed lost in a world of what sounded like a car race. "I hope that's what Bo sees in me." A flash of concern crossed her features. "I come with some baggage of my own. I'm not too quick to let people in after my last relationship. Physical intimacy…can be daunting after years spent with Ray."

"I can understand that." I nodded, and my heart squeezed in sympathy for Amy. I couldn't imagine what she must have gone through, married to a monster like Raymond Martindale.

"Bo's been so patient with me. So tender. I know I haven't made it easy for her." She touched a hand to her heart. "I'm lucky."

"My sister's a good person, Amy. I'm so happy you've found each other." I hadn't missed her message, though. She was advocating for Parker and me, for taking the time we needed to work through our issues. I wasn't sure how to do that. In so many ways, it felt like our ship had sailed, and as much as I longed for her, I'd also built a wall around myself and vowed never to give her the power over me again.

"Hannah?"

"Yep?"

"I hope I didn't overstep."

I smiled at Amy. "You didn't. I find it hard to imagine that even if I did reach out to Parker, we wouldn't just end up in the same spot again."

"Let me ask you this." She met my gaze. "What if you didn't?"

The idea knocked the wind right out of me. I'd not let myself toy with the what-if because doing so felt dangerous. Hell, it seemed ill advised to even crack open the door, but talking to Amy *had* cracked it, and now I had a damned cracked door on my hands, and who wanted a cracked door?

"She'll run again," I said.

Amy inclined her head from side to side. "She may. Or maybe the next time that instinct kicks in, you're there to hold her hand and talk her through it, so that the time after that, it's not quite as scary when it hits. Maybe over time, she'll grow to trust in you as a constant in her life, someone who's not going to bail on her the way others have." She smiled. "Maybe she gets on the elevator."

"How do you know so much?"

Amy shrugged. "I don't. I just know what I've lived. It took me months to believe that Bo was as good and as kind a person as she first presented to be. I held her here," she said, demonstrating an invisible person at arm's length. "Old habits die hard, but they can die. It takes time, understanding, and a little bit of a gamble. She gambled on me."

The knock at the door startled me. Amy smiled and headed off to answer it. "Speak of the devil."

"Wait," I said, calling after her in a panic. We were done? "What do I do? I'm lost."

She walked back a few steps. "The way I see it? You have to decide if she's worth the risk. No one can answer that question but you."

I dropped my head and stared at the countertop, my mind racing as I felt the door crack a little more. I needed a lock, a deadbolt, and Amy's words erased from my brain. Behind me, I heard Bo's voice, then Amy's, and the sound of a kiss followed by a quiet, personal exchange. They were in love. I knew it plain as day, but apparently, it hadn't been as easy as it looked from the outside. In my quest to avoid their blissful coupledom, I'd stayed clear of any deep conversations with Bo that involved the L-word. *Sure, I'll babysit. Did you guys have fun this weekend? How's Amy? Did she get those radishes to grow in her garden?* When beneath the surface, they quietly struggled with their own issues. In the midst of them, Bo kept at it. They'd tinkered away in the manner Amy had talked about.

I sighed.

"Why are you sighing already?" Bo said, coming into the room. "The night is young. There's Monopoly to play."

I laughed and hugged my gorgeous sister. "Oh, and we will." I'd already been briefed on Nash's affinity for board games and his plans for us that evening. I came prepared, and ready to snatch up Marvin Gardens. I was no fool.

Nash tossed his game onto the couch and raced over to Bo, who offered him a high five. "Hey, I was fourth in the Grand Prix just now," he told her. "And me and Hannah are gonna hang out tonight while you and Mom are gone."

"I heard something about that." She smiled down at him. "You finish higher every time on that game. Amazing. What about the spelling test? How'd that go?"

"I only missed one, and it was the hard one with the silent g."

"Gnat. I remember it well. We'll forgive the hard one," Bo said with a smile. "Silent g's are overrated, and you still did great."

I listened as the three of them chattered away about their days, their plans for the weekend, and what Nash was allowed to have for dessert that night: two scoops of ice cream, not three. This time I didn't turn away or zone out or shove thoughts of their blissful existence right out of my headspace. I allowed myself to take in their happiness fully. It hadn't started out blissfully, and maybe, in the end, there was still a lot of work to be done, but they were willing to put in the effort. Bo thought Amy was worth the gamble, and Amy thought so right back.

"Hannah?" Bo was speaking to me.

"Yep?" I straightened and realized I'd drifted from the conversation.

"I was just asking if midnight was too late."

I made a face that said midnight was nothing. "Stay out as long as you want, you kids. I have a Monopoly game to get to and a bag of books for when Nash here"—I grabbed him in a headlock—"gets clobbered and falls asleep."

"Not gonna get clobbered," he informed me.

I smiled and tightened my grip. "We'll see."

Bo and Amy headed for the door, holding hands. I let myself enjoy the sight. Once they were gone, and Nash ran upstairs for the game, I pulled up my favorite photo of Parker and me, the selfie we'd taken one night, lying on the couch, relaxing. I was smiling at the camera as she was kissing my cheek. Us at our best. I'd not looked at the photo since the week I was released from the hospital. Seeing it now brought so many competing feelings. I took them on.

"Ready to do battle?" Nash asked, scampering behind me to the kitchen table. His question resonated more than he knew.

"I think so," I murmured, my heart already starting to gear up.

❖

The next day I went to the shoe store, because that was where all problems were solved. I wish I knew what it was about shoes that called to me when my head was a mess. I didn't seek them out the same way in normal stretches of life. But walking along the rows of leather and canvas centered me in a way nothing else could. I didn't even have to buy any. I simply wanted to hang out with them and revel in their simplicity. Shoes didn't come with expectations, or points of view, or even, necessarily, a high price tag if you shopped smart. Now that it was firmly autumn, with September pushing into October, I got to wear tall, comfortable boots that I could tuck my jeans into and just go. I took a seat on one of the benches and stared at the contenders as I let my mind work itself out. I hadn't slept that night after my talk with Amy. She and Bo had come home glowing and slightly disheveled. I remembered what that used to feel like.

"Can I help you find something?" a man-child of about twelve asked. He had an earpiece in his ear, most likely for shoe emergencies. I wanted to witness one come over the airwaves.

"No, thank you. I'm just browsing today. Searching for inspiration." That wasn't a lie.

"Take your time."

No choice, I wanted to tell the shoe-selling youngster. I operated more cautiously these days and needed time to ruminate among the footwear. I hadn't been on that bench six minutes before a text message from Luna hit my phone.

Have you seen this?

Below she'd pasted a link to a breaking news story: *Novelist Parker Bristow Reported Missing to Police.*

Well, that sentence made no sense. I stared at it, paralyzed. My blood pressure went into standby mode, and I clicked furiously for more information. When the article appeared on my screen, however, my blood pressure leapt into overdrive. It wasn't a prank, as I'd momentarily hoped. The website was a legitimate news outlet. Details were scarce, just what had gone into the report itself. There was a side note that sources reported her publisher had called it in to police after the writer couldn't be located.

I looked up at a pair of combat boots on sale for $49.99 and realized my hands were shaking, which caused my phone to tumble onto the bench next to me with a loud thud. I retrieved it and stood but wasn't exactly sure where I would go. What exactly was I supposed to do? I couldn't sit with the shoes any longer, not if something had happened to Parker. And if that was the case, I needed to fix it right now so that she was fine and everything could be all right again. As I raced out of the store, I got the idea that I needed to reach out to people who would know more so I could relax and it wouldn't feel like the world was crushing me with all its might.

"Pinky? It's Hannah Shephard from A Likely Story." Pinky and Co. knew about my relationship with Parker, but I still felt like I needed to clarify my identity.

Pinky didn't miss a beat. "You probably saw the headline. I'm sorry about that. We did everything we could to handle this discreetly, but somehow it was leaked."

"Have you heard anything?"

"No. We're worried, Hannah. Have you talked to her in the last week?"

I grappled with the calendar. "I saw her at the bookseller's conference, but nothing since."

"Yeah, that's when she went MIA. Don't get me wrong, this isn't exactly new. She's been going on and off the grid for six months, but this one has me worried." Since my accident, my brain supplied.

"Why is that?" I started my car. "Why is this time different?"

"Because she's always answered me before to say she's not doing this interview or not doing that appearance if she didn't feel up for it. She was supposed to be in New York two days ago and she didn't show up. She's a responsible person. The silence is scaring me."

It was scaring the hell out of me, too, and all I wanted to do was find Parker, look her in the eyes, and make sure she was safe. The rest didn't matter. We could sort that out, right? A pause. I looked around the parking lot, unsure what I was supposed to do with myself now. There was really only one option.

"Hey, Pinkie? Have you tried her place in Austin?" I slammed on my brakes, nearly running a stop sign.

"I let the police know, and they were going to have the local officers down there stop by her place for a wellness check. I'm not sure if they've done that yet. It's been hard to get answers."

That did it.

"I don't think we want to wait. I'm grabbing a flight."

CHAPTER TWENTY

I had to become a full-on detective in order to locate Parker's lake house once I landed in Austin. She'd sent me photos in the past, and Pinky had a few more details to help me along, including the tidbit that the house was located on Lake Austin not far from a restaurant called the Oasis. I wish I could report that I'd enjoyed my drive through Austin, which turned out to be full of sunshine and beautiful hills, but I was too worried about what I'd find, or not find, when I located the lake house.

An hour passed in the car. Then another. There were a lot of houses near the Oasis. I decided I needed to seek external help.

"Oh, yeah. I know that place," a man walking his dog along the lake told me when I showed him a photo. He turned around and squinted. "Back that way about half a mile. Double balcony in the back, and wooden steps down to the water. Pretty place. Away from everyone."

I sent a silent prayer of gratitude to the heavens. At last, some direction. "Incredibly helpful. Thank you." I wondered if he could hear the amped-up thudding of my heart. I didn't stick around to ask him. I followed the main road set back from the lake and studied each home in the vicinity, sometimes dodging pesky trees, until I found the house that matched not only his description but the photos I'd seen. I worked my way around to the front, taking note of the fact that there was no car of any kind out front. Parker could be halfway across the country for all I knew, but my last check-in with Pinky an hour before told me no one had heard from her yet. The police were putting out feelers but didn't seem as concerned as the rest of us.

I climbed the many steps that led to the front door, fueled by adrenaline. I'd have needed a break by now without it. I knocked, exhaled slowly, and waited. Nothing. I knocked again to the same silence. Finally, I found the doorbell and rang that a few dozen times, pleading with God to make Parker be okay. As the silence stretched, an overwhelming feeling of dread washed over me. I understood that I probably wasn't going to find what I hoped. In fact, the answer to what happened to Parker might be worse than my brain was willing to accept. I sat down on the step as everything I'd felt for Parker since the moment I'd met her bombarded me from every angle. Admiration, lust, like, love, frustration, anger, love, amusement, resentment, love, love, love, love.

Everything slowed down.

I could hear the sound of air entering and leaving my body. The Austin sunshine touched the porch with gentle light. The breeze lifted my hair and set it down again. I finally understood, with startling clarity, that the love I had for Parker topped everything else, simply all of it. The lust was staggering, the hurt was palpable, but it didn't compare to the all-encompassing love. I pressed my palms flat and hard against the concrete of the porch, understanding that this lightbulb of a moment might have come too late. A scream from deep within rose in my throat. Tears took over before it could escape. My body shook, and I reached out and touched one of the columns of the house for support. If something had happened to Parker, how would I possibly survive? Why had I waited this long to understand that there would be struggles, but she was it for me? For once in my life, I should have put it all on the line. I shouldn't have *let her* walk away from me. I should have assured her that she had nothing to be afraid of. Instead, I'd let her go, and now she might be gone forever. I covered my mouth as a sob tore from my throat.

From somewhere in the distance, a banging sound joined the chorus of my cry. I took a breath as another sob hit. More banging.

A sob.

A bang.

I didn't understand.

I looked to the left in curiosity, tracking the sound. It seemed louder when I turned, so I followed that instinct, wiping my tears as I walked around the house and down the steps to find a deck overlooking the lake.

Maybe it was a mirage. Maybe this whole ordeal had caused me to lose my mind.

Either way, the world, which moments ago hung upside down, righted itself when I saw the most beautiful woman in the world raising and lowering a hammer.

Another bang.

Parker was all right.

I picked up my pace and hurried to her, tears still falling. Only they were happy tears this time, infused with relief, happiness to see her, and a firm understanding of why I couldn't just get over Parker Bristow. I was so hard-core in love with her I could barely breathe, and you didn't just pick up and move on from that kind of love. You do exactly what Amy had insisted; you work like hell to fix the problem, whether it takes days or years. I could see that clear as day. Now.

"Hannah?" Parker stood from the kneeling position I'd found her in. She looked behind me, confusion written all over her face. "I don't—what are you doing here? How did you…"

I made quick work of the remaining steps until I landed on the deck not far from her. She wore faded jeans and a gray knit top. Her hair was partially back and the rest fell in lazy curls around her face and shoulders. I had no idea what kind of project had her so engrossed, but it clearly involved wood. "First of all, you weren't answering your phone or email, and everyone is panicked."

She furrowed her brow and dropped the hammer onto a nearby patio chair, still seemingly shocked to see me. "I just…I needed to unplug. Had to."

"Unplug? You have to tell someone that kind of thing." I heard the intensity in my voice. I hadn't meant to scold her. Hell, I was just so happy to see her, but the scolding came out anyway. "We were scared to death. They filed a police report in New York."

"They did what? Oh, no." Her expression morphed into guilt.

"The Austin PD was supposed to come out and check on you."

"I haven't seen anyone."

"But they had no updates." I was talking too fast. I could tell. "Getting information was like pulling teeth, and I couldn't wait anymore, so I just got on a plane." I raised my arms and let them drop to my sides. "Here I am."

"Hannah. No, I'm so sorry. I just needed some time. I didn't have any deadlines or appearances scheduled, so I shut everything down for a while. I didn't realize anyone would notice." She glanced behind her at the house, and back to me. Alarm struck when she saw my face. "Are you crying?"

"Yes, I'm crying, and I'm not even sure why." I brushed the tears away in embarrassment. "It's all of the feelings. All together." God, it was just so good to see her.

"I'm sorry I worried you. I'm safe and sound." She gestured to the pile of wood in front of her. "Just trying my hand at a little furniture building. It's therapeutic. I have three end tables, if you're in the market for one." Parker tried a smile. It faded when she looked at me. "I don't like seeing you cry." She walked closer. "You must have really been scared if you flew all the way out here."

"Of course I was scared, you idiot. It's *you*. Nothing can happen to you. Do you hear me?" Fresh tears now. I was apparently an untapped well of them.

"Hey, I'm okay. I promise. Stop that. I'm serious."

Parker was moving toward me, and in response I took a decided step back. If she touched me right now, I'd come undone. I was an unraveling ball of emotion already, all of them held in for too long. I couldn't let myself get any further out of control because I had things to say, damn it. I pointed at her. "Hold on a second."

She held up her hands in apology. The softness of her features rescinded, as she likely remembered where we currently stood. "I'm sorry. I didn't mean to cross any lines."

"This is a mess," I told her.

"I know. I apologized. What can I do? I can call the police department. Let them know I'm okay." She turned around to likely do just that.

"Please, wait."

She paused, turning back to me curiously. "Okay. Hannah, you seem very—"

"Off-balance? No. I'm not anymore. I'm not confused either, and I've been that for a long time. My heart hurts. That part's true, because I've been apart from you for so long."

I watched as her expression shifted. Her lips parted slightly, and her eyes went wide. I had her attention. "Is this about me disappearing?"

"Put that on hold," I said, and brushed the annoying hair from my eyes. "I have to talk about the rest first."

She nodded, and I shook my head at the magnitude of love rushing through me. It had always been there. I'd just gotten really good at keeping it dammed up.

"I know you left that day in the hospital because you were scared." A pause.

Parker's face fell in recrimination, and she touched the back of her neck the way she sometimes did when uncomfortable feelings bubbled up.

"It gutted me. I won't pretend otherwise, and I thought, after that day, that we couldn't go back. I didn't feel safe with you anymore."

"I hate that I did that to you. To us. I won't ever forgive myself."

I took a step toward her. "Well, I have, and I want you to work on doing the same. Do you know why?"

"Why?"

"Because we're like a shooting star. You don't see them every day, and when you spot one, you have to treasure the gift."

"That's exactly the reason I've stayed away. I'm not going to do any more damage."

I shook my head. "I don't think you will. Do you know why? We're in this together."

She seemed taken aback, and of course she would be. I'd not answered her letter, I'd rebuffed her in Portland, and now I'd shown up unexpectedly at her home and fussed at her for being irresponsible. "What are you saying, Hannah?"

"I'm saying that I love you, and I'm late. I should have chased you when you left, let you know that your fear was something we could work through together."

Parker blinked. "You love me after—"

"Yes. Before. After. Always."

She shook her head adamantly and her green eyes glimmered brightly with conviction. "What I did was awful."

"Do you plan to do that ever again?"

"What? God, no." She touched her chest and moved straight to me. "I would never, ever hurt you that way."

"Then use the elevator next time."

She smiled briefly. "I will forever embrace elevators. You have my word. I'll get a tattoo of one."

We stared at each other.

"Do you love me?" I asked.

She didn't hesitate. "You know I love you. I will always love you. That hasn't changed for a second."

"I love you, too."

We stared at each other. I inclined my head to the side and sent her a smile that I hoped communicated everything I was feeling. Instead of returning it, she walked away to the railing overlooking the lake. I gave her a minute, let her be with her thoughts, before slowly following her there. I slid my arms around her waist from behind, and her breathing hitched at our contact. I held her for several minutes, gently, just like I used to back in Providence, when we'd stare out at the night from my balcony. She didn't ask me to stop. She didn't step away from my touch. Instead, as the seconds ticked by, she relaxed into it.

Finally, I spoke quietly. "We're both afraid. That's not an excuse to give up what we want in life." I gave her a squeeze. "There's no one for me but you, Parker. I've tried convincing myself otherwise. I'm done now."

She sniffed, and though I couldn't see her face, I could tell there were tears. It was an emotional day all around.

"If you love me back and tell me you want this as much as I do, then we work through the rest together."

"I love you. No question." She turned in my arms and rested her back against the railing but hadn't let go of me. That was something. "You're the first thing I think about each morning and the last thing on my mind when I go to sleep. But you deserve more."

"Can you give it to me?"

That seemed to pull her up short. She hadn't expected another chance, and I hadn't expected to give her one. "Yes. I think I can, but what if—"

"I get clubbed over the head again?" I meant for it to be a lighthearted comment, but the sadness that came over her face had me rushing to reassure her. "You can freak out all you want. As long as you plant your feet. I'll be there to talk you down."

"When you were first brought into the hospital, I was worried you wouldn't make it." She whispered the sentence, emotion strangling her voice. "But do you know what I've realized since then?"

"What?" I asked.

"That if I lost you, then I still would have had the best moments of my life because I met you. And I then understood that I'd made the biggest mistake of my life in not spending every second I had with the woman I love, the woman who had become everything to me." She paused. "If I live my life trying my best to avoid any kind of major loss, in the end, what will I have to show for it?"

She dropped her face onto my shoulder and held me tight. "I'm so sorry, Hannah."

"I know." I pulled her in close. "Remember that night at Harry's when we argued about romance and idealism?"

She laughed, and lifted her head. "How could I ever forget? The poor bartender."

"You were right. Fantastical, novel-worthy romance exists." I gestured between us. "I wouldn't be standing on a lake in Austin, Texas, if it didn't. Everything in my life propels me toward you, and when we're together? Everything is better."

She nodded and pulled my hand to her chest just like she had that first night I'd met her, back at my apartment. The gesture released such a warmth in my chest that it was I who moved into *her* arms this time. We hadn't come to any formal conclusion, and there was work to be done, but standing along that railing overlooking that lake, we shared a long, slow, and tender kiss.

"This might be scary," she said.

"It might be."

"You know what, though?" She offered a tender smile. "Doesn't feel scary at all. In fact, in the last five minutes, I've felt more like myself than I have in a long time."

"Good."

She wrapped her arms around me tighter. "I love you so much. Do you hear me?"

I relaxed into her, savoring her warmth, her scent, her being. "I love you, too." A pause. "We should probably call the police now."

"One more of these first," she said, and brushed her lips to mine.

"Maybe two," I whispered back.

❖

"Good morning, baby," were the words I woke up to the next day. Parker, back in the most amazing robe in the world, stood next to the bed with two cups of coffee. I pushed myself up and accepted the mug she handed me.

"I slept in?"

She winked. "We were up pretty late." She sat on the bed with her own cup and smiled at me. "I was thinking."

"What were you thinking about?"

"Well, after reliving everything we did last night, and everything we said to each other before we did it, I want a firmer plan for the future."

I took another sip. "And what have you come up with?"

"I want to move to Providence."

I hadn't expected that. I figured we'd do the long distance, travel to see each other thing for a little while before settling on something more workable. Her plan was infinitely better.

"You would do that?"

She nodded. "You can't leave the shop, and I don't want us to be apart. Especially now. If you don't want me to move in with you yet, I can get my own place nearby. I want to hold on to the lake house for getaways. For you and me, when you can steal time away from the shop. But I'll sell my apartment in New York. I won't need it."

My heart swelled, and the smile on my face followed suit. "Live with me. It would be insane not to."

"Are you sure?"

I nodded, remembering how perfectly we'd fit together the last time she'd stayed with me for an extended time. It had been the happiest time in my entire life.

Parker set her mug on the end table, retrieved mine, and set it next to hers. "What are you doing?" I asked with a giggle, and she slipped out of her robe, naked and beautiful, and climbed back into bed with me.

"I think this is called a lazy morning. Prepare for lots of them in the future."

The future.

I marinated in the promise of that word and looked forward to everything the future brought with it. That morning was a memorable one full of warmth, laughter, pleasure, and above all, immeasurable love.

One chapter in our romance down, so many more to come.

Epilogue

One Year Later

"Do you think I should hang the witch reading Edgar Allan Poe in the front window or the back of the store?" Luna asked, twirling her currently bright orange strand of hair. "I want to capitalize on her seasonal relatability."

I glanced up from the inventory order I was constructing on my laptop and attempted to regroup. Luna was in full-on Halloween decorating mode and already had the place looking like a spooky little wonderland full of black cats, pumpkins, and ghosts—all with a penchant for reading, of course. "Let's hold her for inside, so she doesn't detract from the monster-mash book club meeting in the front window. I don't feel like they would have invited her, you know?"

She nodded. "Maybe a monster/witch rivalry thing?"

"Yeah, I just can't imagine them necessarily socializing on a regular basis. There would be tension."

She pointed at me. "I feel you."

The bell above the green door rang and Parker walked in like a woman on a mission. She held up one hand.

"Your fiancée is here," Luna said in a singsongy voice.

How long until someone tweeted that she was in the shop? I grinned, as it had become a fairly common occurrence. We'd started taking bets on how much time would pass before it happened. The end result was we were blessed with extra customers that Parker then had to smile and sign for. Not that she ever seemed to mind. I definitely didn't.

Parker approached the counter with a determined stare. "Hear me out."

I raised a shoulder. "I'm definitely willing to hear you out, except I was told in no uncertain terms when I left this morning that you were not to leave your writing desk or our apartment until you had three thousand words, and I wasn't to speak to you as leverage until that happened. You were very firm."

"I remember saying that. I meant it at the time. Things have changed."

I raised an eyebrow. "Have they? Because I'm not in the habit of breaking rules. Am I allowed to talk to you or not?" I passed her a hopeful look because anytime she showed up at the shop, my day was instantly brightened, and I wanted nothing more than to talk to her and find out about her day so far.

She waved off my concern. "Rules are made to be broken."

"Aha, so a no-go on the writing progress." I closed my laptop. The order could wait. I had a more important conversation.

"Well, I couldn't concentrate." She dropped her voice. "I started remembering all those adorable sounds you made last night, and then that got me thinking about our wedding night."

"Parker! Not here." I glanced around.

She didn't even pause. "And then the wedding itself. We haven't made any definite arrangements yet."

"True." I felt the blush recede. We'd decided on late spring but still needed to hash out the details and hire a knowledgeable planner, pronto.

But Parker had her idea face on, which I happened to love.

Her features popped with extra excitement, as if she'd stumbled onto something that had amazed her. To her credit, her ideas were generally fantastic, and I often benefited from her creative side, so I listened eagerly.

"Okay, this is the hear me out part. Remember the first night we met, when you told me you enjoyed learning about wine?"

"Yes, and you asked if I'd been to Napa, then declared that I would go one day."

She paused, building anticipation. She was excellent at that. "What do you think about a Napa wedding?"

I stared at her. "As in…actually in Napa?"

She nodded, beaming.

The wheels in my head began to slowly process the concept. "It's an interesting idea. What about our friends? Do you think they'd be able to come? I wouldn't want them not to be with us." We'd already decided on a small wedding, but I wanted the key players present for sure.

Parker shook her head. "Not a concern in the slightest. I'll make sure they're all there. What's the point of having tons of money if you can't spend it on the people you love? It's the biggest day of our lives. A very worthy cause."

I could see Luna practically vibrating as she prepped her decorations not far away. She'd clearly heard every word, having perfected the art of eavesdropping. The idea of getting married somewhere as beautiful as Napa almost seemed too good to be true. Was this my life? I imagined my parents there, Bo and Amy, Parker in a dress standing among the vines. The daydream demanded that I sit down. I had to. Then I stood back up again. There was no universe in which I could say no to her proposition.

"Ms. Bristow, I think you have yourself a destination wedding to plan."

Parker clapped her hands once. "Future Mrs. Bristow, I could kiss you right now."

I laughed at the use of my soon-to-be name.

She joined me behind the counter and wrapped one arm around my waist. "We're getting married in Napa," she said quietly. "You and me. Vineyards in the spring. We'll probably have to take anniversary trips there. Then take our kids. Show them where it all happened."

I sighed dreamily. "I love this idea, but not as much as I love you. And wine."

"I love you, too. What do you want for dinner tonight?"

I grinned. "I'm easy."

She raised an eyebrow, and I laughed, knocking her one on the shoulder for the cheeky insinuation. "How about a good burger? Extra sloppy."

"You know my heart," Parker said in happy approval. "Have a good day at work, sweetheart, and I will be waiting with a glass of wine for you when you get home."

"Okay, but I'm only accepting it if you've finished your words."

She sent me a smile over her shoulder. "Deal."

I watched Parker leave the store and couldn't help but marvel at the difference two years had made in my life. I'd opened up my heart to someone new, gone through the storms of heartbreak, only to emerge happier on the other side. I was in awe of how wonderful giving yourself to another human could be. I looked back in amusement at the time I didn't want Parker's book in our one and only display because romance was silly and idealistic. I was someone who could admit when she was wrong, and I'd never been more off base about anything in my life.

A text message hit my phone. *PS. You look so beautiful today. I love you.*

I smiled, because I was living out my own romance novel every single day, and I knew now without a shadow of a doubt that it came with the happiest of endings.

About the Author

Melissa Brayden is a multi-award-winning romance author, embracing the full-time writer's life in San Antonio, Texas, and enjoying every minute of it.

Melissa enjoys spending time with her family and working really hard at remembering to do the dishes. For personal enjoyment, she throws realistically shaped toys for her Jack Russell terriers and checks out the NYC theater scene as often as possible. She considers herself a reluctant patron of spin class, but would much rather be sipping Merlot and staring off into space. Coffee, wine, and donuts make her world go round. Visit her online at melissabrayden.com.

Books Available From Bold Strokes Books

A Moment in Time by Lisa Moreau. A longstanding family feud separates two women who unexpectedly fall in love at an antique clock shop in a small Louisiana town. (978-1-63555-419-9)

Aspen in Moonlight by Kelly Wacker. When art historian Melissa Warren meets Sula Johansen, director of a local bear conservancy, she discovers that love can come in unexpected and unusual forms. (978-1-63555-470-0)

Back to September by Melissa Brayden. Small bookshop owner Hannah Shepard and famous romance novelist Parker Bristow maneuver the landscape of their two very different worlds to find out if love can win out in the end. (978-1-63555-576-9)

Changing Course by Brey Willows. When the woman of her dreams falls from the sky, intergalactic space captain Jessa Arbelle had better be ready to catch her. (978-1-63555-335-2)

Cost of Honor by Radclyffe. First Daughter Blair Powell and Homeland Security Director Cameron Roberts face adversity when their enemies stop at nothing to prevent President Andrew Powell's reelection. Book 11 in the Honor series. (978-1-63555-582-0)

Fearless by Tina Michele. Determined to overcome her debilitating fear through exposure therapy, Laura Carter all but fails before she's even begun until dolphin trainer Jillian Marshall dedicates herself to helping Laura defeat the nightmares of her past. (978-1-63555-495-3)

Not Dead Enough by J.M. Redmann. In the tenth book of the Mickey Knight mystery series, a woman who may or may not be dead drags Micky into a messy con game. (978-1-63555-543-1)

Not Since You by Fiona Riley. When Charlotte boards her honeymoon cruise single and comes face-to-face with Lexi, the high school love she left behind, she questions every decision she has ever made. (978-1-63555-474-8)

Not Your Average Love Spell by Barbara Ann Wright. In this romantic fantasy, four women struggle with who to love and who to hate while fighting to rid a kingdom of an evil invading force. (978-1-63555-327-7)

Tennessee Whiskey by Donna K. Ford. After losing her job, Dane Foster starts spiraling out of control. She wants to put her life on pause and ask for a redo, a chance for something that matters. Emma Reynolds is that chance. (978-1-63555-556-1)

30 Dates in 30 Days by Elle Spencer. In this sophisticated contemporary romance, Veronica Welch is a busy lawyer who tries to find love the fast way—thirty dates in thirty days. (978-1-63555-498-4)

Finding Sky by Cass Sellars. Skylar Addison's search for a career intersects with her new boss's search for butterflies, but Skylar can't forgive Jess's intrusion into her life. Romance is the last thing they expect. (978-1-63555-521-9)

Hammers, Strings, and Beautiful Things by Morgan Lee Miller. While on tour with the biggest pop star in the world, rising musician Blair Bennett falls in love for the first time while coping with loss and depression. (978-1-63555-538-7)

Heart of a Killer by Yolanda Wallace. Contract killer Santana Masters's only interest is her next assignment—until a chance meeting with a beautiful stranger tempts her to change her ways. (978-1-63555-547-9)

Leading the Witness by Carsen Taite. When defense attorney Catherine Landauer reluctantly becomes the key witness in prosecutor Starr Rio's latest criminal trial, their hearts, careers, and lives may be at risk. (978-1-63555-512-7)

No Experience Required by Kimberly Cooper Griffin. Izzy Treadway has resigned herself to a life without romance because of her bipolar illness but wonders what she's gotten herself into when she agrees to write a book about love. (978-1-63555-561-5)

One Walk in Winter by Georgia Beers. Olivia Santini and Hayley Boyd Markham might be rivals at work, but they discover that lonely hearts often find company in the most unexpected of places. (978-1-63555-541-7)

The Inn at Netherfield Green by Aurora Rey. Advertising executive Lauren Montgomery and gin distiller Camden Crawley don't agree on anything except saving the Rose & Crown, the old English pub that's brought them together. (978-1-63555-445-8)

Top of Her Game by M. Ullrich. When it comes to life on the field and matters of the heart, losing isn't an option for pro athletes Kenzie Shaw and Sutton Flores. (978-1-63555-500-4)

Vanished by Eden Darry. First came the storm, and then the blinding white light that made everyone in town disappear. Another storm is coming, and Ellery and Loveday must find the chosen one or they won't survive. (978-1-63555-437-3)

All She Wants by Larkin Rose. Marci Jones and Tessa Dalton get more than they bargained for when their plans for a one-night stand turn into an opportunity for love. (978-1-63555-476-2)

Beautiful Accidents by Erin Zak. Stevie Adams doesn't believe in fate, not after losing her parents in a car crash. But she's about to discover that sometimes the best things in life happen purely by accident. (978-1-63555-497-7)

Before Now by Joy Argento. The instant Delaney Peyton and Jade Taylor meet, they sense a connection neither can explain. Can they overcome a betrayal that spans the centuries to reignite a love that can't be broken? (978-1-63555-525-7)

Breathe by Cari Hunter. Paramedic Jemima Pardon's chronic bad luck seems to be improving when she meets police officer Rosie Jones. But they face a battle to survive before they can find love. (978-1-63555-523-3)

Double-Crossed by Ali Vali. Hired thief and killer Reed Gable finds something in her scope that will change her life forever when she gets a contract to end casino accountant Brinley Myers's life. (978-1-63555-302-4)